Rising Shadows

By
Ashley Townsend

Ink Smith Publishing
www.ink-smith.com

Ink Smith Publishing
710 S. Myrtle Ave Suite 209
Monrovia, CA 91016

www.ink-smith.com

In Loving Memory
Ruth Elizabeth Wimpy Smith
July 2, 1927 to February 22, 2011

*"He who dwells in the secret place of the Most High
shall abide under the shadow of the Almighty."*
Psalm 91:1

Acknowledgements

To my mom for being the first to read The Shadow in its earliest stages and still thinking it was worthwhile, and especially for giving me the push to do something with it. Thank you, Mommy! Dad, thanks for all the crazy inside jokes that make others stare and for always encouraging me to dream. And to my incredible big sisters, DeAnna and Elizabeth, for never letting me think those dreams were out of reach. To my roommate and not-so-little sister, Katie, who put up with the glare of the laptop screen and my incessant typing at one in the morning when inspiration struck. Thanks, Kiddo, for getting so attached to these characters and inspiring new ones. And inexpressible thanks to my Heavenly Father and the Author of all creation for allowing my wildest dreams to become a reality. May this bring glory to Your kingdom!

To all the dreamers out there who imagine the impossible—this one is for you. Never stop believing.

Prologue

The young man crept silently through the corridor toward the torch flickering at the next bend. He would most likely get in trouble with his father if he were found down here, wandering around where he was not supposed to be. But when he had found the secret passageway leading into this musty and rarely used underground path, the excitement of his discovery had prompted him forward against his better judgment. Besides, his father had always encouraged him to leave nothing undiscovered, so he was really just obeying his wishes. These excuses were meant to assure him that all was well with his plan, but they did little to assuage the guilt that troubled his conscience.

He stopped at the next cross section. The passage split into four different directions. The adolescent gnawed on his lower lip and glanced down each corridor in hopes that one of them led to the end of this maze. Unable to see more than a few feet down each dimly lit tunnel, though, he took a moment to think about his current situation. He had been called intelligent and crafty by young admirers and disapproving adults alike, yet he was unsure if he'd be able to find his way out if he continued further into the maze.

His shoulders sagged as his common sense won over his adventurous spirit. He decided it was better to cut this adventure short and leave while he still knew the way out rather than risk being trapped inside the dark labyrinth until someone found him.

He turned around and started back in the direction he had come from. The boy managed to take two steps before stopping abruptly, startled by the sound of voices raised in anger somewhere behind him.

"Just keep going," he mumbled to himself. He made no move to leave, though; he knew it was futile to fight his curiosity. Rolling his eyes, disgusted over his lack of self-control, he spun around on his heels and quickly walked toward the sounds of an argument.

The flames of the torches mounted on the walls flickered in the dark hallway, throwing eerie shadows onto the cold stone floor. But he hardly noticed the disturbing feel they gave the empty passage as he focused his eyes ahead, slowing his steps so he crept silently along.

The wall he was following curved around to the left, and he stopped, peering around the corner to see what was happening. He was surprised to find his father standing in the dim corridor with his arms folded across his chest, staring down at the plump man before him. The boy couldn't make out the man's face because he had his back to the light, but he recognized his raspy voice the moment he spoke.

"The king's brother demands that you remain silent about this matter," the castle gatekeeper hissed between his teeth, his voice dripping with irritation. His hushed words echoed off the walls of stone and drifted through the corridor to the boy's awaiting ears.

"You know I cannot," his father said firmly, standing his ground and not showing the least bit of fear—an emotion that most men exhibited in the vile man's presence.

Even without seeing his face, the boy could feel the gatekeeper's hatred.

"You weren't supposed to overhear our conversation," the gatekeeper replied, "so it is your duty to forget what was said and step aside when the time comes."

"My duty is to the king," his father replied, not even wincing when the large man struck him across the side of his face. The young man had to resist the urge to strike the man himself for laying a finger upon his father.

"You will pay for this," the gatekeeper threatened in a low, menacing voice, sending a chill up the youth's spine. The nasty man stalked away into the darkness, leaving the young man and his father alone in the castle hall as they watched the man's retreat.

The young man hesitantly walked around the corner toward his father, half expecting the gatekeeper to return and send him to the racks for eavesdropping. He stretched out a hand toward his father, but instead of touching flesh, he grasped at nothing but air. Alarmed, he stared at his tingling fingers and then glanced up as his father turned toward him. The young man watched in stunned silence as the details of his father's face became a blur, his frame slowly dissolving into a cloud of vapor.

Terrified but unable to move or call for help, the young man only watched as wisps of translucent smoke curled from the hazy mass, extending toward the walls like a hand reaching for help. He stood frozen in horror as one of the ghost-like tendrils broke away from the cloud and floated lazily toward him.

When it was mere inches away, the tendril transformed into a spitting flame that leapt toward his face. He jumped back to avoid the spray of sparks as the flame burst just inches away from him before calming once again into a wisp of vapor that faded into the air. A chilling breeze suddenly stirred the fetid air in the passageway, and he watched helplessly as the draft carried the smoke that was once his father lazily down the tunnel and out of reach.

The young man instinctively reached a hand out to stop all that remained of his beloved father. He tried to follow the mist down the passage, but his legs refused to obey. He collapsed to his knees in anguish as the fog moved out of sight.

ℭℛℰℴ

The young man opened his eyes slowly, though they begged him not to. Smoke assailed his senses, and he felt a cool hand upon his forehead. He was lying on the ground outside with a canopy of night stars overhead. It had all been a dream. A vivid and horrible nightmare.

"Are you all right, son?" His uncle stooped over him, his brow knit in worry. The boy didn't answer as his attention was drawn toward the terrifying sight of the burning house.

"Where are my mother and father?" he whispered urgently, dread evident in his voice. His uncle started in surprise at the question, and then his horrified gaze wandered to the blazing inferno.

"Please, God, no!" He jumped to his feet and ran toward his sister's home. A gust of wind came over the hill, and the hungry orange flames grew larger as they leapt toward the sky, feeding off the wind's presence. Before the boy's uncle could take more than a few steps toward the house, the roof caved in, and the walls followed in a rush.

The house collapsed into a large heap as the fire engulfed the fallen building, flames reaching their angry hands toward the heavens, momentarily lighting the darkness in a flash of fury and brilliance. The flames settled just as quickly as they had grown out of control; they calmly crackled over the fallen house, acting as though they were no more threatening than a small fire in a stove.

"No!" his uncle cried out as his knees buckled beneath him.

The boy covered his ears to block out the sound of the snapping flames and his uncle's cries. He began to sob as he watched the burning rubble hiss and pop, consuming the two people he loved most in the entire world.

Chapter One

Bethany Lane was usually a calm and peaceful street, but today rain poured down from dark clouds, and strong gusts of wind blew debris in all directions across the deserted lane.

Eighteen-year-old Sarah Matthews watched the storm through her bedroom window, sighing when it grew worse. This was one of the wettest Oklahoma summers in over a century; the weatherman with the overly large smile had said so on the news last night, proclaiming that they had also experienced record-setting heat for so much rain. The combination of heat and water had resulted in delightfully high humidity levels that wreaked havoc on Sarah's auburn waves, turning them into a halo of unmanageable curls.

Having grown tired of the bouncing ringlets poking her in the eye, Sarah scraped her hair back from her face and secured it with the elastic band she always wore around her wrist. She tugged the ponytail at the back of her head, satisfied that her hair was temporarily out of the way.

The door opened slowly, and Sarah turned to see her ten-year-old sister, Lilly, poke her head around the doorframe.

"Can I stay here with you?" Lilly asked timidly, her eyes darting nervously around the room as a flicker of lightning momentarily lit the sky.

"Fine," Sarah answered her tersely, turning back to watch the storm from her position on the window seat. She wasn't in the mood to entertain her only sibling, and she wished Lilly would just leave so she could go back to her thoughts.

Before she was interrupted, she had been thinking about the start of college at the end of summer, which was just a little over a month away. She wasn't worried about the distance between her home and Southwestern Christian University—it was one of the closest colleges she could find. Located in the small city of Bethany, Oklahoma, SCU was only an hour's drive away in good weather (although there hadn't been much of that this summer), and she planned to drive back home on the weekends and for holidays. All of her friends from her graduating class, at least those who had plans for further education, were going to Southwestern, so she would have plenty of people there to keep her company.

No, college wasn't the source of her current dilemma; it was the end of summer that she was mulling over in her head. She had graduated from high school a semester early, and over the past seven months, her life had felt pretty mundane: she'd worked at her dad's hardware store in town, hung out with friends when the weather permitted, worked, made lists of things she needed for her dorm, and worked some more.

She wasn't exactly complaining—working so much had helped her buy her first car, which she would need to make the trips back home from her dorm. She even had money left over for spending and living expenses. No, the thing that was causing her to be so pensive on this dreary day was the fact that nothing exciting had happened over the summer. She had wanted an adventure before she went off to college, one last escapade before she lost her freedom to endless hours of classes and piles of homework.

Her friend, Tanya, had been gone the whole summer on an exotic trip to Maui with her family. Sarah couldn't help but feel left behind. And she certainly had not gotten the chance at a sweet summer romance like Janice had, though Sarah didn't feel like she had missed out on that too much— she doubted the relationship would last through the fall.

Whenever people discovered that Sarah was single, which was more often than she liked, they gave her those irritating looks of pity. She always told them that she was perfectly content and just wanted to focus on her studies. And that was completely true; she hadn't yet found that man who made her toes curl or her heart skip a beat. And though she was fairly sure she wouldn't find him anytime soon, she'd kept a secret hope that maybe, just maybe, she'd be surprised.

But now, knowing that she would be leaving soon, she figured her chance for adventure and romance had been lost. Reluctantly, she had accepted the fact that mundane was inevitable, and she had given up the hope of enjoying her last few weeks of childhood before the start of her new life.

"I wish Mom and Dad weren't in Texas right now," Lilly said, bringing Sarah out of her reverie. She had completely forgotten that her sister was there. "Do you think Grandma's hip surgery went all right? Can we call them?"

Sarah watched as Lilly sat down on the floor, crossed her legs, and began twirling a strand of her shoulder-length brown hair around her finger. Sarah cringed whenever Lilly paused to nibble on the end of the strand. It was a nervous habit Lilly had picked up recently, and it never failed to grate on Sarah's already raw nerves. Lilly's blue eyes were wide as they stared out the window at the raging storm, and Sarah had to bite her tongue to keep from kicking her distraught sister and her irritating habit out of her room.

"I'm sure everything's fine there," Sarah assured her in a calm voice, though her heart wasn't in it. "And, no, we can't call; the phone lines are dead. I'm just glad that the storm didn't knock out the power lines, too."

The moment the words left her lips, the lights in the room flickered, then went out.

Lilly let out a startled screech that made Sarah cringe. *Figures*, Sarah grumbled to herself. Now the darkness in the room reflected her current brooding mood. She knew how much her only sibling hated thunderstorms. She didn't want to have to deal with the hysterics of a ten-year-old while their parents were away in Texas. They had left two days ago to stay with Sarah's grandparents while her grandma recovered from surgery. They wouldn't be back for a few more days, so it would be up to her to calm her frantic sister.

"It's probably just a downed line," Sarah said, trying to comfort the younger girl, whose breathing rate had increased noticeably in the darkness. "I'm sure once the storm passes, they'll have it fixed in n—"

Sarah's sentence ended in a gasp as the floor beneath her rippled and quaked, throwing her off the window seat and to the ground. She planted her hands and knees firmly on the floor, trying to pull herself back up, but the whole room seemed to dip from one side to the other. It was impossible for her to do anything but remain crouched in that position and hope that she could remain upright.

Lilly screamed as lightning flashed brightly across the dark sky. A clap of thunder cracked so loudly that Sarah wanted to throw her hands over her ears, though she didn't for fear of falling face-first into the floor. A strange ripping sound was heard over the thunder, and a horrible whirring noise made Sarah think that a tornado might be on its way. She prayed that wasn't the case, since they were currently unable to walk or even crawl to the basement to seek shelter amidst the bucking and shaking of the house.

Sarah squeezed her eyelids together to block out the sickening motion of the room and clenched her teeth to keep them from chattering as the quaking continued. Her stomach lurched with each jerk of the house, and she fought the rising nausea, wondering how she would get to Lilly if they did need to make a break for the basement.

The room suddenly lurched to the side, throwing Sarah off-balance and sending her tumbling across the floor. Her forehead connected with one of the heavy oak legs of her bed before the room tossed her carelessly onto her back. Stunned, she could only lie there like a helpless turtle on its back and stare up at the blackness above her, fighting for breath. Lilly was still shrieking with each flash of lightening and clap of thunder, but Sarah felt too disoriented to move toward the sound of her sister's cries.

After what seemed like an eternity—though it was only mere seconds—the shaking abruptly ceased, the lightning no longer illuminated the blackness, the thunder stopped, and even the rain no longer pelted against the window. Total darkness enveloped them.

Chapter Two

The silence was unnerving.

Sarah groaned as she sat up and gingerly touched her throbbing forehead. It didn't feel like she was bleeding, but she wouldn't be surprised if she had a mild concussion.

She shivered. The temperature seemed to have dropped. The heater must have turned off when the power went out. Sarah tried her best to push away the troublesome voice reminding her that her family never ran the heater during the hot Oklahoma summer.

"Are you all right, Lilly?" she asked, crawling across the floor toward the sound of her sister's erratic breathing. She thought about standing, but she wasn't sure her shaky legs could hold her. She paused, hands on the ground. Hesitantly, she moved her hands over the rough wood floor, then began searching more anxiously for her bedroom rug. It was oversized and extremely shaggy, taking up most of the floor space in her room. After shuffling wildly around on her hands and knees for several moments in search of it, she gave up. She couldn't find it.

"Where are you?" Lilly cried frantically, sounding near hysteria.

Sarah tried to calm her nerves so she wouldn't worry Lilly when she spoke. "I'm right here. Calm down, it was just a freak earthquake. Are you all right?"

"Yes! Oh, please turn on the lights, Sarah. I can't see anything, and it's freaking me out."

You and me both, Sarah thought to herself; she didn't dare voice her thoughts—they would only upset her sister further.

"I can't turn on the lights right now because the storm knocked the power out," she replied with as much calm as she could muster, though Lilly sounded as shaken as she felt. "That was a bad one. I'm sure we'll have some cleanup, but I can't really be positive until I have some light. I think there's a flashlight in the kitchen," she mumbled to herself as she felt her way along the wall. When her fingers brushed the cold doorknob, she breathed a sigh of relief, though she would never admit to her younger sibling that the darkness had begun to unnerve her, too.

"Stay here," she commanded.

"No, Sarah, don't leave—" Lilly protested. But Sarah turned the knob and pulled the door open anyway.

She gasped, shielding her eyes from the sudden light that poured in through the doorway. The roof must have caved in, she realized with dismay. But then she remembered that it had been nearly dark just a moment ago.

Sarah blinked several times and squinted against the light. She took a step through the doorway and looked behind her to motion for Lilly to follow, but she froze when she realized her wide-eyed sister wasn't standing in her room any longer; instead, she was in the doorway of a moldy looking shed. Sarah took a step back in surprise, then spun around to find that they were in the middle of forest clearing, surrounded by trees.

She staggered backward, stunned. Her mouth formed a silent "O" as she gaped at the clear blue sky and the bright sun visible through gaps in the dense foliage above. Her eyes drifted, and she started at the sight of a young woman standing before them.

The young woman's hands were clasped in front of her, and she wore a friendly expression. Her silky red hair was pulled back in a neat braid, and she wore a snow-white dress with a tapered bodice that hung off her pale, slender shoulders. The ends of the sleeves flared around her wrists, looking like large white bells dipping toward the ground, and she quickly fastened something onto her right wrist under the sleeve. The tip of a brown leather boot peeked out from beneath the hem of her dress, and a thick leather strap of the same color rested on her hips, accentuating her thin waist. She reminded Sarah of what a medieval heroine would look like.

Sarah shook her head. She had to be hallucinating from the bump on her head. That, or she was having a serious mental breakdown from the stress of planning for college. She hoped it was the former.

The girl's smile faded as she examined them for a long moment. Sarah shifted uncomfortably beneath her intense scrutiny. The girl's emerald eyes suddenly widened, and her hand flew to her mouth. "Oh, no! What have I done?" she cried.

"Are you looking for someone?" Sarah asked curiously, taking another step toward the distraught girl as her eyes darted about their strange surroundings. She could at least be a Good Samaritan in this crazy dream. That's what this was—a dream. It had to be.

"Yes, the professor!" the girl said, sounding as though this should be obvious. Her next words were hurried, and Sarah had to strain her ears to make sense of her frantic ramblings. "When I saw the flash, I thought maybe he had gotten free or was coming back. He's been gone so long, I thought—" She pressed her hand to her throat and furrowed her brow. "I'm so sorry! I never meant to bring you two here. It was an accident!"

Sarah paused as the girl's words sank in. She narrowed her eyes suspiciously and tried to keep the accusation from her voice. "What do you mean you 'never meant to bring us here'?" She glanced at Lilly, whose blue eyes bulged and mouth hung open wide as she absorbed their surroundings. Sarah looked back to the girl.

The redhead chewed on her lip and hesitated, which only piqued Sarah's curiosity and suspicion. "Um, well . . . it was an accident," she repeated, the words suddenly coming out in a rush again. "The professor and I are the only ones from our time who have been here, and we didn't think it could work like that. It never should have pulled anyone back this far, especially not someone who didn't have the transporter with them."

Sarah held up a hand to stop any further explanation. She was baffled enough without the girl's jumbled words adding to her confusion. "Slow down; you're not making sense. Are you saying this is your doing?" She couldn't keep the disbelief from her tone as she motioned to their surroundings with an exaggerated gesture. How did the girl expect her to take in all this?

The redhead inhaled a calming breath through her nose and said more slowly, "I was just trying to tell you that there's—"

Sarah jumped as a flock of grey and brown birds abruptly took flight from their perches among the trees, interrupting the girl's explanation as they scattered in the air with warning calls to one another. The sound raised the hairs on Sarah's arms.

"This way," someone suddenly called through the trees. Sarah turned her head away from the fleeing birds and focused on the rustling branches just past the clearing. The sound of approaching horses sounded like thunder in the quiet woods.

"We have to hide," the girl whispered urgently, her wide green eyes darting about the foliage.

"What? Why?" Sarah asked, her own eyes roaming the thickness surrounding them. Her stomach began to churn at the thought that these riders might pose some kind of threat—at least enough to cause the girl fear.

"There's no time," the girl hissed between her clenched teeth. "Quick! Over here." She ducked down and dashed to the edge of the clearing opposite the approaching horses, looking like a strange, long-necked bird with her awkward gait. She listened for a moment to the men's shouts, then frantically motioned for them to follow.

What other choice was there?

With only a brief hesitation, Sarah turned around and grabbed Lilly, who was still frozen in disbelief and confusion, and dashed toward the tree line. She practically had to drag her sibling through the dirt and fallen leaves that littered the ground.

Even in her panic, Sarah couldn't help feeling amazed. A few minutes ago, she'd been ready to throw Lilly out of her room for seeking company during a thunderstorm, and now her only thought was to get her younger sister to safety. She could feel the adrenaline pumping through her veins as she dove toward the bush the girl had disappeared behind. Lilly remained in the open, dumbstruck. Sarah snatched her hand and yanked her down beside them just as six large horses appeared in the clearing.

Chapter Three

"Should we run?" Sarah whispered from her crouched position behind the bush. Her voice sounded breathless after their mad dash for cover, and she shifted uncomfortably on her hands and knees to move away from the jagged rock that was digging into her leg. She stared at the rock, feeling uneasy as she contemplated whether the pain felt too real for this to be a dream. *If this isn't some concussion-induced delusion,* she thought with growing apprehension, *then we're in serious trouble.*

The girl pressed a finger to her lips to silence her.

Please, Lord, Sarah prayed silently, a sickening feeling turning her stomach to knots. *Let us not be in any danger. I'll never forgive myself if something happens to Lilly.* She didn't always get along with her sister, but she still loved her and was responsible for her well-being.

Sarah peered anxiously through the leaves and branches to the men on horseback. The largest of the riders stretched in his saddle, his ample abdomen bulging over his belt as he extended his arms over his head. Sarah felt brief pity for the poor horse beneath him. Then she took note of the large sword attached to the man's belt and swallowed hard.

"Well," the man said, his gruff, raspy voice matching his scruffy appearance. "I don't see her anywhere, do you?"

The man riding beside him snickered. The two other men seemed to be made of stone as they stared at the trees, their faces expressionless. The fifth rider was older, with dark hair graying around the temples that made him appear wiser than the rest of them. He stared at the first man, sitting up straighter in his saddle as he spoke. His voice was soothing, as if he were talking to a child.

"I know she came this way, sir. We must have just missed her. If we keep following the trail—"

"Thomas," the large man interrupted, slashing his hand through the air to silence him. He looked annoyed that he should be talked to in such a condescending manner. "Maybe you should just accept the fact that your skills are not what they used to be."

Thomas's look remained impassive, and his tone didn't change. "Maybe if you did not insist that you knew a short cut at every bend, or if you did not have to rest every hour when your backside gets saddle-sore, Gabriel, then maybe we—"

"That's Captain Dunlivey to you," the man shot back, his face looking like a plump tomato as it reddened. "And maybe you're just losing your skill in your old age! If the king didn't value your tracking ability, then I would have—"

He stopped mid-sentence and gasped for air, his face reddening with every passing second as he struggled to breathe in his state of rage.

"Are you all right, sir?" the man next to him asked, looking worried. The rest of the riders appeared uninterested in the man's plight.

"I'm fine, John" Dunlivey snapped when at last he was able to catch his breath.

A small smile stretched across Thomas's mouth. "Don't get so worked up about it, Gabriel," he said in that same soothing voice. "I do not see the threat she poses; she is only a girl."

"Exactly!" Dunlivey cried, his face turning crimson again in his obvious frustration. "She's just a girl. How difficult can it be to find her? And if you don't see the threat that witch poses, then you shouldn't be here!" He glared at the older man as though daring him to defy his authority.

All right, this is getting ridiculous, Sarah thought as she stared at the group. She wondered when she was going to wake up from this psychotic, albeit realistic, dream. She tried to ignore the uncomfortable feeling of dried pine needles and twigs beneath her legs that caused her to question this theory. Believing this was a dream was the only thing holding her sanity together; if she began to believe that it was real, she was sure to panic.

"But she is merely a child," Thomas continued, clearly unaffected by the glare with which Dunlivey was trying to spear him. "I do not see how she can be such a serious threat against the kingdom."

"Just because she is a child does not mean she can go around practicing her witchery. What happens if the people find out that the royal guard made an exception because of her age? There will be ruffians running about the streets causing trouble for us at every turn!"

Thomas shook his head but remained silent, obviously deciding it was futile to argue with the crazed man.

Sarah gazed nervously at Lilly out of the corner of her eye. The girl appeared to be completely baffled by their current circumstances, her mouth still hanging open as far as it had been earlier. Sarah's eyes shifted to their companion, who was glaring at the heavy man, looking like she might jump out of their hiding place and push him right off his horse at any moment.

"Let's not get ahead of ourselves," a deep voice said. Sarah started at the sound. She hadn't paid any attention to the hooded figure before now. In fact, she had hardly even noticed the sixth rider until he spoke, his dark green cloak allowing him to blend in with the trees and bushes behind him. She had been so distracted by the seriously disturbed Dunlivey that she hadn't taken notice of much else. But now that she'd seen him, she could only stare.

Robin Hood.

Everything about him caused her to think of her favorite masked hero from the movies and childhood storybooks. The dark green cloak that provided camouflage against the foliage, the large hood that was pulled forward so that it dipped down over his head and caused only blackness where his face should have been, the arrows in the pouch slung over his back. And the bow! He even had a bow grasped in his right hand, which rested lightly against his horse's side. Everything simply screamed Robin Hood.

Sarah had to squelch the untimely giggle that tried to bubble out of her mouth. Her parents had always said she found humor in the oddest of circumstances. That had gotten her into trouble numerous times; more than once, she had inadvertently insulted someone by allowing one or two giggles to escape her lips when she should have been serious.

She struggled to compose herself. This was one of those times when she needed to remain serious. If she laughed and revealed their hiding place, who knows what would happen? Thoughts of the potential danger sobered her, and she put away her twelve-year-old fantasies of Robin Hood rescuing her in a forest much like this one.

"We need to have solid evidence before we convict her of anything, let alone witchery." The hooded man's voice pulled Sarah from her wandering thoughts, and her eyes focused on him once more.

" *'Solid evidence,'* " Dunlivey said in a mocking voice that didn't come close to sounding like Robin's melodiously deep one. "I don't need solid evidence. I am the captain of the guard and—"

"*Temporary* captain of the guard," he corrected. "When the captain is over his illness, he will lead the guard once more. We should not have to wait long, considering the castle physician said his health has greatly improved." He leaned forward and crossed his arms, casually resting them against the black stallion's neck, his bow still in hand. Sarah noticed that he never relaxed his grip on it.

"And when he returns," he continued, "we will just see what he thinks about your little crusade after a young girl none of us has ever seen, and whom you claim is a witch. Now, what do you think he will say to that?"

For the first time since entering the clearing, the two stoic guards cracked a smile; Sarah thought one of them might have coughed to cover his laugh.

Dunlivey's face turned red again, and Sarah wondered if he would have a heart attack on the spot.

"I saw her!" he cried, leaning threateningly toward Robin. "She was wearing a white dress, she has long red hair—yes, yes, it was red!" It sounded like he was convincing himself as much as the others that she was real. "And she had something on her wrist. It was shiny and thin and black. One minute there was no one around, and then she appeared out of nowhere!" He waved his hands wildly in the air as he described the girl, pausing to take a breath. Out of the corner of her eye, Sarah saw the girl they were hiding with slowly put a hand over her wrist.

The Robin Hood man straightened in his saddle and grabbed the reins with both hands.

"Well, at least now we have a description," he said, sounding like it didn't make a difference anyway. "I suppose we should split up, and if all is as you say it is, we will find her and straighten this out."

Without another word, he pulled on the reins and turned his horse around. Even atop his large mount, he seemed stealthy as he rode into the thickness of trees, disappearing from sight within seconds. Thomas followed silently, and the other two men galloped through the trees to the right of the direction the others had gone, leaving Dunlivey and John alone in the clearing.

"Which way, Captain?" John asked, sounding like a loyal dog awaiting his master's command.

"How dare he," Dunlivey hissed, ignoring the other man as though he had not spoken. "I do not understand why the prince even asked him to come along. I never expected the prince to send him as well as the old man." He snorted, running a gloved hand through his thinning hair.

John appeared to be at a loss as to how he should handle the ranting man.

Dunlivey rolled his eyes. "Fine. Let's go this way." He pointed to the bushes in the opposite direction the hooded man and Thomas had gone.

When the sound of their retreat could no longer be heard, Sarah released the breath she hadn't realized she'd been holding. Turning to their companion, she took on an authoritative tone and said, "I think you have some explaining to do."

Chapter Four

The girl paled slightly. Sarah felt pity on her and decided to go easy. She asked the first question that came to mind.

"What's your name?"

The girl appeared relieved that the question was so easy to answer. "Karen Ashmore," she answered.

"Okay, and who were they?" Sarah asked, motioning toward the empty clearing.

Karen's eyes darted about the forest. "I'll answer all of your questions the best I can, but we have to move before they circle back around, otherwise we might not have a chance at losing them in the forest." She paused and smiled grimly. "We're not out of the woods yet."

Her words caused Sarah to stiffen. Normally a pun like that might have made her chuckle, but this time it was true enough to squelch her humor. She nodded silently and stood.

Karen motioned for them to follow her as she made her way deeper into the forest, pushing limbs and leaves out of her path as she went. Sarah silently encouraged Lilly to go in front of her with a nod of her head. She made sure that she trailed behind the two, wanting to keep an eye on her sister and their mysterious trail-blazing guide.

"Are you going to answer my question?" she asked impatiently, her voice louder than she intended. Karen stopped abruptly and raised a hand to silence her. Sarah pinched her lips together and silently reprimanded herself for being so careless.

Karen's voice was quiet when she spoke. "Those men are the castle guard. Well, four of them, at least. The older man, Thomas, is a tracker."

"A tracker?" Sarah asked, unfamiliar with the term. Karen resumed walking, and the two siblings scrambled to keep up with her hurried pace.

"A specialized hunter. He follows people," Karen answered over her shoulder. "He's able to pick up on a trail, hair, clothing, prints in the ground, anything, and follow it until he finds whatever he's looking for. Anyway, he's extremely good at what he does and has served the king well for many years."

"How long?" Sarah asked, her curiosity getting the better of her.

Karen thought for a moment before answering. "I heard that he started working for the king when he was twenty, so I would say he's been tracking for about twenty years or so. I'm not exactly sure, but that sounds about right. King Josiah truly values him, and the prince must have insisted

Thomas go along on the search while his father is unable to attend to the kingdom."

"Why is that?" Lilly asked, speaking for the first time since they had arrived in this strange place. The sound of her voice surprised Sarah. Karen glanced back at the younger girl briefly before turning her eyes back to the trees ahead.

"The king has been ill, and very few people have been allowed to see him—only the doctor and the king's brother, Cadius. The doctor isn't sure what's wrong with him, so he won't even let the queen and prince see him until he can diagnose his illness. If it's contagious, they don't want the entire royal family bed ridden all at once.

"He's been sick for quite some time and is only getting worse, so the prince has had to take over his duties. He's only twenty-three; I can't imagine how much pressure there must be on his shoulders. The king was always in good health, and everybody expected him to rule for many more years. It must have been a shock for the prince to have so much responsibility all of a sudden."

She stopped and turned to face them so abruptly that Sarah almost bumped into her. Karen lowered her voice and leaned closer, a conspiratorial look in her eyes. "You know what I think? I think the king's brother is poisoning him."

Sarah looked at her and tried to determine whether she was joking. Karen's stare never wavered, and her green eyes remained serious. Sarah cleared her throat and glanced around nervously, feeling uncomfortable beneath Karen's intense gaze.

"Why would he try to kill his own brother?" she finally asked.

"The king is five years younger than his brother, who's already in his sixties and the rightful heir to the throne. When their father passed away, Cadius was terribly ill with typhoid and no one knew if he would recover. Even though he was the rightful heir to the throne, they made Josiah king. They needed someone to rule, and it looked like Cadius wouldn't make it." She shrugged.

"It took him three more months to recover and even longer to get back his strength, but by then Josiah had already been king for long enough that nothing could be done—not that anyone would do anything about it. The people loved him; they still do. In that short time before Cadius got well, King Josiah had already done so many good things that the people didn't want a different king.

Karen's expressive eyes shone with the intensity of the story. "Could you imagine how that would make Cadius feel? And now, thirty-some years later, a strong, healthy king suddenly becomes ill after dinner one night. Don't you think that Cadius could have just gotten fed up with the circumstances and is now trying to get rid of him so he can take the crown?"

"Well, it does make sense," Sarah mumbled. She had actually gotten caught up in the story. "It just doesn't make sense, though," she continued. "What about the prince? Wouldn't he be next in line?"

What am I saying? Why am I encouraging Karen's theory? Sarah shook her head, deciding that this was no longer a dream; it was just some kind of incredibly realistic delusion brought about by stress. She imagined she'd be in a psych ward by the end of the week. She thought wryly that at least if she fell off her bed in a psych ward, she would have a nice padded floor to land on.

They resumed their progress, and Karen held back a tree branch to let them pass. She released her hold, and the limb snapped back, releasing a shower of leaves that fluttered to the forest floor.

"I'm sure Cadius will deal with the little issue of the prince, as well," Karen said. "Do you have any more questions?"

"What was Robi—" Sarah caught herself and tried again. "Who was the man who wasn't a part of the guard? You know, the guy with the hood?"

Karen grinned slowly. "They call him the Green Shadow, or just the Shadow, since some people argue that shadows can't be green." She shook her head slightly at the absurdity of the argument and then continued. "He's a good guy, goes around helping people, appearing out of nowhere in the nick of time. No one knows who he is, though—or those who know his identity are loyal enough to keep it a secret.

"Some people want him dead because he could thwart them someday. And believe me, people have tried to stop him. But they say he can evade anything—sword, dagger, arrow—almost as if he weren't real. That's why they call him the Shadow; he always slips away unharmed, just like an illusion."

Sarah caught sight of the redhead's face and thought that she looked completely engrossed in her own story.

Karen went on. "Some of his followers speculate that he was trained in fighting as a weapon for those who control him, since he can supposedly drop an armed man in combat with only his bare hands like that—" she snapped her fingers in the air, and Sarah jumped at the sound. Karen grinned good-humoredly. "But that sounds a little farfetched to me. I do believe he's an amazing shot, though. Those who've seen him shoot an arrow say he never misses."

Just like Robin Hood, Sarah inwardly confirmed with satisfaction, trying to hide her grin. Her mirth faded, though, as she thought about what Dunlivey had said earlier.

Karen eyed her warily. "There's more, isn't there?"

Sarah nodded and bit her lip, unsure if she should even ask her next question. She glanced at Lilly to see if she was paying attention to their conversation; the girl's mind was obviously elsewhere as she stared in awe at their surroundings. Sarah lowered her voice.

"It's you they were talking about, isn't it? Are you really what they say you are?"

Karen shook her head vehemently from side to side, her eyes wide at the mere thought of it. "No! Well, I mean, yes, he was talking about me. But I'm not a witch. Dunlivey saw me use my watch a couple of days ago and freaked out. He tried to capture me, but I was able to escape, though I lost track of the professor because we had to split up. I've been trying to find him ever since."

"The professor?" Sarah asked, squinting her left eye in confusion as she sometimes did when something baffled her.

Karen opened her mouth to speak, then snapped it closed so fast Sarah heard her teeth smack together.

"Someone's coming. Quick!"

Without looking behind her to make sure they followed, Karen darted ahead, her red hair swinging behind her as she fled. Sarah's heartbeat quickened at the girl's reaction to the noise. The two sisters looked at each other and then ran to catch up. Lilly got a head start before Sarah could even react. Then they were sprinting through the forest once again.

As they ran, Sarah listened intently for the sound of approaching horses or shouts coming from the guards, but she didn't hear anything other than the crunching of leaves and twigs beneath her own feet. She was about to call out to Karen that they could stop for a while when her foot caught on an exposed root. She stumbled, and a shriek lodged itself in her throat as she plummeted, face-first, toward the ground. She instinctively put her hands in front of her to cushion her fall and landed with a thud. The leaves she stirred up in her landing settled around her in a shower of gold and brown. She quickly lifted her head off the ground and searched for any sign of Karen or Lilly, but she didn't see them anywhere.

She groaned as she rolled off of the arm that had gotten caught under her in the fall. The wind had been knocked out of her, and she lay on her back helplessly as she worked on breathing normally. She tried not to panic. She could find them if she needed to, she assured herself. She would search for clues, track them down, and find them. If that man, Thomas, could hunt down thieves who were trying to cover their tracks, certainly she could find her sister and their helpful, albeit jumpy, companion as they carelessly tromped through the woods. She wouldn't be left behind in a strange forest. She didn't even want to consider it.

Sarah stared at the canopy of trees above her as she lay on her back, her breath slowly returning to her. Was it her imagination, or was it getting darker? She resisted the nearly overpowering urge to scream for help and slowly brought herself up to a sitting position. She busied herself with brushing the dirt and leaves off the front of her shirt and jeans. While she was picking the twigs and greenery out of her hair, she noticed that the leaves around her stirred slightly. Her hand slowly dropped to her side.

She stared at the muscular black legs and felt the beast's warm breath on her face. Fear raced through her. She stiffened, and an involuntary shudder slithered up her spine. Her pulse quickened as her gaze traveled over the sleek legs and broad chest of the horse, and finally into the darkness that was the face of the Shadow.

Chapter Five

They stared at each other for a long moment. Sarah had to remind herself to breathe as the initial shock began to fade, though her pulse continued to race as she stared up at him from her position on the ground. The silence stretched on, and she swallowed against the sudden dryness in her throat. If she made a run for it now, she might have enough of a head start to lose him in the deepest parts of the forest.

As she began to form a plan in her head, Sarah realized how absurd it sounded. Even if she did manage to rise clumsily to her feet and run into the woods, she doubted that she would get even a few feet before he could practice his finely tuned archery skills on her. Karen had said he was trained to kill, and Sarah prayed he hadn't gotten his license just yet.

A bush to her right rustled. Sudden adrenaline raced through her veins and allowed her jump to her feet in record time, though she winced as pain coursed through her left arm. A small squirrel scurried out of the bush and up a tree, hurrying out of sight. Sarah chastised herself for being so excitable and willed her heartbeat to return to normal.

She rotated her shoulder slowly and gently massaged her sore arm. From her experience as an active child with numerous broken bones and a dislocated shoulder, she could tell it wasn't broken or sprained. But she knew she would be in pain for the rest of the day and wake up with some nasty bruises tomorrow.

"Are you all right?" the Shadow asked in a deep voice that startled her.

Sarah directed her attention back to him and shivered. She didn't like the fact that she was unable see his face. She tried to anticipate his next move.

As if sensing her thoughts, he leaned forward in his saddle. She took a frightened step back to put more distance between them.

"I am not going to hurt you." His soothing voice calmed her frayed nerves slightly, but she refused to let her guard down just yet. "What are you doing in the forest alone this time of day?"

"I–I wasn't alone," she said, trying to stop the tears that threatened to spill over at the reminder that she was alone now. She clenched her jaw to quiet the chattering of her teeth. She hadn't even realized she was cold, but her jeans, tennis shoes, and T-shirt were no longer appropriate for the rapidly dropping temperature. She hugged her arms close to her side to stave off the chill of evening. Her muscles tensed as she tried to keep herself from shivering.

The man suddenly stiffened in his saddle, and Sarah wondered for a moment what had caused him alarm. Then she heard it. She spun in the direction of the sound of crunching leaves and low, murmuring voices heading their way.

Sarah's heart sped up, and her thoughts immediately turned to Lilly. What would happen to her only sibling if she was captured or killed? How would the young girl fend for herself in this foreign place? Sarah knew she had to find a way out before it was too late for both of them. She turned back to the man on horseback, her only hope.

"Please," she whispered desperately, her blue eyes wide and pleading.

She could not see his eyes but knew he stared at her silently for a moment, appearing to contemplate her request. Leaning toward her again, he spoke in his low voice. "You are not the one they are looking for."

His voice was so quiet that she almost didn't catch his words. He sat up straighter and turned his head in the direction of the approaching men. "You need to go now before they catch you. I will hold them until you are safe."

Sarah could only stare at him, too surprised to move. He was actually going to help her, a stranger? Her overactive imagination took over, telling her that he had agreed far too easily. She'd seen the movies: the so-called hero would allow the maiden to leave, but before she was able to seek shelter, he would sell her out for the right price, tell the wrong people, and she'd be dead within the hour.

Among these ridiculous thoughts that raced through her head—the products of too much time spent watching spy movies—one voice spoke clearly. It was merely a whisper.

Go.

She was startled by the sudden thought and wondered if she'd heard right. God certainly wouldn't want her to risk her life and turn her back on a potential assassin, would He? Then again, her only other option was to wait for the guards to find her and pray they wouldn't mistake her for the girl they were hunting. She knew there was no arguing with the owner of that voice, and she took a deep breath to steady her nerves.

"Thank you," she said quietly, praying the man would keep his word and allow her to escape.

"All in a day's work." If she hadn't known better, she'd have thought she detected a hint of amusement in his voice. "I will tell them you went in the opposite direction. Now go; the sun is setting and you will not have much time."

Sarah nodded and forced herself to move before someone found them together. Running as fast as she could away from the approaching guards, she dodged trees and swatted branches aside, making her way further into the thicket and away from danger. She waited several moments before giving in to the temptation to look behind her. Through the thickness of branches and leaves, she could still make out the form of the Shadow.

And he was still watching her.

She quickly spun back around, picking up her pace. She needed to find Lilly and Karen and get out of there as fast as possible.

CRWSO

He watched as the woman dressed like a man fled. When she turned her head to look back at him, he didn't turn away in embarrassment but stared boldly back at her. She seemed flustered at his gaze and tripped over something in her haste to leave.

The other guards were nearly upon him, and he needed to give them some wrong directions before they picked up her trail. Even as he turned his horse around and headed deeper into the woods, he knew he wouldn't be able to get a certain clumsy brunette off his mind for the rest of the day.

CRWSO

Sarah stumbled through the forest in exhaustion. She'd been running for several minutes, and she felt like she was getting nowhere. Every tree and bush looked the same, and she was beginning to wonder if she was ever going to find her way out of this mess. The sun dipped closer and closer to the tops of the trees, seeming to descend a little farther each time her feet hit the ground, reminding her that she didn't have much time.

Please let me find them, she pleaded silently. She was trying to avoid becoming hysterical when she heard a noise. She froze in her tracks, her breath catching in her chest. Terror filled her, feeling as though an invisible hand were choking the air from her.

"Psst, Sarah, over here!"

Sarah jerked her head toward the sound of her sister's voice. Her breath released in a rush when she saw Karen and Lilly crouched behind a bush, motioning her over. Sarah looked around at the trees before diving behind the bush.

"We thought we'd lost you," Karen said, looking worried.

"We turned around and you were gone!" Lilly's face had paled and she looked ready to cry.

"I'm fine," Sarah said, panting. She was still winded from her run. "I just tripped and got a little disoriented." She decided to leave out the part about her encounter with the Shadow.

"Do you need to rest a moment before we move again?" Karen asked. By the way her eyes shifted uneasily across the trees, Sarah could tell she wanted to keep moving.

Sarah's arm still ached from her fall, and a rest would certainly help clear her mind and make her more alert, but she shook her head. "No. We need to keep going."

Karen looked relieved and stood quickly. Sarah and Lilly dutifully followed her through the forest again, being careful to stick together as the evening light faded. They came to a well-beaten path just as the sun disappeared behind the trees and turned the horizon a muted pink.

"Is it safe to follow a trail?" Sarah asked uncertainly.

Karen nodded. "It's too dark for us to be conspicuous, and besides, this is the only way to get to where we're going. The trees are too thick in this part of the woods."

Sarah felt like asking where they were headed, but she decided it was best to keep her mouth shut. They would be there soon enough, and maybe then she could get some answers to her questions.

CRSO

A little over an hour later, Karen slowed her pace, then stopped. Placing her hands on her hips, she smiled. "This is it."

At first Sarah didn't know what she was referring to. She squinted through the darkness and was just able to make out the shape of a house in the middle of a grassy field a few hundred feet in front of them. The way she was feeling, that small distance might as well have been the hike to the top of Everest.

"We'll be there soon enough." Without allowing them a chance to catch their breath, Karen sprinted off toward the dark house. They had no choice but to follow.

Lilly groaned in protest, and Sarah grabbed her hand.

"Come on," she muttered, pulling her reluctant sister along. As they neared the house, Sarah noticed a faint glow coming from one of the upstairs rooms. The thought of a warm bed and something to eat caused her to walk a little faster. She was surprised when Karen veered off the path to the house and made her way to the barn behind the main building instead.

Lilly glanced at Sarah in confusion. Sarah shrugged in response to the younger girl's unspoken question.

Swinging the barn door open, Karen motioned for them to follow her inside. Lilly's grip on her hand tightened as they stepped into the barn, and Karen quickly closed the door behind them, cutting off the dim light from the moon and enveloping them in complete darkness.

Chapter Six

Lilly began to whimper, and Sarah inwardly groaned. She could hear their forest guide fumbling around in the darkness. There was a faint clicking noise, and a small flame illuminated the outline of a lantern. Karen lit the wick inside. The light threw long shadows on the wooden floor and only served to illuminate a small circle around them, fading away as the darkness overcame it in the deeper recesses of the barn. Karen leaned over and quickly tucked something into her boot.

"Can't you just turn on the lights?" Lilly asked, shivering against Sarah's side. Sarah was watching Karen closely and thought she looked taken aback by the innocent question, but she quickly schooled her features and shook her head.

"There's no electricity in this ti—" She paused, then started again. "It's a barn. There's no electricity in here. But don't worry. I made a bunch of lanterns that we can light tonight. I always keep lots of blankets out here, too, just in case. And—"

"In case of what?" Sarah asked, noting that Karen appeared slightly flustered and seemed to be trying to get them to settle down for the night without any time for argument.

"Well, um, some nights I stay out here when I don't want to wake the house by coming in late."

Sarah could tell there was more to it than she let on, but she decided to let it go—for now.

"It's getting really late, and we should probably head to bed." Karen faked a yawn, stretching her arms overhead in what Sarah thought to be an overly exaggerated gesture. Karen let her arms fall to her side and eyed the two siblings from head to foot, looking dissatisfied with their appearance.

Her face suddenly brightened in the dim light. "I have some clothes you can borrow for the night. Do any of you have to use the facilities before we go down, though?"

Lilly nodded. "Where's the bathroom?" she asked, peering around the dark barn.

"Um, outside," Karen said cryptically, avoiding eye contact with either of them as she shuffled her feet. It took Sarah a moment to realize exactly what she was talking about. She heaved a frustrated sigh and motioned over her shoulder for her sister to follow.

Karen ran ahead of them to hold the large door open.

"Can we at least have a lantern?" Sarah asked.

Karen shook her head. "We can't risk drawing attention to ourselves by taking the light outside. We're more vulnerable at night."

"Great," Sarah mumbled as they made their way outside. Thankfully, the overcast sky hadn't decided to cover the moon completely in its eagerness to make it feel like autumn. When her eyes adjusted to the pale light outside, she was able to spot a bush large and full enough to allow them some privacy. When she walked up to it and waited, Lilly gaped at her with wide eyes.

"You've got to be kidding me." She wrinkled her nose in disgust.

When Sarah didn't answer, the younger Matthews girl timidly walked over to the bush and ducked behind it. She appeared a few minutes later, her dainty nose still wrinkled. Sarah quickly took her turn and emerged from behind the bush, chewing on her lower lip. She probably should have made sure those leaves weren't poison oak or poison ivy before they both used them. Not like she would be able to tell anyway; she had failed wilderness training. Twice.

They walked silently back to the barn and entered through the open door. Karen had lit several more lanterns and spaced them out on the floor to brighten the large room. They found her fumbling around in a large weathered wood trunk, her upper body completely hidden in the depths of the large chest. She emerged holding two plain brown dresses and a victorious smile.

"These are for you." She handed a dress to each one. "You can use the empty stalls to put them on." She turned back to the trunk, and her head disappeared inside once more.

Sarah clenched her jaw to keep from telling her where she'd rather put the dresses. Karen's nonchalant tone annoyed her. She worked on masking her irritation as she made sure that Lilly was set up in an empty stall, then went to find one of her own.

Two of the stalls held several goats, and she wisely decided to leave them alone. She glanced inside a few empty stalls as she passed them. Her curiosity about what other animals would be their companions that night propelled her forward.

She went over to the other side and spotted a brown and black dog in the first stall there. Six young puppies vied for their exhausted mother's attention all at once, causing Sarah to smile as she moved onward. She stopped when she reached the last pens on that side. Two large horses stared back at her, though the golden mare in the last stall simply nibbled at her hay, disinterested in the newcomer.

Sarah had been fascinated with horses since she was a young girl, and that fascination had grown to love over the years that followed. Simply seeing the brown and gold beauties caused her to wonder what it would be like to ride one of them, feeling the wind in her hair, the pounding of the horse's hooves on the hard earth beneath her.

There was just one problem: she'd never actually had a successful riding experience. Though she loved to stroke a soft coat and run her fingers through a silky mane, her fear of actually climbing onto the large animal had kept her from riding, especially after the accident.

Lilly's stall door opened, and Sarah dashed into one of the empty enclosures on the opposite side. She hadn't realized how long she'd taken inspecting the animals. She removed her tennis shoes and quickly changed out of her jeans and T-shirt. She tossed her clothes over the side of the stall to keep them out of the hay and caught sight of the yellowing bruise that was beginning to make its appearance on her arm.

Now that the adrenaline had faded, she could feel the ache in her arm and gingerly touched the discolored skin, wincing in pain. She quickly pulled the soft dress over her head to cover the mark; she didn't want to cause Lilly unnecessary worry. The dress was a little snug around her hips, but Karen was only a few inches shorter than Sarah, so the length was no problem at all.

Sarah picked up her clothes and shoes and made her way out of the stall in her socks. Lilly was standing behind Karen, who was still half inside the chest. She was holding large fleece blankets in her arms, the stack nearly covering head. The dress pooled on the ground around the younger girl's feet. Sarah set her clothes down in the corner and took the quilts into her own arms, relieving her sister of the burden. Lilly's face relaxed in relief.

"I think that's all we need for tonight," Karen said as she emerged from the trunk. She closed the lid before turning around. "We can set them up over here." She walked over to a large stack of hay. Karen took the blankets and laid one over the other, creating a thick padding that nearly covered the fresh hay. She set two blankets aside for them to use in the night and smiled.

"That should do. If you need anything, just let me know. My bed is up in the loft."

Lilly's eyelids drooped in exhaustion. She looked ready to drop at any moment.

"Come on," Sarah whispered in her ear. "Let's get you into bed." She helped the younger girl onto the haystack and spread the remaining blankets over her. Karen blew out all of the lanterns but two. She left one on the floor near the girls and carried the other light up the ladder to the loft. Sarah crawled in beside Lilly, surprised at how comfortable the makeshift bed was. She could feel her aching muscles relax, the tiring day lying heavy upon her. But she couldn't fall asleep. Not yet.

"Sarah?" Lilly whispered tiredly. Sarah turned her head to the side to see the outline of Lilly's profile in the darkness. She couldn't make out her sister's expression, but she could tell by the sound of Lilly's voice that the younger girl was already half-asleep.

"What is it?" Sarah whispered back, propping herself up on her elbow to better see her sister's face.

"Can we go home now?" Lilly's mumbled words hung in the darkness for several long moments, and she sounded like she was fading quickly into sleep.

Sarah rolled slowly onto her back and stared up at the outline of the rafters. She steadied her voice before she spoke, knowing the younger girl would be afraid if she showed fear. "Not just yet, kiddo." Lilly settled deeper into the covers to get more comfortable. Sarah's next words were more of a promise to herself in the shadows of the barn; they were almost indiscernible as she whispered them to the darkness. "But soon."

CR&SO

She waited until the sound of Lilly's breathing became rhythmic. She didn't have to wait long. Sarah tried to make as little noise as possible as she crept out of bed, retrieved the lantern beside the haystack, and tiptoed over to the ladder that led to the loft. She looked up the length of the rungs, wondering how exactly she was going to manage the lantern while she climbed to the top. She placed her left foot on the lowest rung and began her awkward ascent. Using her sore arm to hold the lantern and the other to pull herself further up on the rickety old ladder took more talent than she had originally guessed.

When at last she reached the top, she hoisted herself into the loft, giving a sigh of relief that she hadn't fallen backward and broken something—namely an arm or a leg. Leaving the lantern on the floor, she slowly walked over to where Karen sat looking out a large cutout in the side of the barn. It was positioned three or so feet above the floor and seemed to be used as a window.

Karen's body was turned away from her, but the glow from the lantern gave enough light for Sarah to see the girl's profile. She appeared to be concentrating very hard on something and didn't notice her approach. Sarah took another step forward, and the board beneath her feet creaked noisily. Karen whipped her head around at the sound, appearing both surprised and frightened.

"What are you doing up?" she whispered, her expression relaxing when she realized who it was. Sarah searched her face for some sign of apprehension or anger, but Karen's expression appeared open.

"I couldn't sleep," Sarah said. She made sure to keep her voice low, though she doubted that an armored truck busting through the side of the building would have woken Lilly. That girl could sleep through just about anything, including her alarm every morning.

Karen patted the empty space beside her. Sarah sat down, trying to get her thoughts in order so that they didn't come spilling out at once.

"Did you need anything?" Karen asked when the silence stretched on.

Sarah sucked in a deep breath for courage and nodded. "An explanation."

Chapter Seven

Sarah didn't quite know where to begin. She had a hundred questions floating through her head. The first one that came out was, "Where are we?"

She couldn't be sure in the dim light, but she thought she saw Karen wince at the question.

"Um, what do you mean exactly?"

"I mean, whose barn is this?"

"Oh," Karen said slowly. Her look became slightly guarded. "A couple named Sam and Ruth Jones own this property. They have three kids, Joshua, Leah, and Seth." The way her voice softened when she said the last name stirred Sarah's curiosity, but she pushed it away. That question could wait for another time.

"Do they mind that we just took up residence in their barn without asking?" Sarah asked, biting her lower lip and wondering what the odds were that Sam Jones owned a shotgun. Maybe he would tie them up and hang them by their toes on the porch as a souvenir. Wasn't that what hunters did to deer? Maybe they did the same to trespassers here.

"Oh, no. Not at all." Karen's eyes widened innocently. "They're like family to me. I stay here whenever I visit."

"Okay," Sarah said slowly, her next question already forming in her mind. "How did we get here?"

Karen appeared confused. "Well, there's a path once you exit the forest. It leads pretty much straight h—"

"No, no. That's not what I meant. I mean, how did we get here?" She motioned around the enclosure with a sweep of her hand. "I mean, we're obviously not in Kansas anymore."

Her quip fell flat. Karen paled and wouldn't look Sarah in the eye. It took a moment for her to answer.

"This is going to sound crazy," Karen whispered, shaking her head. She looked at Sarah. "How much do you want to know?"

"Everything," Sarah said simply. "From the very beginning."

"That might take a while." Sarah raised her brow and gave Karen a look that said she had all the time in the world. Karen inhaled a shaky breath.

"Well, my parents died in a car accident when I was eleven," she began slowly. "Thankfully, a good friend of my parents, Charles Ashmore, came to my rescue. He was a physics professor at the college that my dad went to and later taught at. Anyway, he adopted me, and I went to live with him. He's the one who led me to the Lord." Tears filled her eyes, and Sarah smiled slightly at this insight. At least they shared the same faith.

It was a moment before Karen spoke again, her voice growing steadier as she continued in her explanation. "That was eight years ago. Over that time, the professor has been working on a project that I've been assisting him with. We worked on it day and night for years. Finally, we actually made it work!"

"Made what work?" Sarah asked incredulously.

"The time machine." Karen's eyes darted about the barn as though the walls would share her secret. She leaned closer, and Sarah raised a brow. "We figured out a way to actually travel through time."

She must have noticed Sarah's astounded expression because she went on hurriedly. "It sounds crazy, I know. I thought so too when he first introduced me to his theories and ideas. But the two of us tested the hypothesis and—" She halted midsentence and shook her head. "That's just a bunch of information that I can leave out for you.

"Anyway, it took several years, but we eventually created a large machine in our basement. It hooked up to a super-powered generator that could light up all of Minneapolis. We tested it several times, placing our subject inside the machine. Though our test subjects got to their destination completely, they . . . well . . . let's just say they never came back in one piece."

Sarah's mouth fell open in shock. Karen's green eyes widened.

"Don't worry. We didn't use any living thing until it was stabilized." She shook her head. "Well, except for a guinea pig we sent in the earlier stages of development. We never saw him again."

She raised her hands in front of her at Sarah's expression of disbelief as if to ward off her disapproval. "But we're positive he got there okay. Anyway, after we fixed the machine, we realized that all of the monitors and large tools we had strapped to the subjects to keep track of them were weighing them down. Sometimes they didn't even make it to their destination because they were too heavy. This was the biggest problem, since it trapped them . . ."

She appeared to search for the right words. Her hand motions had become more pronounced and exaggerated as she spoke, growing even more animated as her explanation went on.

"Well, they got stuck in a sort of limbo—not here, not there. So we had to find a way to concentrate all of the power from the machine and energy source"—she cupped her hands together as though crumpling a heavy piece of trash—"and most of the data that we had stored on the monitors into something small enough to fit in your pocket . . . or on your wrist."

She grinned conspiratorially as she rolled up her sleeve and extended her arm toward Sarah. A square watch was strapped to her wrist by a piece

27

of sleek black leather. The dark glass of the face reflected the dim light from the lantern. There weren't any buttons or dials that were visible, only a small silver knob on the side; it looked like any other watch.

"At first," Karen continued, her green eyes glowing, "we could only travel to different cities within a certain range, but time was still the same. That was one of the large problems that we encountered. We didn't just want to make travel faster and easier; we wanted to find a way to travel back in time. And finally, we did."

"A time machine? Time travel?" Sarah shook her head, her face expressing her obvious skepticism. "That's a little hard to believe."

Karen motioned around the loft with her hand. "How much more proof do you need?"

Sarah opened her mouth to answer, then stopped herself. That would explain how they got there. It wasn't logical, but how could she deny what was right in front of her face?

"It's just a little hard to digest, thinking that all this was impossible for the past eighteen years." What was she thinking? Of course it was impossible, wasn't it? "How exactly does it work?"

Karen grinned. "That part is a little more complicated. Ideally, the watches were designed so that wherever you are, you can program a date and time into it and go. Our computer can override the watches in case of emergency and pull someone out from wherever they are. It also works as a monitor so that whoever is in the lab can keep track of the one traveling. It serves as assurance that if someone loses a watch, they can get back home."

Sarah raised a hand to stop her from going any further. "Okay, I get that part. But how did we get here? I certainly didn't use one of your watches."

Karen shrank back almost imperceptibly. "Oh, well, that wasn't supposed to happen. You either have to be wearing a watch or touching someone who is. I accidentally dropped my watch in a puddle while I was running from the king's guards a few moments before you got here, and I think it must have malfunctioned," she admitted guiltily, looking near tears.

"I freaked out when I saw you and your sister in the clearing because I realized what had happened. When I saw that bright light, I had hoped that maybe it was the professor. I had no idea it was capable of pulling someone else here. I'm so sorry."

"It's okay," Sarah said instinctively. Actually it wasn't—not in the least—but she didn't want Karen to feel any worse than she already did. "We can just go back, can't we? I mean, couldn't you just program your watch for home and beam us up?"

Karen stiffened visibly, and Sarah knew whatever news she was about to hear would not be positive. She braced herself.

"That's the problem," Karen said, chewing on her lower lip. "When I dropped my watch, something went wrong internally and the battery power drained almost completely. The watch will still work, but the battery power has to build back up to where it should be. It takes a while to get enough power to transfer one person after it's been damaged this badly, let alone the both of you."

"How much power do you think you'll have by tomorrow?" Sarah asked, trying not to let her irritation show.

"Not enough." The words were said quietly and with regret. Sarah's anger drained from her, and a feeling of defeat took its place. "Sometimes it gets enough power to send something—a very small something—back to where it came from within a few hours. But we'll have to wait and see. It could be a day, maybe a week."

"So we're stuck here?"

Karen nodded solemnly.

"Great." Sarah glanced out the window at the night sky. She frowned. "Where exactly is *here*?"

"Well, that's one of the problems we encountered with the machine. Whenever we programmed a date into the watches and then sent something out, it couldn't arrive at the time we specified. The objects became lodged in time and were unable to move further back than that.

"We couldn't figure out why. There seemed to be this gap in time that they kept falling into. We tried everything we could think of, but traveling freely through time just isn't possible yet. For some reason, though, this time is accessible. No other place in history, just this. Currently, we're somewhere in the twelfth century. Someplace called Serimone."

She leaned closer to Sarah, her eyes bright with excitement. "But this is the weird part: there's nothing about this place recorded in our history, absolutely nothing! We tried to glean information from some of the townsfolk, and they seem to know the history of their country, but history has never heard of them. No one has."

"What are you saying?" Sarah asked.

"I'm saying," Karen said as though the answer should have been obvious, "that this place technically doesn't exist. Somehow, we accessed a place in time that doesn't exist and never has. We assumed it was the time machine that opened passage and created this location, but after talking to some people, we realized that they have a past—a very intricate and old one—dating back to just after Christ's death. They have lived, Sarah. We're still not positive, but it appears to be, well, another world, a whole other time that no one knew existed. Until now."

Sarah stared at her in open-mouthed shock, gooseflesh making the hairs on her arms stand at attention. She cleared her throat.

"Another world?" she asked slowly, her tone expressing her doubt.

Karen groaned. "I know it sounds insane; I thought so too, at first. But you being here now . . ." She trailed off. "Can't you see that you're living proof that it is possible?"

Sarah closed her eyes and rubbed her temples. She couldn't process everything that she had been told, let alone believe it. But what choice did she have? She was living proof and could hardly deny it.

"So," she began, hoping to make sense of her thoughts, "is this place stuck in the twelfth century? Does time move slower here and just keep repeating itself?"

"Not exactly. As far as we can tell, time seems to be moving forward here normally, so we can only assume that they will eventually reach the thirteenth century and so on. But with nothing in the history books or anything recorded about them. . . ." Karen lifted her shoulders in a shrug. "We can't really be sure. But everything we've observed—their dress, lack of certain technologies, and way of life—would point to that era."

Sarah took a moment to digest the information she was receiving.

"So you've obviously been here before."

Karen nodded. "I don't really socialize; I try to keep a low profile for the most part. But mingling and knowing certain people has helped in certain situations. However, there are some things from home that they really can't help with."

"Can't you just bring them back with you?"

Karen shook her head. "The professor says it's best not to. If this is somehow the past, then it's better not to change the course of history by introducing electricity too early, you know?" She bit her lower lip guiltily. "I have brought stuff back before, though. I'm not very good at smacking two rocks together to get sparks, so I carry a lighter in my boot with me all the time. It's saved my rear end more than once."

"That's how you got the lanterns started!" Sarah whispered excitedly, the wheels in her head spinning as small pieces of the puzzle began to come together.

"We need to get to bed," Karen said suddenly, breaking into Sarah's excited thoughts. "I promise that if you have more questions I'll answer them in the morning, but we both need sleep. It's been a long day. Oh, and you don't need to worry about what you're going to wear tomorrow; I have several dresses for you to choose from."

"How did you get so many?" Sarah asked curiously.

Karen giggled. "Flea markets and thrift stores, even yard sales back home. I buy them whenever I can find them. This ended up being my favorite"—she motioned to the white fleece dress she wore—"and I have a couple more in different colors. It kind of helps me to blend in. Plus, it's really comfortable—even to sleep in."

Sarah understood the hint and raised her hands in mock surrender.

"All right, I'm going." She rose and walked to the edge of the loft.

"Oh, and Sarah?" She looked back over her shoulder at Karen. "I might need your help with something tomorrow."

Sarah didn't know what to say, so she simply nodded. As she descended the ladder, she wondered exactly what she was caught in the middle of.

You're the one who wanted an adventure, she chided herself.

As she collapsed into bed next to a still-sleeping Lilly, Sarah thought about that old adage Mom always recited to her when she wanted something on a whim: "Be careful what you wish for."

She sighed and closed her eyes, exhaustion suddenly conquering her. Too late, she realized she should have specified exactly *what* kind of adventure she was wishing for.

CRSO

It hadn't been hard to find them. He had traveled behind at a good distance, picking up on their trail here and there, and followed them to the clearing. Now all he could do was wait.

He could see the two girls talking side by side, but he was unable to hear what they were saying from his perch on a small hill some fifty feet away.

A twig snapped. He spun around and stared at the trees behind him, ready to take on any foolish trespasser who dared surprise him. No one appeared, and aside from the crickets calling to each other in the field, all was silent. He shook his head as his heartbeat began to return to normal.

What was he doing here, anyway? His eyes returned to the small window. The redhead's back was to him, but he could see the brunette clearly. She appeared surprised, irritated, and confused all in a matter of seconds. He couldn't hear their words, but her face expressed every emotion she felt, making him wonder what they were discussing. He shook his head again at his own foolishness, knowing he should leave before he was caught spying.

But he didn't move. There were plenty of men who wanted these girls captured—even burned at the stake if it came to that. And that's why he would stay.

Watching. Waiting.

Chapter Eight

Sarah awoke disoriented. She blinked hard to clear her eyes of the fog that refused to lift. It took several moments for her to remember that she was in a barn, in the middle of nowhere, almost nine hundred years in the past. Her conversation with Karen the night before came flooding back. The realization that someone might want her and Lilly dead for associating with a supposed witch erased all trace of grogginess.

Just your typical summer vacation, she thought wryly.

The sun was just beginning to peek over the sill of the upper window, and she watched it rise as she lay on her back. She kept still to keep from disturbing Lilly, who lay on her side and was starting to drool in the throes of sleep.

Sarah was working on making sense out of the events of the previous day when she heard the small door on the backside of the barn creak open. She froze, her breath catching in her throat. Heavy boots clomped slowly across the wood floor, and Sarah pulled the blankets up to her chin, trying to make herself as small as possible beneath her covering.

What am I doing? She realized she was cowering in the corner to save her hide when she should be distracting the intruder before he found her sister or Karen. With great determination and courage that she did not feel and prayed would not fail her, Sarah slipped out from under the thick blankets and slid slowly to the floor. Her feet landed silently on the wood, and she breathed a silent prayer for strength.

Tiptoeing as quietly as possible, she peeked around the stall that shielded their bed from the view of the barn's center aisle. A man stood not more than twenty feet away with his back to her. Her heart beat faster as she took in the size of the intruder. There was no way she could overpower him, she realized with dismay. Her only option was using her head to outsmart him. But what could she do?

The man leaned the large pitchfork he was wielding against the wall and bent over into the vacant stall he was standing near. Sarah recognized the opportunity to sneak up behind him and shove him into the stall, then lock the gate. Giving herself no time to think over what she was about to do lest she change her mind, she quickly slipped across the barn toward the man. Her pulse pounded in her ears, and she wondered for a moment if he could hear it as she approached.

Instinctively, she grabbed the pitchfork he had set aside, watching him carefully as she grasped the handle and noiselessly pulled it away from the wall. The man was still searching for something, but Sarah knew she would not have long. She held the tool in front of her like a sword, ready to jab him as she edged forward. She took a deep breath and prepared herself to knock him off balance as she came up behind him.

Before she could react, the man straightened and turned around, startling her so badly she nearly dropped the oversized fork to the floor. Her heart pounded wildly against her ribcage, and her hands began to perspire. She instinctively gripped the handle tightly and held it aloft, hoping she looked more threatening than she felt.

The intruder's expression registered shock as he came face to face with her, and he stumbled back in surprise, landing on his backside in the pen. His fall disturbed the hay littering the ground; it fluttered around him in a golden rain that landed noiselessly on and around him. Sarah mirrored his backward steps and prepared to scream if he attacked her. His eyes darted from the pitchfork to her face, then back to her weapon.

"Seth!"

Sarah spun around and saw Karen making her way down the ladder, smiling like nothing was amiss. She hopped gracefully to the floor and walked toward them, looking amused by the scene.

Seth glanced up at her and grinned, his shock seeming to melt away as he stood and brushed himself off.

"I should have known you'd be here." His gaze came back to rest on Sarah as he plucked stray hay from his hair. "Are you going to introduce me to your friend? I figure I should know the name of the girl who nearly had my head a moment ago."

Karen laughed. "Seth, this is Sarah Matthews. Sarah, this is Seth Jones. His family owns the property."

Sarah nodded slowly, feeling foolish as she lowered her weapon to the ground, though she didn't relinquish her hold on it altogether.

Karen seemed to sense her hesitation. She must have found great humor in Sarah's actions, as her easy laughter echoed through the barn.

"Were you going to poke him to death?" she asked, her brows raised. She grinned at Seth. "Not that I haven't thought about doing the same thing, but what made you try and bludgeon him?"

"Well," Sarah began, shyly, "I thought he had broken in and was going to take us all as his prisoners." She shrugged as though it were no big deal. Karen and Seth burst out laughing, and Sarah felt her own smile emerge as she realized how silly it all had been.

Hoping to smooth things over and start fresh, she extended her hand toward Seth, still smiling. "It's very nice to meet you, Mr. Jones."

Seth looked surprised by the gesture at first, then his grin returned. He grasped her outstretched hand with his strong, calloused one, shaking it firmly. "It's a pleasure to meet you, as well. But my father is Mr. Jones. You can call me Seth, and I hope I can call you Sarah."

"Of course," she said, still feeling idiotic over the way she had overreacted earlier. Seth's grin stretched across his face.

"We are very informal here where names are concerned, you see. I'm sure even my parents will insist you call them by their Christian names." His eyes twinkled, and Sarah couldn't help smiling at his friendly nature.

"Does your mother need help with breakfast?" Karen asked, looking pleased by the amiable exchange between them.

"Oh, no. We can't have breakfast here," Sarah said. Years of her mom's training suddenly returned, reminding her that she should politely refuse. "We shouldn't have even stayed here last night, and we certainly can't impose on your family's breakfast."

Seth's hearty chuckle and Karen's laughter surprised her.

"Well," Seth said, looking amused, "you could certainly learn a thing or two about etiquette from her, Karen." Karen grinned. Turning to Sarah, Seth said, "Don't worry about it. Karen stays here all of the time and is always welcome, as are you. And my mother always makes more than enough for our family at breakfast."

Seth leaned closer to her and glanced around. He grinned conspiratorially. "She'd hang me if I turned the two of you away. We don't get too many people coming through here, and she thoroughly enjoys company; you would actually be doing me a favor by coming to eat with us. That way she won't tan my hide."

Sarah found herself smiling over his cocked brow and mock fright.

"Sarah?"

She spun around to see Lilly behind them in her nightgown, looking surprised and dazed. Her hair was tousled and her eyes squinted at the early morning light as she wiped at the corner of her mouth.

"It's okay, Lilly." Sarah motioned her over. The younger girl complied with obvious hesitancy in her steps. She stopped just behind her sister and seemed to be sizing up the large man. "Seth, this is my sister, Lilly."

He leaned down, placing his palms on his bent knees so he was at eye level with the young girl. He smiled kindly. "My mother will be doubly pleased to have all of you for breakfast. And I suspect my sister, Leah, will be ecstatic. She doesn't have too many playmates around here."

Lilly perked up at this, and her eyes brightened. "Is she my age?"

"She just turned eleven, so I assume you're close." Seth chuckled at the excited look on her face. He straightened and smiled at Sarah a moment longer than she thought necessary.

Karen cleared her throat and said, "We'd better get inside before your mother comes looking for us."

Seth nodded. He stood aside and allowed them to go ahead. Then he closed the door behind them and walked with long strides toward the wood house. Sarah and Lilly hung back slightly from the two friends as they talked and reminisced. Much laughter was exchanged between them, and Sarah suddenly felt out of place as she took in their surroundings.

It had been too dark the night before to make out any details about the house, other than its size. Sarah now saw that it was larger than she had originally thought. The dark wood porch in the front of the modest two-story home matched the rest of the house. A handcrafted rocking chair on the porch swayed in the light breeze, and a field of wildflowers that varied in color, shape, and size surrounded the small garden just behind the house. The morning sun shone brightly above the hills, making the flowers and tall grasses look as though they had been sprinkled with flecks of gold.

Sarah blinked slowly. She couldn't remember ever seeing something so simple and beautiful.

The arm that she'd fallen on the day before began to ache slightly, and she massaged the tender spot on her shoulder. She remembered the mysterious Shadow who'd helped her the previous night. Thinking about him brought more questions to her mind, and although she wondered why he had let her go without alerting anyone to her presence, one question had haunted her in her sleep: Who was the masked hero?

Her desire to uncover his true identity was spurred from reading too many mystery novels and the fact that she never liked being left out of the loop. But—and she hated to admit it—he also intrigued her.

"Are you okay?" Lilly's whispered question brought her out of her reverie.

Sarah mustered a smile to reassure her sister and relaxed her shoulders. "I'm fine."

Seth stepped onto the porch and opened the large door, escorting them into a small living room. Sarah let her gaze wander over the room. A rocking chair identical to the one out front had been placed on the right wall beside the fireplace, which cast a warm glow over the room and made it feel inviting. A colorful wool rug covered a large portion of the wood floor, and a staircase on the right led up to a second story. Directly beneath the window on the wall opposite was a wooden bench paired with a chair on either side. Except for a small round table in the corner with an oil lamp atop it and the candles lining the mantle over the fireplace, the decorations were sparse, though the modesty of it all appealed to Sarah. A smile tilted the corner of her lips. The cozy space was as welcoming as she had expected from the appearance of the house's exterior.

"Mother?" Seth called as they entered the kitchen. Copious amounts of pots and pans were scattered throughout the room, and baskets of fresh baked biscuits sat on the wooden counters. The petite, curvy woman he addressed was bent over a small fireplace and had her spoon dipped into the bowl before her. When she heard her name, she straightened and smiled at the newcomers.

"Well, what have you brought me here?" the woman asked. She clasped her hands to her ample chest in obvious pleasure. "This is a real treat! It's not often we get guests out here, you know."

Sarah smiled at the older woman's genuine pleasure at seeing them. Her thick, curly red tresses were piled on top of her head in a messy bun, and her face was flushed from the heat of the fire, making her bright green eyes stand out. Sarah instantly took a liking to the woman.

"Mother, these are Karen's friends, Sarah and Lilly" Seth said, motioning to each girl as he introduced her.

"It's very nice to meet you, Mrs. Jones," Sarah said. Lilly hid behind her shyly, but she still smiled at the woman.

"Oh, call me Ruth, dear," Ruth Jones said. The grin that spread across her face was infectious.

"They'll be having breakfast with us this morning, Mother," Seth said, walking over to her and kissing her cheek.

"Well, glory be!" The flushed woman looked as though she might burst with excitement. "It would be a true delight. I always make plenty and just take the leftovers to the horses and goats." She turned to Karen and smiled. "Come here and give me a hug, dear." Karen chuckled but obliged the older woman without hesitation.

"Now, Seth, will you fetch your brother and sister for me? Pa is coming in from tending the fields, and then we'll be ready to eat."

Seth left them and went out to find the rest of the clan.

"Is there anything we can help with?" Sarah asked, still feeling like they were intruding.

Ruth appeared surprised at the offer, then beamed at her. "Well, dear, that is too sweet of you. Leah helps where she can, but with just the two of us feeding three hungry, hard working men—"

She placed a dainty hand upon her flushed cheek. "Oh, dear. Look at me, rambling on and on. Yes, if you wouldn't mind placing the biscuits on the table, and Karen, dear, you know where the apple butter is. And I think that should do it."

The girls had only just finished their tasks when Seth came back into the kitchen, grinning from ear to ear. Behind him appeared a tall, broad-shouldered boy with copper-colored hair; he sported the same easy smile as Seth. The girl that followed her brothers into the kitchen could have been a much younger clone of her mother, though her curves hadn't quite caught up to her long frame yet. She smiled shyly at the newcomers. Sarah looked back to the small woman bustling about and wondered who the Jones children got their height from.

Her question was answered when Mr. Jones came in from the fields. His body filled the kitchen doorway, and he had to duck beneath the frame to avoid grazing the top of his head on it. The man shook hands with Sarah, and his large hand seemed to swallow hers.

"How pleased was my Ruth when she found out we had guests?" he asked, glancing at each of his children in turn. He stood next to Seth, and Sarah was struck by how alike they looked, though the older of the two was a few inches taller. They had the same ruddy brown hair, matching brown eyes, and equally infectious smiles.

"Well, stop your bally-ragging and let the poor children eat. They must be half-starved!" Ruth shook her head in mock exasperation and set the last pan on the large rectangular table.

Sarah felt awkward as everyone gathered around the table, wondering where she should sit. Seth held out a chair for her, and she cast him a grateful smile. He took the chair on her right, and Lilly plopped down at the end of the table on Sarah's other side. Karen took the last available chair next to Seth.

They all joined hands, and Mr. Jones prayed over their food. Seth's large hand was rough and calloused from hard work, though his grip on Sarah's hand was gentle.

"Amen," the family said when their father concluded his thanks.

Everyone began passing the large bowls and wooden trays around the table. Ruth had prepared fresh biscuits, large slices of warmed ham, and a mixture of eggs and chopped potatoes. The smells wafting from the plate in front of Sarah caused her mouth to water, and she ate the delicious meal gratefully. She enjoyed listening to the easy conversation around the table, laughing as Mr. Jones told his guests about Joshua's first experience milking goat.

"It took him nearly an hour of chasing that thing around before he realized that it wasn't even a female goat," he said with a grin. Sarah couldn't help laughing. Joshua seemed to take it all in stride, smiling the whole time and sharing some stories of his own.

After everyone ate their fill, the men headed outside to work in the fields, and the girls went about clearing the table. Ruth sent her daughter outside to collect water from the well. When the girl returned with a full pail, the older woman poured it into a large pot and set it over the fire to boil so they could clean the morning's dishes.

Sarah couldn't imagine living without a dishwasher and having to wash every pan and utensil by hand after each meal. The again, if they had never known anything other than this way of life, then it probably just became a routine part of the day.

"Breakfast was delicious. Thank you," Sarah said sincerely to the lady of the house, who was busy dunking plates into the hot water.

Ruth glanced up at her and fairly beamed at the praise. "Why, thank you. Do you ladies have anything planned for this morn?"

"We were hoping to go into town on some errands," Karen answered quickly, surprising Sarah. She didn't remember making any plans for the day, but she decided to remain silent about the matter and let Karen handle things.

"I believe Seth was going into town, dear," Ruth said. "Why don't you have him take you girls?"

"Oh, no," Karen said, shaking her head. "We couldn't impose like that. We'll simply walk."

Just the thought of walking caused Sarah's legs to ache from their run last night.

Ruth swatted the air with her hand as if the idea of them walking to town were an annoying pest. "It's no imposition for him to accompany you. He can take you girls in the wagon. Now go and get some proper clothes for town on before the day gets away from you."

Karen nodded her head slowly. When the older woman turned back to the fire, Karen leaned closer to Sarah and whispered, "It's probably best if Lilly stays here with them."

Sarah looked over to the two young girls who stood idly by the table, chatting away while their unsoiled cleaning towels hung limply from their hands. Leah laughed at a joke Lilly made; the two appeared completely oblivious to the conversation going on around them.

Sarah turned back to Karen. "I don't think that will be a problem."

Chapter Nine

On the way into town, Seth chatted about his family. Sarah listened intently as he told her about how his father had traveled out of the country to look for cattle and ended up meeting his mother.

"Mother was the daughter of the man he was supposed to purchase the cattle from," Seth explained, taking his eyes from the road for a moment to glance at Sarah before looking ahead again. "You see, it was supposed to be a quick trip, but he ended up staying for longer than necessary. My parents married there, and then my father took her back home to his farm, although he did forget to purchase the cattle and bring it back with them." He chuckled. "I guess he was a little distracted at the time. The way he likes to tell it, he returned here without any cattle, but he certainly wasn't empty handed." He grinned and wiggled his eyebrows.

Sarah laughed at his antics and looked at the young woman next to her to see her response to his story. Karen sat in between the two of them on the wagon's bench seat and appeared occupied with her thoughts. Not wanting to be caught staring, Sarah sat back in her seat and focused her attention ahead for the remainder of their ride into town, which took the better part of an hour.

She felt a small stirring of anticipation as they entered the tall wooden gate that was left open for travelers coming down this road. The mass of thick trees that had lined the road abruptly ended at the gate, leaving nothing but a canopy of blue sky over the small town. Sarah's eyes scanned the cobblestone streets and the varying structures that lined the main drag and curved down the numerous neighborhoods and side streets that were set back from the noise and excitement of the square. There appeared to be no separation of classes in this town; some of the larger, more opulent brick buildings and businesses were situated between rough-hewn or dilapidated buildings that were made of peeling sideboards and straw roofs.

Sarah gaped in surprise at the jumble of people crowded together on the busy street hawking and purchasing various wares. Venders stood beside their carts in front of some of the buildings and bartered loudly with their customers. People rode by on horseback and wagons similar to the one they were in.

She caught sight of a man who was a probably a butcher, adorned as he was in a heavily blood-splattered apron. She watched as he reached into the coop at the side of his shop and removed a squawking brown chicken. The bird flapped wildly in panic as the man tucked it firmly against his side and walked to the bloodied stump next to the coop. He situated the desperate animal on the block of wood and steadied it as he reached for the ax leaning against the side of the stump. Sarah's eyes widened in shock, and she quickly turned her gaze away just as the ax sliced through the air; she still managed to hear the thump of finality as the butcher brought the shining blade down on the bird's neck, effectively cutting off its cries.

Though she knew that chickens came from somewhere before they reached the freezer section, Sarah still felt sick at the startling sight; she never had any desire to see her dinner before she ate it. In an attempt to keep her gag reflex from acting up, she focused on two small boys chasing each other around the legs of a horse; they startled the animal, causing it to jolt its rider. The opulently dressed man atop the animal shouted a curse at the boys, and they ran away, laughing as they continued their game.

A woman shouted nearby, and Sarah turned to see that a mother and her daughter had narrowly missed having a pale of slops tossed on their heads as the woman in the room above them carelessly tossed the contents out the window. She ignored the mother's shouted obscenities and closed the window without ever glancing down.

All these things occurred within the first few minutes of their ride through the square, making Sarah's head spin as she tried to absorb it all. But what caused her mouth to hang open was the large stone castle at the far edge of the small town.

The imposing structure had been built so that it was perfectly center with the main drag. Although there were a few buildings nearby, it seemed to be set apart from the rest of the town. Four large towers were situated at the corner of four walls, forming a fortress surrounding the castle. Sarah couldn't see much of the inside from her vantage point, but it was impossible to miss the steeples and towers of the castle that rose high above the walls.

A large wooden gate was situated at the front between the fortress walls; it was decorated with long purple flags emblazoned with the symbol of a gold crown. The tall logs of the main gate were spaced a few inches apart, and the tops were sharpened to spikes in order to keep intruders out—or prisoners in. She shivered at the thought of being desperate enough to escape to risk getting impaled on one of those poles.

Seth guided the horses to the front of a large wood structure and pulled back on the reins. The wagon slowed to a stop. The sign proclaiming "Livery and Blacksmith" in faded black letters waved in the slight breeze as he helped Sarah down. When he released her, she self-consciously brushed her hands over the front of her dress.

She still couldn't believe how extravagant the gown was as the dark green velvet reflected the sun's light. The sleeves puffed slightly on her shoulders, small tuffs of white fabric peeking out from beneath the loose threads that secured the sleeves to the bodice. The small gold band that encircled the bottom of each sleeve glittered as she moved her hands over the thin ties that cinched up the front of the bodice. It had taken Sarah several minutes of struggling to realize that the ties were not made to close the front of the dress completely; rather they were meant to crisscross over the white fabric sewn into the front of the gown. When Sarah had protested against wearing the beautiful garment, Karen had assured her that the dress was perfectly fine for town.

"I never wear it, so it deserves to get out once in a while," Karen had said with a shrug.

She had opted for wearing a dress similar to the one she had worn the previous day, except this one was made of a deep green that matched her eyes and was adorned with a hood. Her long red braid swayed from side to side as she made her way toward the livery. Seth excused himself to run his errands and jogged across the road, stepping inside a small shop that looked like a general store. Karen stopped in front of the open door to the livery when he was far enough away. She glanced over her shoulder to make sure he was gone before turning to Sarah.

"I need to check something out," she whispered, pulling the hood over her head. "Stay inside of here for a little while until I come and get you. Remember, no one can know I'm here. I'm not sure how much has gotten around town yet about my run-in with Dunlivey, but I'm pretty positive you will be fine because we haven't been seen together yet. I'll be back as soon as possible."

Sarah nodded as she tried to absorb the hurried instructions. Karen looked back and forth across the street, probably to make sure she wasn't being followed, then darted across the road.

Sarah stared at her back until she disappeared from sight. She touched the braid she had managed to pull her hair into earlier and took a deep breath before entering the livery. The smell of horses and wood mingled together in the large open room. An unattended anvil and welding iron sat off in the far corner near a fire that was encased in a small brick enclosure. The mock fireplace had been built into the side of the building to allow the smoke to be released outside. Blacksmith tools littered a bench nearby, but no one appeared to be inside the building, which caused Sarah to relax. *Good*, she thought. *The fewer people I encountered while I'm here, the better.*

Just then, she heard a noise behind her and turned to see a man standing in one of the stalls. He glanced up and noticed her, then exited the stall, leaning his rake against the side of it and closing the door. He didn't look much older than her, and his sandy hair gave him a boyish appearance. He didn't look dangerous. Then again, appearances could be deceiving.

"Can I help you?"

"Oh, I was just, um, looking around," she replied lamely.

"Anything in particular?" he asked, his eyes brimming with amusement.

"Horses," she blurted, then mentally kicked herself.

He nodded again, looking like he was trying hard not to smile. He took a step closer. "Do you have any specifics in mind?"

She said the first thing she thought of. "Something fast and big. Black, maybe."

He brightened. "I think we may have just the thing. Right over here." He led the way toward the back and said over his shoulder, "I'm Allan, by the way. Allan Miller."

"It's nice to meet you." Sarah wasn't sure it was entirely safe to give her name, so she offered nothing more. Allan didn't seem too worried about it as he stopped in front of a stall at the back of the building that was set apart from the rest. The door only came up to her chest, so she could clearly see the large black stallion that watched her from inside.

"He's beautiful," she murmured, fighting the desire to reach out and stroke its mane.

"Thank you."

Sarah started and spun around. The owner of the voice stood a few feet behind them. She shrank back slightly at the sight of the tall man who had somehow snuck up behind them.

"That one isn't for sale, though." He stared at Allan as he spoke.

"Sorry, sir," Allan said, not looking the least bit repentant. "I just wanted to show the lady what kind of fine horses your establishment boards."

The man nodded and walked forward. "Why don't you go finish those horseshoes you were supposed to have done by now, Allan?"

That man looked disappointed, but he nodded and disappeared out the door, stealing one last glance over his shoulder at them before exiting the livery.

"Are you in the market or just looking?" the man asked, drawing her focus back to his face.

Sarah felt uncomfortable to be left alone with the tall, dark haired man, but she knew she would only draw attention to herself if she suddenly fled from the building.

"I'm just looking right now," she said, hoping Karen would come for her soon.

His gaze moved to the horse, then back to her. She was struck by the way his dark blue eyes seemed to bore straight into her soul.

"I'm William Taylor. This is my shop, so any questions you might have, I can answer them." She was momentarily taken aback by the fact that someone his age owned a business this size. He only looked to be in his early twenties, with his long, lean frame and broad shoulders of youth. There was something in his eyes, though—a certain weary and jaded look—that suggested he knew more of the world's realities than most people his age.

"How did you come to own this place?" she asked. She hoped her attempt at casual conversation might cover her nervousness. His face seemed to darken, though, and she realized that she might have insulted him in some way. She glanced away awkwardly. "I'm sorry. That was prying."

He shook his head. "It's all right. Actually, it was a gift from my father."

"Isn't owning a livery a lot of work?" She looked back up at him again.

He shrugged, his face giving away nothing. "I have Allan, and my uncle occasionally assists me in running this place, so I do have help." He studied her intently as if he were trying to decipher her character simply by looking at her. She shifted uncomfortably beneath his gaze and turned her attention back to the large beast.

"Is he yours?" she asked, still looking at the horse.

He paused before answering. "His owner boards him here most of the time." He clicked his tongue, and the horse's ears pricked up at the sound. Sarah nearly jumped back when the large animal walked toward them and hung its head over the front of the stall, wanting their full attention.

"Oh, my," she breathed. The horse was as large as the beast she'd encountered last night, and just as intimidating. When his large eyes flicked to her, she took a small step closer to William.

He eyed her, his expression hard to read. She didn't appreciate not knowing what was going through his head.

"You've never been around horses, have you?" he asked.

She shook her head no. Before she had time to think of an excuse as to why she was shopping for an animal that she had hardly spent any time with, Seth entered the livery behind them. He appeared surprised when he saw her there, and then he frowned and crossed his arms across his chest, his gaze flickering between the two of them standing so close together.

"Do you have those shoes I requested, Will?" His voice was gruff, and Sarah wondered what had him so rattled.

William nodded, but didn't move. "Allan has them out front."

Seth turned to her. "Are you ready to go, Sarah?"

She looked between the two men and then to the horse. Gazing at the black stallion longingly, she sighed and nodded. Though she had been afraid of the large animal, she realized that Seth might have interrupted her only chance to confront her fears and stroke the silky black mane like she'd desired to do last night.

"Thank you for your time," Sarah said to William.

He nodded his head but said nothing.

"Goodbye, Will," Seth said curtly as he led Sarah out of the shop.

"Goodbye, Sarah." The whispered words floated to her as they left, and she wondered if she might have imagined them.

CR80

Seth was quiet on the drive back to his family's house, and Karen seemed consumed by her thoughts as she twiddled her fingers anxiously in her lap. Sarah was grateful for the silence in the wagon because it gave her time to contemplate the things that she hadn't yet had a chance to think over.

As Seth halted the horses in front of the barn, she began to realize that no matter how much time she spent trying to sort out her current predicament, her thoughts got mixed up and ran into each other in a confusing pile of tangled thoughts and theories. She couldn't make sense of any of them, and that frustrated her to no end; she was a fixer by nature, and she had to make everything right.

Sarah wondered if everyone might notice that she seemed a little preoccupied, but Karen was the one who seemed to be consumed by her thoughts for the remainder of the day. She made little conversation with anyone and answered questions with one or two words. The Jones family seemed to know better than to question her, so Sarah decided to follow their example and remain silent about it until she could get her alone.

She got her opportunity after the evening meal. While Leah occupied Lilly's time by teaching her how to knit a wool scarf, Sarah stole away in search of Karen, pushing aside the guilt of leaving her sister alone again. She found the redhead standing behind the house staring up at the star-speckled sky.

"Wow," Sarah said, eying the heavens as she came up beside her. She didn't remember there being this many stars back in Bethany, and they certainly weren't as bright or as large as the ones that hung above them. They stood in silence for several minutes before Sarah spoke.

"Are you going to tell me what you did in town today?" she asked, keeping her face to the night sky. She glanced at Karen out of the corner of her eye to judge her reaction.

Karen sighed heavily. She stared at the ground for a long moment and answered without looking at her.

"I found the professor."

"You did?" Sarah asked in surprise. Anticipation coursed through her veins at the prospect of returning home. "That's great! Now you can send us back, right?"

Karen glanced up at her, and Sarah saw that her eyes were filled with pain.

"He's being held by Cadius as the castle sorcerer."

Sarah blinked. "What? How do you know that?"

"When I left you earlier, I passed the castle gate and saw him inside." She paused and took in a shaky breath. "One of the servants had witnessed him using something that he'd brought back from our time. Apparently, the servant told his master that he had seen a man doing some strange trick, and Cadius had him brought to the castle. He said that he would stay in the dungeons until he performed some kind of 'miracle.' Cadius allowed him access to some chemicals, and since he's a scientist, he was able to dazzle him." She gave a rather unladylike snort.

"So instead of releasing him," she continued, "he made the professor the castle sorcerer. He's nothing more than an amusing distraction from the death and destruction that Cadius is planning."

Sarah heard the rancor in her words and shivered. "But won't they figure out that he's just faking it, that he's not really a sorcerer?" she asked.

Karen shook her head. "Cadius doesn't use him for anything other than entertainment for himself and his pompous guests at castle parties. These people have never seen a smoke screen before, so all he has to do to keep them amused is mix a few chemicals. The professor said that they're treating him well, but he needs to stay there for right now because he's the only one we have on the inside. He's been asking some questions, and most of the staff seem more scared of Cadius' power than the king's. That makes me think that something is up."

"His power doesn't scare you?" Sarah asked curiously. "I mean, you're planning on revealing the guy's plan to dominate the kingdom, and you aren't even a little intimidated?

Karen shook her head. "I'm not scared for myself; I'm worried for the professor."

"But he's okay right now," Sarah reassured her, trying to hold back the questions that burned her throat. She didn't want to seem insensitive toward Karen's feelings.

Karen smiled sadly at her, seeming to understand what was on her mind. "Cadius had the watch taken from the professor when they threw him in the dungeons. I'm sorry about that, Sarah. But I do have one bit of good news." She extended her wrist toward Sarah and pressed one of the buttons. The square face glowed brightly, but Sarah couldn't make out any of the numbers on the screen. A short green bar at the top blinked on and off.

"What is that?" she asked, pointing.

"That's the energy bar. It registers how much power the watch has. Right now it has enough to transport."

Sarah's eyes widened. "Really? You mean we can go back? Both of us?"

Karen nodded slowly. Sarah opened her mouth to question her further, but Karen interrupted before she could say anything more.

"We'd better get inside before it gets too late. They'll come looking for us if we take too long out here." Something in her tone caused Sarah to feel guilty, but she wasn't exactly sure why. It wasn't her fault that they had come here, nor was it her fault that they could go back.

And leave her to fight this battle by herself.

The thought came out of nowhere. Sarah tried to brush it off, but it left her shaken inside.

Her earlier feelings of celebration were nowhere to be found as they walked silently toward the house. They could hear the laughter from the group gathered inside. It was strange that she could be so tormented by her thoughts, while the rest of the world seemed to go on without a care. She stared at the back of Karen's head as she walked in front of her, and she suddenly realized what she needed to do.

CR&O

Late that night, after everyone had gone to sleep, Sarah stared down at Lilly's sleeping form. Her mind was made up.

"You don't have to do this, you know," Karen whispered beside her. "If we use it to send her now, it may never regain enough power to transport again." She paused to let her words sink in. "If that happens, you'll be stuck here until we can figure out how to fix it."

Sarah's throat tightened with the unshed tears she held at bay. "I told you I would help, and I intend to keep my promise. Besides, we'll find a way back," she said hopefully. She waited a moment before asking, "How much time do you think will go by before we see each other again?"

"Honestly?" Karen lifted her shoulders in an uncertain shrug. "A day here could be a week, a month, or it could be exactly the same day as your time. It's never predictable."

Sarah nodded and took a deep breath to steady her nerves. "If she stays here, she'll be put in danger, so this is the best thing for her." She wondered if she spoke the words to reassure Karen or herself.

Karen stared at her for a moment more; she sighed when Sarah nodded her head decisively. The redhead pressed several buttons on her watch, and Sarah felt the earth move beneath her. It was nothing like the quaking that had thrown her to the floor in her bedroom, but she still grabbed hold of the nearest post to steady herself against the swaying of the building. She closed her eyes against the blinding light that engulfed the barn. When the light faded, she opened her eyes again. Lilly was gone.

Chapter Ten

When Ruth Jones asked where Lilly was the next morning after breakfast, Sarah stubbornly remained silent while Karen explained that Lilly had had to leave for home because of a family emergency.

"Oh, dear, I do hope everything's all right," Ruth said, fanning herself with a towel in the warm kitchen.

"She'll be fine," Karen said, darting a quick look at Sarah out of the corner of her eye.

"How on earth did she get back? She didn't walk, did she?" The concern in the older woman's eyes was genuine.

Sarah gave Karen a look. She realized it was unfair for her to be upset with Karen when she herself had made the decision to send Lilly back and remain behind, but she felt desperate to blame someone. She had to get her mind off her own regret, and the redhead had the misfortune of being an easy target.

"Well, you see," Karen said, stumbling over her words until she seemed to come up with a scenario that fit, "we all walked to town yesterday where Mr. and Mrs. Matthews were waiting."

Sarah rolled her eyes to the ceiling.

"Dear heavens, you lasses walked into town in the dark?" Ruth looked completely aghast. "You should have just taken the wagon. Seth would have been more than happy to take you."

"We needed the exercise," Karen said, grabbing a stack of wooden plates off the table and dumping them into the washing basin.

Ruth clicked her tongue. "You and your loony notions, walking alone in the dark. You're lucky nothing happened to you all."

Karen nodded, as though she were grateful that they had returned from their walk unscathed.

"Anyway," she continued, "it was very sudden, and Lilly said to tell you how sorry she was that she couldn't say goodbye. But you know that there's no time for formalities in the wake of an emergency."

Ruth nodded sympathetically. "I do hope everything is all right." She turned to Sarah. "You didn't need to go back home with her?"

Karen shook her head quickly from side to side. "They just needed Lilly."

She grabbed Sarah's arm suddenly and pulled her toward the door.

"We'll be going into town this morning, so we'll be back before the evening meal," she called over her shoulder as they exited the house.

CRBO

They kept walking until they were out of earshot.

"What do we need to go into town for?" Sarah finally asked, yanking her arm free. It was the first time all morning that she had actually said more than a few words at a time. Karen looked surprised that she had spoken, but she recovered quickly.

"I just need to check on a few things. We're going to go alone, though. Seth isn't going to drive us this time."

As if the sound of his name had caused him to materialize, Seth walked around the back of the barn and spotted them. He smiled and made his way over. Karen straightened and pasted on a smile, obviously putting up a happy front to show that nothing was amiss.

"We need to go into town," she said before he had a chance to greet them. He looked amused at her sudden declaration.

"If you give me a few minutes, I can finish getting these bales of hay into the barn and then drive you myself."

"I think it will just be Sarah and me this time. But you can secure the horses for us." Not waiting for his reaction, Karen bustled ahead toward the barn.

Seth looked at Sarah in confusion. She simply shrugged, just as confused as he was. The two trotted toward the barn, trying to keep up with Karen's quick stride. She pulled the door open and waited anxiously for them to follow her inside. Karen's odd behavior made Sarah wonder where the urgency to get to town had come from.

Seth entered the building reluctantly and led the two brown bays they'd used before to the front of the wagon. He worked on tying the horses to the wooden contraption, shooting the girls speculative glances from time to time. Karen tapped her foot impatiently on the hay-strewn floor.

Seth stopped his task and folded his arms across his chest. He stared at her, looking exasperated with her impatience. "What's the hurry, Karen?"

"I have an appointment in town that I forgot about, and I need to get there quickly. That's all."

He didn't look convinced, but he nodded reluctantly and went about securing the horses. He gave each of the girls a hand up as they stepped into the wagon.

"Don't do anything stupid," he said, looking Karen straight in the eye. She smiled reassuringly, and Sarah wondered if he could see straight through her false pretense as he walked up behind one of the horses and smacked its rump to get it moving. The wagon lurched forward, and Sarah was forced against the back of the hard seat as they rolled out of the barn.

When they were far enough away to speak without Seth hearing, Sarah asked, "And what appointment are we so late for?"

Karen used the reins to steer the wagon onto the dirt trail that led away from the Joneses' property, not bothering to slow down for the tight turn. She seemed to be in a hurry as she forced the horses to speed ahead, making Sarah grip the side of the wagon to steady herself as they lurched over a rut.

"Could you slow down?" Sarah asked, feeling her stomach tighten in protest at being jarred around. "I haven't thrown up since I was seven from ice cream overload, and I'd like to keep it that way."

"I need to find a way to get into the castle," Karen said, almost to herself. She glanced at Sarah out of the corner of her eye before directing her attention back to the road in time to swerve around a fallen log. She hardly seemed to notice as the wagon lurched to the side, nearly spilling its occupants. "I have to help the professor find some evidence against Cadius. If that means I have to sneak inside each night or become a castle servant, I'll do it. He has to be stopped before he has the chance to do anything else."

The determination in Karen's voice made the hairs on Sarah's neck stand on end. She sounded like she would take on anyone who got in her way. Her resolve against Cadius made Sarah wonder how far she would go and what danger she would face in the process.

"But what if this really is the past and he's supposed to succeed?" she asked. "Maybe you're just messing up the future by trying to stop him." She shook her head. "You're playing with fire here, Karen."

"I know this sounds crazy," she said, "but I feel like it's my *purpose* to stop him, like that's why I'm here. I have to do this. Can't you understand that?"

When Sarah looked into those green eyes, she thought of Lilly. Somehow, though her heart had told her to go with her sister and leave this foreign place behind, she knew the right thing had been to stay. Though the odds were against her, she knew that they would be reunited. Someday. She had felt compelled to stay, and she now saw that same determination in Karen's eyes. There was no changing her mind. Sarah breathed a heavy sigh.

"I do get it, Karen. Just please understand that you're all I have here. I realize that we've been here for three days now, but if something happened to you, I'd be completely lost. I have no idea what I'm doing as it is."

Karen suddenly pulled the reins back, and the horses came to a stop at the edge of the forest. Sarah could see the town and the tallest spires of the castle with their flags waving high above the rest of the buildings. She looked at Karen and noted her serious expression.

"Don't say that, Sarah. If something were to happen to me, you'd be fine. You seem very resourceful, and I have no doubt in my mind that you could find a way. Sam and Ruth would be more than willing to let you stay, so you would at least have a roof over your head."

Sarah decided not to mention the fact that she'd still be stuck here with no way to get home. There was no sense in bringing up something that couldn't be fixed at the moment.

"But if for some reason everything doesn't go as I planned, I want you to find the Shadow. He'll help you figure this out." She put up a hand to silence Sarah's protest. "I'm not asking you to put yourself in danger, but I would like you to see if the two of you can finish what I've started, at least while you're here. I know that's a lot to ask, but can you do that for me?"

Sarah stared up at the overcast sky in surrender. She felt no need to mention the fact that several of her pet goldfish had died at her hands because she had neglected to follow through in her responsibility to feed them. But this was different. It wasn't goldfish she was being asked to feed; there was more resting on her answer than she could have ever imagined.

"I'll do my best," she promised. "But I can't give you any guarantees."

Karen visibly brightened at her response and turned back around in her seat, looking like a huge weight had been lifted from her shoulders. She flipped the hood over her head and flicked the reins, and the horses pulled the wagon the rest of the way into the busy town.

People milled about in the square and went in and out of shops. On this trip, Sarah focused on the people milling about. The women wore an array of clothing, from ragged gowns to simple yet fine dresses that conveyed their wealth and social standing. They walked about with baskets dangling from the crooks of their arms, and some toted children behind them. Boys played in the street, tossing rocks at each other or observing their fathers haggling with the butchers and conversing with other men.

Karen halted the wagon in front of the livery. Sarah inwardly groaned.

"So I guess this is something you're doing alone, since you're dropping me off at the babysitter's," she said sarcastically. She hated the sting her words carried, but she disliked being cast aside and excluded from something, especially when it was as important as what Karen was trying to do.

"Just try not to distract the blacksmiths with that dress. They might lose a hand." Karen smiled teasingly.

Sarah covered her blush by turning away and jumping to the ground. She had observed that even the wealthier of the townsfolk mostly wore grey or black to the markets. The soft blue fabric and white detailing around the neckline of her dress seemed extravagant in the sea of everyday apparel. Karen had said the dark blue color accentuated her eyes, and she had insisted that Sarah wear the dress, saying she enjoyed dressing her up and making her look like a princess. Sarah had rolled her eyes in good humor at the comment, but now she wasn't so sure it was a good idea to stick out like this—especially considering the glances she was getting from a few of the men strolling across the road.

"If anyone catches on to who I am," Karen was saying, drawing Sarah's attention back to her, "you run as fast as you can and don't look back. Do you understand?" Her serious expression conveyed the importance of her words.

Sarah nodded reluctantly and received a look of relief in return. She watched as Karen moved the wagon past the livery in the direction of the castle. She breathed a prayer of safety for Karen as she fingered the blue silk sash tied about her waist to ensure that it was secure. She glanced around and observed the male eyes that followed her as she quickly ducked inside the building. The warmth from the room where the fires were kept burning enveloped her as she stepped inside. Allan looked up from his task of sweeping the floor and smiled.

"Hello again."

Sarah held back a groan. She had hoped that maybe the livery would be empty so she could pray in peace. And she hadn't even stepped under any ladders or broken any mirrors today—not that she believed in that sort of thing.

"Hello," she answered, avoiding eye contact and hoping that he would leave her alone. "Don't mind me; I'm just browsing."

He nodded, looking regretful. "I would love to help you, but I have to run a few errands around town. I was just finishing up here."

Sarah tried to hide her pleasure. "I won't keep you, then." She turned around and pretended to study the reins and horseshoes hanging on the wall. It took several moments before she heard him walk across the floor and leave out the front door. She risked a glance behind her and saw that she was finally alone. Turning back to the wall, she took a deep breath and began to pray for safety in whatever it was Karen was doing. She also prayed that she would be able to find a way home when this mess was over.

"Amen," she breathed when she finished.

"The church is further down the road." Sarah jumped at the voice and spun around. William stared back at her, a large black saddle slung over his arm. His gaze didn't falter, and she felt like a kid caught with her hand in the cookie jar, though she knew she'd done nothing wrong.

He walked over to her and laid the saddle across a post that had been driven into the wood floor.

"Is there anything I can help you with?" he asked. Sarah didn't note any hostility in his tone, and he didn't appear irritated, so she decided to answer him honestly.

"I'm sorry, no. I-I just enjoy looking at the horses. I can leave, though."

He frowned and opened his mouth to answer, then closed it as a commotion sounded from outside. A masculine voice yelled something that Sarah couldn't make out, a child cried, and a woman's scream rent the air.

William pointed a finger at her. "Stay," he commanded. Then he bolted for the door, his long legs carrying him quickly outside.

The blood in Sarah's ears was pumping, and her heart beat at a rapid pace. She had heard him tell her to remain inside, but her instincts told her that something was wrong.

She ran out the door and came to a stop just outside the entrance. William stood further out with his back to her, staring at the large group of people that had assembled in the street. Her eyes slid past him and became riveted on the young girl fighting against the grip that two guards had on her arms. Her hood fell back, revealing long red hair.

Karen.

Chapter Eleven

"No."

Sarah had meant to scream the word, but it came out weakly and strained in her current state of fright. How had they found her? And what would they do to her? Sarah looked around her helplessly, not knowing what to do.

She heard the guard holding Karen cry out as she kicked him hard in the leg in an attempt to free herself. The offended guard landed a hard blow to the side of her head, stilling her movements as her body sagged in his arms. For one horrifying moment, Sarah thought that he might have killed her. Then she saw the girl roll her head up long enough to spit at the guard's boots.

The anger Sarah felt over seeing him land another blow on Karen's head seemed to free her from the spell that kept her in her place, giving her sudden strength. She shouted Karen's name, but the sounds and cries coming from the growing mob drowned her out.

Gabriel Dunlivey suddenly emerged from the throng, glaring at Karen. He pointed a scraggly finger at her.

"Witch!" he cried, his face contorted in rage. Sarah could almost sense Karen's thoughts from her vantage point behind the crowd. She imagined that they mirrored her own ill feelings toward him.

"We've been trying to find her, and now we've captured the witch!" he cried out again, more victoriously this time. Most of the men in the gathering seemed to scoff at his outburst, but the children cowered in fear, and some of the women cried out in terror, obviously believing his ridiculous accusation.

"What proof do you have?" someone shouted. Sarah thought it might have been William, but she didn't know his voice well enough to identify it among the sea of onlookers. Dunlivey sneered at the crowd as he searched for the owner of the voice. When he couldn't locate him, he motioned for the guards to take Karen away. Her eyes looked over toward the livery and locked on Sarah's face. Karen must have read her expression because she shook her head frantically.

"Don't," she yelled.

Dunlivey must have thought that she was crying out in anguish at her fate because he smiled wickedly. Sarah knew that Karen was warning her not to do anything, but when they started to pull the girl out of the mob, all sense left her, and her reflexes kicked in.

"No!" she yelled, though no one in the dispersing group paid her much mind. Rain began to fall slowly, and then large drops fell from the sky, driving any lingering townsfolk away in search of shelter.

William turned around at her shout and saw her bolting forward. She hadn't even realized that she'd moved, but when she tried to race past him, his strong arms wrapped around her waist and held her back. The action caused her feet to lift off the ground, and she strained against his hold as he pulled her backward. Karen and the guards were nowhere to be seen, but she still fought against his grip frantically.

He pulled her out of the sudden downpour into the livery and closed the large door with his boot. After they were safe, he released her slowly, as though afraid she might run again or turn her anger on him. She might have done just that if her knees hadn't been shaking so badly; she had to press her back against the nearest wall for support.

Sarah slid down slowly until she was sitting on the floor, suddenly feeling like she had been playing a game with the world and had just lost. She began shivering uncontrollably, and William knelt down beside her.

"Are you cold?" he asked. Although water ran down her neck and the dress she wore felt heavy from the rain that had soaked all the way through, she shook her head.

When she looked up, Sarah found herself gazing into the deepest blue eyes she'd ever seen, eyes filled with compassion. Droplets of water hung on his thick eyelashes and dripped from the dark hair that clung to his forehead. His voice had been soft when he spoke, and his expression was concerned. It was the most emotion he had shown since she'd met him, and she found herself asking this stranger the question that burned her mind.

"What will they do to her?" she whispered, her voice strained.

A muscle in his jaw twitched, but his gaze remained unchanged. He took a moment to answer. "If she is found guilty, they will have her burned at the stake."

Sarah's eyes grew large. "Why?"

He searched her face, as though trying to gauge whether she really wanted to hear his answer.

"Please, just answer me honestly."

He hesitated for a split second. "They think that the only way to get the devil out of a witch is to burn it out, so a hanging is not enough."

Sarah nodded her head as if she understood, though she felt more lost and confused than ever. She closed her eyes against the tears that threatened to spill over and shivered, though the building felt cozy from the fire. So many thoughts tumbled around in her head, and she felt numb, empty. She didn't know how to save Karen or stop the king's brother from finishing his evil deeds, and she had absolutely no idea how to get home. Despair suddenly washed over her, chilling her more than the cold rain had.

Please, Father. Help me, she prayed silently. She heard William get up, but she didn't bother to open her eyes as she continued to entreat God to make this easier, or at least bearable. She felt something rest upon her shoulders and glanced at the quilted blanket that William had draped over them. It smelled of hay and wood, and she found the scents strangely comforting.

She glanced over at William, who was adding logs to the fire, shifting them with a long poker. After he was finished, he walked over to her. Sitting on the floor in front of her, his broad forearms resting on his knees, he leaned forward, giving her his full attention. He seemed to be waiting on her.

"Do you believe she's what he says she is?" Sarah asked quietly, staring at the faded quilt as she fingered its threads. She knew his opinion wouldn't change the situation, but she needed the reassurance that someone was on her side.

He scoffed, and the sound surprised her into looking up at him. His eyes narrowed. "Dunlivey is a fool if I ever saw one. The woman he was accusing has come in many times before, and I do not believe what he says about her. The cod should be strung up for what he's done." His eyes darkened, and she shivered, glad that she wasn't on the receiving end of his anger. She looked at his wet clothes and pulled the quilt from her shoulders.

"Here," she held it out to him. "I'm feeling warmer, and right now you look wetter than me."

William stared at the offering. She couldn't read his expression, but it looked like he wasn't accustomed to having people take care of him.

He shook his head. "I thank you, but no. You need it more than I do. I am used to the elements."

A small smile came across her lips. "I wouldn't really call a rain shower an 'element.' Besides, I like the rain . . . under different circumstances."

William stared at her. He cleared his throat and shook his head again.

"No, you may keep it. Thank you."

Sarah nodded and replaced the blanket on her shoulders. For a few minutes, the only sound in the livery was that of the rain pelting against the roof. They both stared out the window, watching the large drops fall in a steady downpour. Some rain had blown in through the window, but neither made any move to mop up the small puddle.

"How long have you known her?" he asked without taking his eyes from the window.

Sarah looked at him, startled by the sound of his voice. She shifted nervously. "Why do you ask?"

He stared at the falling rain outside. "I know you most likely don't want people to know that you are associated with her, but I heard you call out her name, and I can tell by your face that it is not simply a random bystander that you are concerned for." His gaze drifted to her. "Am I correct?"

Sarah swallowed hard and nodded reluctantly. If anyone found out about their friendship, their plan could be ruined—especially if she were burned beside Karen.

William's eyes bore into hers, seeming to understand her fear. "You can trust me." His voice was deep and masculine, and she suddenly felt safe in his presence.

"I know I can."

CRSD

Sarah spent the next hour recounting the entire story to this man whom she barely knew. She told him everything, except for the part about traveling through time to get here, which she imagined would be difficult to explain. The sound of the steady rain began to sooth her, and she found that it was almost therapeutic to talk about the past three days and have him simply listen.

When she told William of Karen's suspicions about Cadius' involvement in the king's illness, his expression suddenly became guarded, and he looked away from her.

"I suppose we will never know if she was right, then," he said.

"Well, that's part of my problem." Over the past hour, Sarah had developed a strange determination to finish what Karen had started, so much so that she felt a stirring of anticipation when she thought about the quest before her. "She asked me to figure out exactly what's going on if anything happened to her. I promised her I would, and I intend to follow through."

William's eyes darkened, and she forced herself to remain in her place and not shrink back at the intensity of his gaze. "Do you realize how dangerous that is?" He didn't raise his voice, but she could feel his anger in each word, which surprised her.

"I'll be careful," she said, stubbornness evident in her words. She could feel herself growing angry, so she took a calming breath before continuing. "I'm going to get help from someone."

"Who?" he asked.

"I was hoping you could help me find him." Out of the corner of her eye, she saw the large black stallion hang its head over the side of his stall. She glanced at it and looked back to William. Lowering her voice, she said, "I know it's his horse. It's the Shadow's."

His face gave away nothing, but the twitching muscle in his jaw indicated that she'd hit her mark.

"I know it is because I saw it the first night I arrived here. You have to tell me where I can find him. He's the only one that can help me sort out this mess."

William sighed and dragged a hand down his face. "I don't know that I can help you."

"Please. I have to save her; she's my only chance to get home." Sarah leaned forward, hoping with every fiber of her being that he would allow her to finish what Karen began. "*Please*, you have to help me. I don't have a choice. I have to finish this."

"Everything is a choice," he said quietly. He stared at her a moment before rising to his feet and offering her his hand.

"I will see what I can do."

Chapter Twelve

Sarah exited the livery several hours later, and William followed silently behind her. After he'd promised to help her, the tension between them had eased. They'd spent the rest of their time together trying to stay out of the storm. William let her watch him make an elongated pair of tongs for placing wood into a fireplace, explaining that the rain couldn't keep him from filling his orders.

Sarah watched him as he hammered the glowing tips of the tongs to better grip the wood, and she couldn't help but observe the way his damp shirt clung to the corded muscles on his arms and his lean torso as he expertly flattened the iron. She averted her gaze when she realized she was staring, and she was careful to keep her eyes on his work rather than him as he finished the tongs and dipped them into a basin of rainwater to cool. He also showed her how to shoe a horse, though she stayed a ways off for that tutorial.

Few people were milling about the square outside, though it was only drizzling now. Sarah looked up at the sky and could see the glow of the sun through the grey clouds. She was surprised to see that the light hung so low in the sky. There were only two or so hours of light left, and she hoped that the Joneses hadn't put out a search party for her and Karen yet.

She swallowed hard at the thought of her friend's predicament. How was she going to explain this to the family that awaited their return?

"I don't know what to tell the people we're staying with," she confessed to William in a small voice. "They treat Karen like a daughter, and I know this will crush them."

"Tell them that she is staying with an acquaintance in town and will be back in a few days."

"I can't lie to them," she said, her eyes wide at the thought.

"It is not a lie." He lifted his shoulders in a shrug. "She is staying in the castle, where Dunlivey is also staying, and you said she had encountered him before."

"And the part about the few days she'll be away?" Sarah asked quietly.

William turned away and let his gaze rested on the hazy clouds that hovered in the sky. He ran a hand through his dark, wavy hair. "You had better go before you lose all of your light."

Sarah nodded her head. "Thank you for listening, William."

"Please, call me Will. Almost everyone does."

She gave him a small smile. "Thank you, Will."

He led her out into the square. She was so distracted by her thoughts and her planning that she didn't even notice where they were until they'd stopped. The wagon she and Karen had ridden into town sat before them underneath the awning of a fruit vendor who had packed up most of his produce in the rain. The two horses shook their heads in irritation at being left alone, but thankfully they were still tied and ready to go. She sent up a grateful prayer that they hadn't run off in the storm.

"I saw Karen leave it here earlier," Will explained. "I thought you should probably take it back with you so you don't have to walk in the rain."

"It's only misting," she said with a grin, and then her expression grew serious. "Thank you again for everything, Will."

He nodded his head, looking uncomfortable at her gratitude. He took her hand gently and helped her into the wagon. When she was seated, he quickly released his hold on her and handed her the reins.

She gave him one last smile before setting the horses into motion. She was so intent upon her potential meeting with the Shadow that she didn't notice how Will watched, unmoving, as the wagon rolled away and out of sight.

CR80

Just tell the truth, it's that simple.

Sarah kept repeating the words over and over in her head as she walked up the porch steps and opened the door to the house. Dusk had settled by the time she had arrived, and the fireplace in the living room had been lit to stave off the night chill. It had been a cold ride through the forest as she tried to find her way back to the Joneses' home in the fading light, and the warmth of the house caused Sarah's chilled body to sag in pleasure.

Leah had pulled one of the chairs close to the fire and sat with a book in her hand, reading intently. She glanced up and smiled when she heard Sarah enter, then went back to her book. Sarah breathed a sigh of relief that Leah hadn't asked where she had been all day.

Seth walked out of the kitchen just as she was about to walk through the doorway. She nearly plowed into him, but she stopped short of ramming him in the chest.

"Where have you been?" he demanded, taking a step back to see her more clearly.

Sarah winced and was momentarily taken aback by his presence and his reaction to her absence. You have to tell him. He needs to know the truth.

He raised his eyebrows at her pause. "Well?"

Her mouth felt dry, but she managed to sound normal and nonchalant when she said, "I got held up in town."

Seth looked behind her. "Where's Karen?"

She tried to stop her legs from shaking. She was tired and emotional, and it took every ounce of strength she had left to remain standing. After a moment, she realized that he was still waiting for an answer.

Just tell him that she's in trouble. Maybe he can even help.

She took a deep breath. "Karen's staying with someone in town." Coward.

He looked surprised at this news. "Really? I didn't know that."

Sarah nodded, thinking hard. "Her appointment didn't go the way she had hoped." Well, that much was true. "It's a little more extensive than she originally thought, so she had to stay behind in town."

"Oh." Was he buying it? She felt a mixture of guilt and relief at this.

"She does that sometimes," Seth continued, nodding almost to himself. "I don't know why I didn't think of that first. She pretty much always leaves without telling us where she's going. But you should have said how long you were going to be out. We were worried."

"There's nothing to worry about," she assured him. "I'm fine? See?" She held her arms akimbo to show that she was unscathed.

"Sarah, is that you?" Ruth Jones poked her head around the doorjamb and smiled. "There you are. Are you hungry? We're just about to have supper."

Originally, she had come into the house in hopes of finding something to eat—she hadn't had anything since breakfast—but now the mere thought of food caused Sarah's nervous stomach to churn. All she wanted to do was sit down and think about her next move for tomorrow. She shook her head at the invitation.

"No, thank you. I am very tired from the day's travels and simply wish to rest." She had seen a renaissance movie for her history class last year, and the main character had said that exact thing to a friend, so she felt it was appropriate—overdone, but appropriate. Sarah had decided that since she was supposed to act like she belonged, she would try to sound more like the townsfolk. Thankfully, she hadn't developed an English accent in her attempt at accuracy.

Ruth looked disappointed at her refusal, but she nodded in understanding. "You must be tired. Why don't you go rest, and we will save a plate for you. I can have Leah bring it to you later."

Sarah smiled and nodded her gratitude. She avoided eye contact with Seth as she turned around and left the house without a backward glance. A knot had formed in her stomach over lying to him. At times like these, she wished her parents hadn't instilled such good morals in her. Maybe then she wouldn't feel like she had swallowed a baseball right now.

CRSO

Once outside, she took a deep breath of the cool night air. It calmed her nerves some, and her stomach began to unwind with each intake of breath. She walked slowly to the back of the barn that faced the hills and hid her from the view of the house. She leaned her back against the wood and wrapped her arms tightly around her middle. The old feelings of loneliness began to seep in again, and she looked up. The stars shone brightly through the light mist of clouds still left from the storm, and she felt silly for thinking that she was ever alone.

"Thanks for staying with me," she whispered to the twinkling lights and felt a smile touch her lips. She knew she would be okay as long as God was there with her.

A sound caught her attention, and she turned, jumping back at the sight of the tall hooded figure. Her heartbeat began to return to normal when she realized who it was.

"It's you," she whispered in relief.

The Shadow took a step closer, and some part of her reminded her that she should be afraid. She was so distracted by her excitement over his sudden appearance that she paid the thought no mind.

"Did Will ask you to come?"

"You need help," he said in answer to her question, his voice as deep as she remembered.

She nodded. "Um, yes. Yes, I do." She stilled her head lest she break her neck from overusing it. She felt suddenly nervous and wiped her palms on her dress. "I—I also wanted to thank you," she began awkwardly. "You know, for helping me escape the other night."

He dipped his head once in acknowledgement.

"Did Will explain everything to you?" She wasn't exactly sure how much he could help if he didn't know what was going on, so she wanted to clear that up first before she continued.

He nodded silently.

"I know it sounds crazy," Sarah said when he remained silent. The silence stretched on, and she felt herself growing uncomfortable; she began to ramble in her nervousness. "It's just an assumption that Karen had, and I have no idea if it's true or not. It seems to make some sense, though, doesn't it?"

"It seems very possible."

She was taken aback by his response. He believed her? The story seemed crazy even now, and she'd had time to get used to the idea.

"Do you know where to begin?" he asked.

This caused her to pause. She hadn't actually gotten that far in her planning. Actually, she hadn't really gotten anywhere in her planning.

"I was kind of hoping that you could help with that," she admitted reluctantly. "I'm new here and don't really know my way around, so I would need to know where to go."

The Shadow nodded, his hood bobbing slightly with the movement. Sarah couldn't help but wonder what was beneath it. Was he disfigured, trying to hide his ugliness beneath the hood? Or maybe he was just a do-gooder who wished to hide his identity from those who wished to destroy him.

He cleared his throat. Sarah realized that she had lost herself to her thoughts once again and that he was still waiting for her to speak. She shook her head and mentally kicked herself.

"I just thought that you might, you know, have some suggestions," she said.

He was silent for a long moment, and she thought she might not receive an answer.

"Scout out the castle tomorrow," he said after a pause. "Stay out of sight and out of trouble."

"What do you mean 'scout out the castle?'" she asked, confused.

"Be observant; see if anything strange occurs. I will meet you just outside of town after dark. Do not tell anyone of our meeting."

She nodded. "But why after dark?" She regretted the question the moment it left her lips, wishing for the millionth time that she didn't always say what was on her mind.

"I am not much of a day person," he answered simply.

Sarah nodded again, feeling foolish.

I think it's pretty obvious that he doesn't waltz around in the daylight, Matthews, she silently reprimanded herself.

"Okay," she said, her voice higher than usual. She cleared her throat. "That sounds good. How will I know where to meet you outside of town, though?"

"I will find you," he said and turned to leave. He stopped and looked back at her. "By the way, welcome to Serimone." Then he disappeared into the shadows, leaving her alone in the dark.

Chapter Thirteen

Sarah tried to sleep, but her anxiety over the next morning caused her to stay up most of the night. After waking for the third time, she began to pray for wisdom in the coming day—and especially peace and safety for Karen.

With Karen gone, Sarah began to realize how much she had come to care for the older girl and how much she valued her friendship. They had known each other for less than four days, but already the barn seemed empty and lonely without her presence to light its dark interior.

Protection for her friend was heavy on Sarah's mind as she fell asleep and when she awoke the next morning. The sun was high in the sky, and although her eyes felt tired and puffy from lack of sleep, she was grateful that she had slept the few hours she did.

She dressed from the trunk Karen had left in the barn, barely even looking at the dark burgundy garment she pulled out. It wasn't one of the nicest dresses, but when it became dark, she wanted to blend in as much as possible. She hadn't bothered to unbraid her hair when she'd crawled into bed last night; when she noticed that her hair framed her face in kinky waves, she realized that her elastic hair band must have fallen off sometime in the night. She stared at the large stack of hay she used as a bed, knowing it was futile to look for it in that mess. Struggling to pull her hair into the same messy braid she had done yesterday, Sarah concluded that she braided her hair now just as well as she had when she was seven. She eventually gave up, deciding to bring the leather strap she had found in the trunk with her in case Ruth or Leah agreed to help her.

Sarah took her time walking to the house for breakfast. She had decided to tell them that she was going to visit Karen in town and wouldn't be back until late. She hoped they wouldn't grow suspicious of her leaving so much; she wanted to figure out this whole mess without their being aware.

Upon opening the front door, Sarah was immediately greeted by the delicious smells that wafted from the kitchen. Her stomach grumbled, and she remembered that she hadn't eaten much the day before. She would have to ask Ruth to pack her a small lunch so she wouldn't starve while she investigated the castle.

She walked into the kitchen and noticed that the lady of the house was the only one in the room. Ruth looked up and smiled at her as she entered.

"Is there any way I can help?" Sarah asked.

"I just finished setting the table, and the food is just finishing up, so all we have left to do is wait."

Sarah nodded and tentatively asked, "Would you mind braiding my hair before breakfast? I tried to do it myself, but . . ."

The older woman smiled. "Of course not, dear. Come and sit over here." She gestured to one of the table chairs. Sarah sat down obediently, and Ruth set to work gently smoothing and twisting her loose curls into a braid.

Sarah thought of all the times her mom had braided her hair when she was young. It had always seemed like a special bonding experience as they giggled and shared secrets that only the two of them knew. But as Sarah had grown older, she had wanted to spend more time with her friends, which left little time for mother-daughter bonding experiences. She had eventually stopped asking her mom to braid her hair altogether since it was faster to leave it down or pull it into ponytail. Sarah suddenly realized that she missed those special times together. She wished that she could turn back the clock and be her mom's little girl again.

She felt herself tearing up at the thought. Why had she wanted to grow up so quickly? Had she really thought that her parents would be around forever and that she could just take them for granted? She realized with great regret that she had.

Ruth grabbed the leather strap that Sarah had placed on the table and tied her hair securely.

"There," she said, taking a step back.

Sarah pushed her sad thoughts aside as she ran a hand over the back of her head, satisfied with the lack of bumps and stray hairs.

"Thank you very much," she said with a pleased smile, hoping her face held no evidence of the tears she had felt a moment ago.

Ruth beamed. "It's not every day I get to braid a girl's hair. Leah usually wears it down, and Karen does it herself." She paused, and her smile faded. She seemed to hesitate. "Speaking of Karen . . ."

Uh-oh, Sarah thought, squirming in her seat and preparing herself for any question the older woman might ask.

"Well, as you know," Ruth continued, "Karen stays with us most of the time, and we're used to her coming and going without notice. But never before has she shown up with a friend."

She raised a hand to prevent interruption. "Now don't get me wrong; you're just as welcome here as Karen is, and we simply adore you, Sarah. But that's part of the problem."

She glanced over her shoulder at the front door and turned back to face Sarah. She bent closer to her and lowered her voice. "Ever since we met Karen, she's been like family. She and Seth are very close, and I had always hoped that they might possibly marry someday. Do you understand?"

Sarah nodded slowly, though she wasn't sure what this had to do with her. "You think that Karen and Seth make a good couple."

Ruth nodded. "I do. And I know that Karen has feelings for my son, but I don't think Seth has ever cared for her in the way I'd hoped. Then you came along."

"Me?" Sarah squeaked. "What does this have to do—?"

Ruth raised her hand again to stop her. She smiled kindly. "Let me explain. I didn't even realize it until yesterday. I very rarely see my son angry, but he was inconsolable while you were gone."

"He was angry with me for going into town?" Sarah asked incredulously.

"No, no, dear. He was worried and didn't know how to show his fear. Instead of expressing what he was feeling, he became irritated with himself for letting you leave, and that frustration showed."

Sarah was silent for a minute while she thought this over. "But I never encouraged him. I do care for him, I guess, but . . ."

Ruth nodded. "I know. That's why I wanted to tell you this, just so that you can be aware of what is going on where Seth is concerned. I just want you to be careful with my son's heart, that's all. "

"What should I do?" Sarah asked, not wanting to make the decision herself.

"I can't tell you that." The older woman looked apologetic. Sarah felt deflated for a moment before an idea popped into her head. The older woman had just given her an excuse to be absent for the day.

"Why don't I give him some time alone today? I'll go into town and visit Karen, and then I can be back after dark."

Ruth appeared surprised. "Oh, dear, I wasn't asking for you to leave."

"I know that, but this way, Seth can have a day to think and come to the conclusion that I'm not the right girl for him; Karen is."

"There's no reason for you to be away." Ruth Jones looked sorry that she had said anything about the matter, but Sarah was relieved that she had. "I honestly cannot say if he has feelings for Karen other than brotherly affection. There's no telling if he might ever feel more than that. I shouldn't have said anything about my hopes for the two of them. It wasn't my place, and I'm sorry."

"Don't be sorry," Sarah said, trying to hide her excitement so she didn't insult the kindly woman. "I can leave as soon as we finish eating."

Ruth seemed to be thinking it over, and Sarah had to bite her lip to keep from grinning in anticipation. "Well, I suppose it could do him some good," she said slowly, if not reluctantly. "But I truly don't want you to be thinking that I do not want you around. We truly care for you."

Sarah nodded quickly, feeling suddenly energized. "I completely understand, but I think this would be better for both of us. When Seth has time to think it over, he'll realize that we're completely wrong for each other."

"But you'll be half starved by nightfall if all you eat is the morning meal." Ruth seemed to kick into mother mode. "I'll fix up a basket for you."

Sarah smiled at the kind woman, thankful that she didn't have to ask. "I would appreciate that."

CRIÑO

Breakfast was strained and awkward for Sarah. Seth sat next to her, and she shifted uncomfortably in her seat every few minutes, though he appeared to be perfectly at ease with the arrangement. Ruth seemed to notice her discomfort and smiled sympathetically when she caught her eye.

Seldom did Sarah join the conversation around the table. She hadn't thought it possible, but she felt more out of place here than she had before. She just wanted to go back home and tell Lilly she was all right. She didn't even mind leaving for school in a couple of weeks, so long as it meant being back home. But she had made a promise, and she would do her best to keep it.

"If you'll excuse me," she said, rising from her seat as soon as she finished eating. Every bite had tasted like sawdust in her mouth. "I'm going to visit Karen this morning and need to leave soon."

"How long will you be gone?" Seth asked. Having anticipated that he would ask that, she had already prepared her answer.

"Fairly late," she said casually, as though it were nothing to worry about. "We'll probably spend some time around town, maybe do a little shopping."

With that, she thanked Ruth for the meal, picked up the basket that the older woman had prepared, and walked out the front door. She waited for the sound of the door closing behind her, and she groaned when she instead heard the hinges squeak as the door swung back open. She heard large boots clomp across the porch behind her, but she kept walking toward the barn. She didn't have to look behind her to know that Seth was following.

"So, you're leaving again?"

"Yes," she said simply, feeling uncomfortable with his concern and the knowledge of his feelings for her.

He caught up to her quickly and stopped in front of her, forcing her to halt in the middle of the grass. She looked up at him defiantly. She was sure her expression dared him to stop her, and she couldn't remember ever feeling so determined. Then again, she'd never had such a large responsibility thrust upon her and been completely alone in doing it.

"Is Karen in trouble?" Seth asked, staring her in the eyes.

Sarah debated how to answer without lying. She decided to redirect the conversation. "Does shopping and chatting with a friend sound like trouble to you?" She forced a grin and received a smile from him return.

"I guess not. It's just that the two of you have been gone so much, and I started to wonder . . . and worry." He placed a hand on her arm. "Just be careful, okay?"

Sarah nodded, feeling increasingly uncomfortable under his gaze. Thankfully, he removed his hand and dutifully readied the wagon without being asked. He didn't speak until he helped her inside.

"You look very nice today, Sarah." He seemed almost shy about saying it, and the comment took her by surprise as she glanced down at her simple dress. Sarah felt a stirring of sympathy for the sweet man; he looked more like a boy with a crush than a grown man who didn't quite know how to express his feelings. She hoped his crush would fade quickly.

"Thanks," she mumbled as she flicked the reins to get the horses moving. She still hadn't quite gotten the hang of driving the wagon, but she had no trouble motivating the animals to move.

During her ride, she thought about the fact that four days ago she had been sitting in her room complaining about the lack of adventure she had in her life.

She laughed without humor as she rode along on the empty dirt road. If only the Sarah from four days ago could see her now, driving through the forest to scout out a castle in order to find out who was poisoning a king. And all this was happening in another dimension almost nine hundred years before she was born.

Yet even though everything around her seemed chaotic and she might be running for her life soon, some small part of her—that crazy, adventurous spirit inside—was secretly enjoying this. Although it was not exactly what she'd had in mind, it was an adventure, pure and simple. And she would have quite a story to tell when she got back home.

If she survived to tell it.

Sarah swallowed hard as she entered the town gate and looked around. It seemed that everyone had come out of their houses to shop or stand on the street corners and talk with friends. Some of the women glanced at her as she drove by and began whispering to one another, their eyes occasionally flicking back to her.

Sarah felt self-conscious beneath their scrutiny. She realized that by standing alone outside of the castle with nothing to do, she might look conspicuous. She couldn't draw unwanted attention to herself—not now. She needed to blend in while she completed the task before her.

Then, she had an idea.

Chapter Fourteen

Sarah entered the building hesitantly, the basket hanging from the crook in her arm. She had left the horses unattended out front—she hadn't had the nerve to get close enough to their faces to tie the reins to the hitching post. She figured that if they had survived the day before alone in a storm, they would be all right outside for a few minutes.

Allan stood with his back to her while he worked on shoeing a horse. She glanced nervously at the large animal he was working on to be sure the beast didn't suddenly charge at her. She spotted Will brushing the black stallion in the stall at the back and quietly made her way over to him, hoping that Allan wouldn't notice her. She wasn't quite sure why, but his gaze and attention made her feel uncomfortable; he seemed like the type of man who went after anything that moved.

Will looked up as she approached and nodded his head once in acknowledgement. He set the brush on a nearby bench and walked toward her.

"Hello," he said. He raised an eyebrow, silently questioning her presence there. It was obvious to Sarah that he had not expected her so soon.

"Hi," she said quietly, nervously folding her hands behind her back. Allan glanced up from his work. He straightened when he saw her and grinned coyly. Sarah felt like rolling her eyes at his arrogance, but she somehow managed to restrain herself.

"Do you have a minute?" she asked Will.

He nodded and turned to his employee. "The new hay came in today and needs to be moved inside. Take care of it, would you?"

"Want her all to yourself, eh?" Allan asked mischievously, that irritating grin still on his face.

"Now." Will spoke the word quietly, but with such force and authority that it surprised Sarah. Allan seemed to take it all in stride and simply shrugged his shoulders before leaving.

Will didn't say anything after Allan left. When she turned to him, Sarah realized that he was waiting for her to speak.

"W-well, you see," she began clumsily. *Why am I always such a nervous wreck around him?* "I wanted to know if you have some free time this afternoon."

He seemed to think this over for a moment, and Sarah shifted her weight from one foot to the other as she waited. She had never been completely at ease with complete silence; she wondered if Will was aware that he had perfected long, awkward silences. She felt uncomfortable waiting for his answer.

"Why?" he asked at last.

"Well"—she glanced around to make sure that Allan hadn't come back in and lowered her voice—"the Shadow came to see me last night. He said that I should watch for anything suspicious or weird at the castle."

"All right," Will said slowly, his expression blank. "What does that have to do with me?"

"There are so many people out that it would look odd for me to just sit outside of the castle gates for the entire afternoon. I thought that if I had someone with me, I wouldn't be quite so conspicuous." She took a deep breath and spoke quickly. "You were the only one I could think of, otherwise I wouldn't be bothering you now."

He was silent for a moment. "You want me to spend the entire afternoon with you?"

And some of the evening, if it comes to that. Sarah decided to keep that information to herself.

"Well, yes," she said. "I have food, if that's what you're worried about." She raised the basket in her hands. She hadn't inspected its contents, but judging by its weight, there was enough for two.

"I'm not concerned about provisions," he said with a shake of his head.

Sarah thought for a minute. "Is it improper for us to be alone together?" It was the only thing that made sense to her. Or maybe he just didn't want to be around her.

"That's not it at all," he said, looking surprised by the idea. "I have never cared much about what other people thought of me."

"Oh," was all she said, feeling confused.

"I was just wondering how long you would need me," he said. Humor laced his words, though he didn't smile.

"Oh," she said again. "Well, I guess for as long as you're free." She waited for him to refuse, but he actually seemed to consider her request. She chewed on her lower lip as she waited, then realized what she was doing and stopped. She did not want to look too anxious.

"All right," he said at last.

Sarah let out a sigh of relief. "Thank you."

Allan entered at that moment and smiled at the two of them. "Alone again, I see?"

"Mind your business, Allan," Will growled. It was the first time Sarah had ever seen someone elicit much emotion from him, and judging by Allan's surprised expression, he hadn't seen it much either.

"I'm sorry," he mumbled and went back to the horse he'd been shoeing, glancing up at his employer occasionally.

"We should go now," Will said. He placed his hand on Sarah's elbow and guided her outside without an explanation to Allan. He didn't speak as they walked toward the castle gates.

"What did he mean by us being alone again?" she asked after they were a good distance from the shop.

"He needs to watch his mouth," he said, avoiding her gaze as he stared straight ahead and guided them around a group of rowdy young men.

"You didn't answer my question," she prodded.

He looked down at her, and for the first time, Sarah realized how tall he was—even taller than Seth, making him well over six feet. Though Seth had built more bulk from his work on his parents' farm, this man appeared to be broader in the shoulders. For a split second, she wondered if he thought she was too short—the difference in their heights was over half a foot. And then she wondered why she even cared. She didn't, of course, not in the least.

Will expelled his breath and looked away. "People are talking."

"About what?" she asked.

"Apparently, they look down upon a young man helping a woman out of the rain." Seeing her confused frown, he continued. "Some people saw me take you into the livery yesterday without a chaperone, and when neither of us emerged until hours later, they began to speculate."

Sarah remembered the women's glances as she came into town, and she quietly murmured, "Oh." Her face turned red at the thought of what so many had assumed. "You mean they think that we . . ." She trailed off, unsure of how to end her sentence politely. "But nothing happened!"

"You and I know that. However, exciting things rarely happen here, so the people snatch up any chance at gossip they can get." He looked at her face and caught her worried expression as she looked around nervously. She noticed for the first time the stares they were receiving and glanced down at his light grasp on her arm; she had forgotten that his hand was still there.

"They don't know either of us personally," he said calmly. He didn't bother to look around him, though he couldn't possibly have missed the looks of disapproval they received. "Who are they to be making rash judgments of people they don't know? There is no need to worry. It will pass as soon as some new scandal erupts. They are easily distracted."

Sarah nodded uncertainly, trying to match his long legged strides. He seemed to notice that she was having a hard time keeping up and slowed his steps to match hers. They approached the gate to the castle, and he released his grip on her arm. She was confused at the sudden disappointment she felt when his strong hand fell away.

"Shall we walk around first?" he asked.

Sarah smiled gratefully, glad that she didn't have to think of their next move.

They walked around the tall barricade and underneath a series of flying buttresses. Sarah gaped at the incredible arches high overhead that created a wide walkway along the outer ridges of the castle walls. She almost overlooked the small gate leading into the wall on the backside of the fortress, which she thought might have been the servants' entrance. When she asked him about it, Will explained that it was the postern gate, or secondary access, and that it could be used as a sally port for defenders to leave the castle unnoticed in the event of a siege.

Sarah had become riveted by the new sights and sounds around them, and her fascination and intrigue only grew with Will's explanation. She saw a guard walking along the top of the wall, and she asked Will about the walkway and the strange design; she thought that she had seen something similar in one of the many medieval-themed movies she had seen, though the movies were nothing like seeing the power of the fortress firsthand.

"He's patrolling the parapet walkway," Will said, pointing at the guard. "The cutout spaces you see in the wall are the crenelated breastwork that protects the parapet."

She absorbed his words and tried to hide her awe over the expertly carved gaps in the uppermost part of the wall. Encouraged by the fact that he didn't seem to mind her constant questions—instead seeming pleased by her fascination—Sarah continued to point out unknown structures as they walked underneath the arches. He would identify, with a note of pride, she thought, the structure she pointed to and explain its use. She was beginning to feel like she was getting the best history lesson of her life, and she tried to absorb every detail.

It took them some time to travel around the entire fortress, and Sarah was almost disappointed when they came around to the front again.

"Do they always leave that open?" she asked, inclining her head in the direction of the gate.

"In the daylight, yes, but it remains closed throughout the night. King Josiah always wanted his people to feel as though they could come to him for anything. Leaving it open is the one thing that Cadius has done the same as his brother, though I doubt that he does it because of his devotion to his subjects." He folded his arms across his broad chest and said under his breath, "I believe he is simply too lazy to change the routine."

Sarah glanced inside the gate as they passed. A guard stood just inside to the left of the gate, and others patrolled the grounds further in. She turned to Will.

"Can we go inside?"

"I would advise against it. The gate remains open to give the illusion of welcome, but Cadius doesn't enjoy company; he has advised the prince against allowing the people to enter freely. Since the king fell ill, the only time when anyone has entered the castle and been received is for the summer ball."

"What's that?" she asked.

"Each season, the castle holds a ball for some of the more respected people in town and the surrounding villages. It's quite the affair."

"Have you ever been?" she asked curiously.

"I have in the past," he said and cleared his throat. "But I haven't attended for some time." He glanced down at her. "If you haven't already noticed, I am not exactly the most sociable man in town."

"I think you're very agreeable," she said without thinking. She felt the heat creep up her neck when she realized how that must have sounded. "Oh, I didn't . . . I just meant that you seem nice." She avoided his gaze by directing her attention to two little boys playing a game in the street. A middle-aged woman, probably their mother, called them to lunch. They hurried inside their small house and disappeared.

Sarah suddenly remembered the basket on her arm and turned to Will. "Are you hungry?"

He shrugged, and she led him to a nearby stonewall that was short enough for them to sit on. She placed the heavy basket between them, opened it, and peered inside. Two skins filled with goat's milk lay inside, as well as two large slices of bread, fresh cheese, grapes, apples, and a few hardboiled eggs. Ruth had obviously packed enough food for her and Karen to eat lunch together.

Her throat tightened at the thought. She had to push back the sudden guilt she felt over the fact that Karen was in prison while Sarah was having lunch with a handsome stranger.

"What exactly are we supposed to be looking for?" he asked, pulling her from her jumbled thoughts.

She heaved a sigh. "I have absolutely no idea." What did she think she was doing, anyway? Was there even a chance that she could save Karen or figure this mess out?

Will must have read her expression because he said, "We will get her out. Don't worry."

She smiled at the way he said "we." Maybe she wasn't alone in this after all.

"Do you mind if I pray before we eat?" she asked timidly.

He looked surprised, but he quickly wiped the expression from his face. "Do you really think He hears?" he asked.

Sarah took a moment to answer. "I know He always hears."

"But does He care?" he challenged.

"Yes," she said softly, staring into his eyes. "He does care. He wants us to ask because He cares."

"But why ask if you simply receive a negative answer? Tell me that." He appeared calm enough, but Sarah knew she needed to tread carefully.

"Because God desires for you to ask. And even though sometimes you don't get what you were hoping for, you have to trust that it was His perfect will. 'No' is still an answer, it just never seems to be the one that we're looking for."

His dark eyes looked pained for a moment.

Sarah could tell that this was more personal than he was letting on. She tried one last time to reach him before he closed the subject. "Even though you've let go and no longer trust God, Will, it doesn't mean that He no longer loves you."

For a long time, neither of them spoke. Then Will broke the silence. "We can see inside the gate fairly well from here," he said, obviously looking for a way to change the subject. Sarah sighed and quickly prayed over her meal in silence.

☙❧

They ate and talked about nothing in particular for the rest of the afternoon, with Will shying away from any personal questions that she threw his way. They occasionally glanced inside the gate, but nothing of importance was going on that day, so they simply resumed their conversation. They tossed around ways they could get inside the castle without bringing too much attention to themselves, but none of their ideas seemed to work. Then Sarah thought of something and brightened at the idea.

"What about the ball?"

"What about it?" he asked carefully, his eyes narrowing.

"Do you still get an invitation for it?" she asked excitedly.

Will paused, eyeing her skeptically. "I believe I am going to regret admitting that I still do."

She grinned. "Then maybe you should bring a guest with you."

He raised his eyebrows. "And what good would that do, exactly?"

"Then we wouldn't have to sneak in. And once we're inside, there will be so many people that if two of them happened to slip away, no one would really notice." The more she thought about it, the more enthusiastic she became over the idea.

Will took a moment to consider this. "As much as I hate to admit it, that might actually be a good plan."

"Thanks." She scrunched up her face and narrowed her left eye. "I think. When is it?"

"The day after tomorrow."

"Two days," Sarah mumbled to herself, wondering if they could plan it all before then. She smiled in her excitement. It could actually work!

"Do you know what we should be looking for?" His question brought her spirits down, but only a little.

"We need to find something that convicts Cadius of what he's doing," she replied, then she paused briefly. "Or we need to find Karen somewhere inside."

He stood and stared at the sky. The sun was inching closer to the tops of the houses, and Sarah knew that it would be dark within the hour. Where had the day gone?

"We should start heading back. Nothing is going to happen today." He offered his hand to help her up. As they walked past the gate, she felt slightly disappointed that she didn't have anything to tell the Shadow when she saw him that night.

She took another step forward, only to be yanked backward by Will's grip on her arm. He leaned his shoulder against the side of the barricade surrounding the castle and pulled her against his side.

"What are you doing?" Sarah asked in an agitated voice, annoyed at being pulled around.

He put a finger to his lips to silence her. Still confused, she had just opened her mouth to ask him to explain himself when she heard two of the guards from inside the gate talking to each other.

"I don't see how he can," one of them was saying. "Won't the king disapprove?"

"Cadius couldn't care less about the people," the other said, disdain lacing his words. "Besides, who's here to hold Dunlivey back? The king's gettin' weaker every day. Not long now."

"But to keep her locked in the dungeon with no evidence against her, it's just not right. And now these rumors about Dunlivey starving her out or burning her at the stake." He shook his head.

"Well, he'd better hurry up with his deeds before the captain catches word of what he's up to. Captain Quinn's been improving and should be back in a few days, so I'd guess that she doesn't have long."

Their voices grew quieter as they walked away.

Sarah heard the guards leave, but she didn't move. Her legs weakened beneath her weight, and she would have collapsed had it not been for Will's strong arm around her waist holding her up.

"We need to get away from here," he whispered in her ear, and he began dragging her along with him, taking them further and further from the castle. After a few minutes, she was able to support herself, and he removed his arm from around her. They walked silently back to the livery, Will lost to his thoughts and Sarah not caring to say anything.

He stopped beside her wagon and looked down at her. She refused to meet his gaze and kept her watery eyes focused on the ground. He gently lifted her chin with his index finger and bent down so that he was at eye level with her. Still, she averted her gaze.

"We will get her out," he said firmly.

"But what if we can't?" she asked in a small voice, letting her eyes rest on his face.

"We will find her. I promise." Dusk had settled around them, but Sarah clearly saw the determination in his eyes.

She breathed a small sigh and glanced away again, though his finger still held her chin. "There is one thing I've learned since coming here, Will: don't make promises you can't keep."

"I do not make a promise unless I intend to see it to the end."

She appreciated his words, even if he was unable to come through with his promise. Amidst the swirling emotions going on inside of her, she keenly felt the gratitude she had for this man who had chosen to stick by her when he could have easily left.

Suddenly very glad of his presence and overwhelmed with appreciation, Sarah impulsively leaned up on her tiptoes and kissed him lightly on the cheek. He appeared as surprised as she was by the spontaneous gesture and stared at her for some time. He straightened abruptly and cleared his throat.

"You need to go," Will said. His voice sounded gruffer than usual, and Sarah wondered if she had upset him somehow. Then she realized that she had probably just caused another scandal between them. What was she thinking? She had let her emotions rule her common sense and had given the townsfolk more reason to murmur and stare.

"I'm sorry," she whispered without looking at him, jumping into the wagon seat before he had a chance to assist her. She stared straight ahead, though the only thing to look at was the side of the livery, while Will untied the reins.

He sighed as he handed them to her. "Don't be sorry, Sarah. You just need to go. Trust me." She didn't know what he meant by that, but she nodded anyway and managed to get the horses turned around and the wagon pointed in the right direction.

"I will meet you at the castle in two nights about this time," he said. "Simply tell the men at the gate that you are my guest for the ball. They will be expecting you."

Sarah nodded her acknowledgement and prodded the horses into a trot. She needed to get out of there before she smudged either of their reputations further. She took a steadying breath as she headed toward the edge of town.

Chapter Fifteen

Sarah struggled to see in the darkness, but after several minutes, she managed to find a clearing large enough to leave the wagon. She debated ripping down a few leafy branches from the tress to camouflage the cart, but she decided against it; the wagon was far enough away from the main road that she didn't think any passersby would spot it in the night.

She jumped down from her seat and walked a few feet away from the horses while they munched contentedly on the grass beneath their hooves. She sat down and leaned against the trunk of a nearby tree, feeling worn out.

No matter how hard she tried to push the terrifying images away, she kept seeing Karen in her mind: emaciated as she rotted away in the dungeons, or tied to a post in the town square, being consumed by hungry flames as she cried out for help. Sarah couldn't save her friend in either scenario.

She squeezed her eyes shut to block out the images, but that only made them more vivid, as though they were part of a movie being played behind her lids that refused to stop. Silent tears escaped and slid down her cheeks, and she wrapped her arms around herself against the cool wind.

Alone in the silence, the doubts that she had been holding at bay began to break free and poison her consciousness. What on earth was she doing? Spending an entire day with a man she hardly knew anything about—besides the fact that he no longer trusted God—plotting to sneak around a castle, and waiting in the middle of a forest in the dark for someone whose identity no one knew. What had happened to her?

She jumped to her feet at the sound of rustling leaves and spun around to search out the cause of the sound. Several seconds passed before her eyes adjusted to the moonlight; when they finally did, she was able to make out the figure standing silently before her. His green cloak caused blended in with the foliage, making him nearly invisible in the night. Her heartbeat slowed, and she wondered if she would ever get used to him sneaking up on her like that. She wiped the back of her hand across her eyes to get rid of any traces of her tears, grateful for the cover of darkness.

"Thanks for coming," she managed to say past her tight throat.

"What did you find out?" he asked, getting straight to the point.

Sarah swallowed hard. "Nothing about Cadius other than the fact that even the guards don't like him."

He nodded, as if this weren't news to him. "Anything else?"

"Well," she began to say. Her voice wavered, and she had to clear her throat before pressing on. "There are rumors going around about what Dunlivey is going to do to my friend, Karen. I don't know if they're true, and I was hoping that maybe you knew."

"I am sorry; I don't."

Sarah nodded as fresh tears formed. She tried to blink them back, but some escaped her lids and fell noiselessly to the ground. Suddenly, she wished that it weren't the Shadow in front of her, but Will with his strength and determination. She had no idea where the sudden desire had come from, and she decided to stay silent until she had a good enough handle on her emotions to speak.

"Have you figured anything out?" Her voice sounded weak.

"Stay out of town tomorrow," he said. "I need to slip inside the castle and do some digging around. It is best if you aren't anywhere near there."

"In case you get caught?"

"No, you just need to be seen as little as possible. Besides, I never plan on being discovered."

"Sometimes things happen that we don't plan on," she whispered to the dried leaves at her feet.

She looked up at him, feeling weighed down with her hopelessness. "Tell me what you find out," she said. Then she spun around on her heels and stumbled tiredly to the wagon, jumping in and riding away without looking back. This time, he was the one left standing alone in the dark.

☙❧

The Shadow watched her go until he could no longer see her. He turned around and walked silently back to where he had left his horse. The stallion was silent and calm as he approached. The animal inclined its head toward him, and he saw an acute intelligence and awareness in its eyes.

He grabbed his bow and quiver of arrows from the saddle and slung them over his shoulder. The familiar feel of his trusted weapons gave him a sense of security; things were always simpler when he was armed.

Mounting his horse, he rode into town in the direction of the livery. No one ever seemed to notice how often he took his horse from the establishment. Then again, he always did it at night to avoid probing eyes. But he was getting reckless. He needed to be careful, especially with Dunlivey and his cronies keeping an eye out for him. No more late night meetings, no matter who was in need of his help. If he were caught, everything would be ruined.

Sarah's words suddenly ran through his mind: "Things happen that we don't plan on." She didn't know how true that was.

He had left the door unlocked when he had removed his horse earlier, and he now opened it with ease. Working quickly to put everything back the way it had been, he unsaddled the animal and led it into its stall. On his way outside, he grabbed two coils of rope from the wall. He draped the large rope around his shoulder and tied the thinner one around his belt. Clicking the door lock back in place, he crept silently toward his goal. As he went, he melted into the shadows, something he had learned to do as a child; he had perfected the art of being invisible.

He reached the east side of the castle—the least guarded side—and stared up at the tall spires that were shadowed by moonlight. His eyes expertly passed over his surroundings until he spotted the old seamstress's shop. At two stories tall, it would have been perfect for his task if the wooden boards weren't too old to use for scaling. Then he recalled the rose trellis the older woman had placed on the side of her shop years ago. The roses had probably overtaken the trellis by now, but it would be easier than trying to get a handhold on those old rotting boards.

The Shadow stealthily jogged across the short stretch of road to the shop. He crouched low beneath the shuttered window on the first floor, though no light or sound came from inside. At the back of the house, he listened for any sound of movement. Satisfied when all was silent, he walked over to the trellis, which was overgrown with a tangle of thorny roses. He frowned; he hadn't been expecting to scale a wall of thorns.

Steeling himself, he placed his leather-soled boot on a notch in the trellis and began to climb. He moved slowly at first as he tried to locate areas where the thorns were less dense, but it was taking too long. Gritting his teeth, he forced himself to move faster, ignoring the thorns that bit relentlessly into his palms. When he finally reached the top, he dragged himself up onto the roof. Crouching low, he crept across the straw roof to the other side.

He dropped the large coil of rope at his feet, ignoring the bloody mark he saw from his scraped palms. Reaching behind him, he searched through his arrows until he found the one with the steel tip. He only had this one steel arrow; the material was more expensive than he liked and weighed too much to carry a whole quiver full. Despite its downfalls, though, the arrow was useful. Grabbing one end of the rope, the Shadow began to knot it around the middle of the arrow.

He heard a scuffling noise below him and ducked lower on the roof to scan the area. When he caught sight of a large cat running through the street, he released the breath that he'd been holding and quickly finished his task.

Knowing that he had to get over the imposing barricade surrounding the castle, the Shadow stood to his full height and let his gaze drift over the fortress. He hoped to find an easier mark than the courtyard inside the walls; it wasn't impossible to shoot an arrow into the inner courtyard and catch it on something, but it would take too much time, and he didn't want to skewer one of the guards patrolling within accidentally. If he just could find a closer mark.

Aha!

He caught the barely discernible glint of a metal ring used to hang banners in the side of one of the buttresses. It was small, high off the ground, and tucked at an awkward angle inside the arch, but he was nearly eye level with it from his vantage point on the roof.

Satisfied with his mark, he took a step back, set the arrow in the bow, and aimed. He paused to inhale a steadying breath as he always did when he lined up a shot, and the world around him was silenced as he concentrated. He pulled the string back in one fluid motion, stepping on the loose end of the rope as he did so.

One shot, he told himself. Make it count.

His fingers released the string, and he watched the threaded rope flap in the wind as it sailed across the road. The surface of the arrow caught and reflected the moon's light, allowing him to observe the piece of steel slice through the center of the six-inch-wide ring.

He pulled slowly on the end of the rope until the arrow, which was too long to fit through the circular opening, caught on the ring, its length overlapping both sides. He gave a firm tug; it held tight.

Working quickly, he made a narrow loop in the rope he held, securing it with several sturdy knots. He glanced around at the dark rooftops until he spotted what he was looking for.

He began to swing the makeshift noose over his head, slowly at first, then more rapidly as he kept his eyes on the target. He released his hold on the rope. Before it was halfway to its intended destination, he could tell he had released the rope too soon. The loop hit the edge of the roof and then slid off, landing in a useless heap on the ground.

Taking a deep breath to steady his nerves, he tried again, taking his time this round. He released his breath when the rope looped around the thin chimney protruding from the higher rooftop nearby—exactly where he'd intended for it to land.

The Shadow pulled the bow over his shoulder and gripped the line with both hands. Feeling that it was secure, he wrapped his legs around it and firmly locked his knees together. The line dipped until his back nearly brushed the straw roof, but it held.

He began to shimmy across the expanse, one hand over the other, ascending at a slight angle as the line led up to the underside of the tall arch. His father had taught him how to shoot his first arrow, but he had mastered the art of climbing and scaling all on his own. His father had called him a natural.

The Shadow did not look down, though; he never looked down. He wasn't afraid of heights, but he knew that a loss of focus could cost even the most daring and skilled man his life. He focused on his hands and feet as they slid over the rough line, each movement bringing him closer to the arch and his next goal: the parapet walkway.

Ignoring the burning sensation in his hands as the rough rope bit into them, he pressed on toward the other side. Halfway across, his shoulders and biceps began to burn. Though the rooftop had only been a little over twenty feet off the ground—a rough landing if he lost his grip, but not a crippling one—he was now nearly double that height, and the line grew steeper with each pull of his hands.

His eyes trailed upward over the corded rope; motivated by the sight of only a few yards remaining, he forced his shaking muscles to close the last stretch quickly. When he reached the end, he allowed his body to dangle freely in the air as he assessed the distance between himself and the walkway below.

He had just started to swing his body forward to jump onto the walkway when he caught sight of a guard patrolling the upper walk. The Shadow froze, muscles tensing as he dangled there helplessly. His hood had fallen back, and a trickle of sweat ran down his neck, cooling in the night breeze. If the man spotted him now, all would be lost.

His muscles cried out, but his grip on the rope only tightened; he would never survive a drop to the cobbled street below at this height. His only choice was to watch as the guard walked past him. If the guard spotted him, he would probably think he was an angel—or a demon—and flee for his life. But that would draw too much unwanted attention, so he held his breath, willing himself to become one with the shadows for which he was named.

The guard moved languidly down the walkway, and the man cursed the patrol and his slow progress. He could no longer hold his breath, and he tried to control his labored breathing as rivulets of sweat trailed down his exposed face. He waited until the next buttress hid the man from view. Counting on the noise from the guard's footsteps, the Shadow swung his tense body forward, releasing his hold and allowing his body to sail through the night.

He soon realized that he had underestimated the distance. He pumped his arms and legs desperately in the air to give his body the momentum it needed, but he nevertheless began to descend toward the ground. As he fell, his cloak fanned out behind him like a lone wing attempting to give the falling angel flight.

He grunted as his chest slammed into the side of the walkway, and he grappled for a handhold as his body slid over the edge. Pain shot through his abdomen, his legs slipping against the slick stones on the vertical drop to certain death. He barely managed to catch hold of the side of the path. His hands were slick with sweat and blood, and his grip quickly began to loosen as he hung.

He could hear the guard's sandals slapping against the stones as he made his rounds back across the walkway toward him. Gritting his teeth, the Shadow tried to remain calm and think of a possible escape. His hands slipped again; he was only hanging on by his fingertips now.

When the guard was nearly upon him, the Shadow took a quick glance at the cobbled street far below and made his decision.

One chance, he thought to himself.

When the guard's feet came into view, the Shadow used the last of his strength to launch his body forward. His grip caught the man off guard, causing him to stumble and fall. The Shadow bolted lithely to his feet.

The guard eventually managed to stand up and looked around. Quickly tucking his body into a roll, the Shadow came up behind him and wrapped his arms around his neck. The man choked and struggled violently in his arms. The Shadow tightened his hold on the man and the guard gasped, making a choking sound as his body relaxed; the Shadow loosened his grip just before the guard went limp. Leaning the smaller man against the wall, he felt for a pulse. Still alive. He adjusted the guard into a sitting position against the wall. He was out cold.

Glancing up, the Shadow caught the faint outline of the rope swaying in the gentle breeze. It would take too long to cut it down, so he left the line alone, slightly disappointed that he would also have to leave his only steel arrow behind. He leaned over the wall so he could see into the inner courtyard. It was too far down for a straight jump; he needed to climb down. His descent was slow and methodical, and he forced himself not to rush. When he was far enough down, he slid to the ground, landing in a crouch noiselessly. He pulled the hood over his head as he rose to his feet and surveyed his surroundings.

A guard patrolling the opposite end of the courtyard turned around and began making his way toward him; his window of opportunity was closing quickly. The Shadow quickly scanned the ground and spotted a trellis leaning against the west wall, just a foot shy from a window. Upon approaching the trellis—his opportunity for escape—he was relieved to find that the roses trailing up it had been planted recently and appeared far less troublesome than the ones at the old seamstress's shop.

He climbed as quickly as possible, trying to avoid being spotted by the guard. He grasped the last slat and paused for a moment to regain his balance. Then he reached up and pressed on the window panel.

It didn't budge.

He pressed harder against the frame, leaning into it as best he could. Finally, the pane cracked and the window swung open. He pulled himself over the sill and instinctively dropped into a crouch.

The room was completely dark and devoid of any life. As his eyes adjusted to the darkness, he felt his way past the many couches and tables in the sitting room. When he brushed past a small table, he accidently upset an oversized vase; he barely managing to right it before it toppled off the table and crashed to the floor.

He exhaled in relief when he found the door without further mishap. Before opening it, he paused to listen intently for any sound coming from the hallway. When he heard nothing, he cracked the door and peered out.

A servant was coming down the hallway carrying a glass goblet filled with wine. The sound of more footsteps came from the opposite direction. When the footsteps paused, the Shadow was only able to see the newcomer's back.

"Where are you headed?" the newcomer asked. The Shadow thought the voice sounded familiar and tried to place it.

"The physician told me to give this to the king," the servant replied.

"Oh?" the man asked, sounding surprised. "Then I'm glad I caught you. I just saw the good physician downstairs, and he told me to have you give this to the king, instead." He motioned to the silver chalice he held.

The servant looked suspiciously at the goblet. "That's odd. I spoke to him only a moment ago."

The faceless man's thin shoulders lifted in a shrug. "He said he gave you the wrong dosage."

A female voice interrupted them. "Excuse me, sir, but could I speak with you?" A maid emerged from one of the rooms. When the older servant turned his head toward the girl, the other man quickly switched the goblets.

So that's his game, the Shadow thought with disgust, pushing back his desire to shove the man over the railing.

"I'll just take this back to the physician and leave you to your business, then," said the man. He hurried in the opposite direction that he'd come.

The servant shook his head and began making his way toward the king's chambers.

Without thought of the repercussions, the Shadow swung the door wide and jumped out of his hiding place. He briefly registered the shocked face of the servant and the startled gasp from the maid. Grabbing the silver goblet from the tray, he tossed the contents on the floor. The murky green liquid splashed across the stones and began to soak into the ornate rug.

"What on earth!" exclaimed the servant, but the Shadow did not wait for him to come to his senses. He dashed back into the room and threw the goblet on the floor behind him as he jumped out the window. He landed on his feet, sending pain shooting up through his legs.

He ignored the discomfort as he ran toward the front gate. When he heard the servant shouting for the guards, the Shadow untied the shorter length of rope from his belt, tied it the end to an arrow, and set it in his bow. He aimed for the sky and hoped that the arrow would hit something that was strong enough to hold his bulk. He released the string, and the arrow disappeared on the other side.

With no time to check if it was secure, he made a running jump for the short rope; his body slammed into the wood just as the guards caught wind of what the servant was shouting. The guard patrolling the courtyard yelled for him to stop, but he ignored him and kept climbing. He hauled his body over the pointed tips of the gate, dropping down on the other side and pulling the rope with him.

The guards had opened the gate and were shouting behind him, but he didn't turn around. Why were they coming after *him*? He had just saved the king's life!

Chapter Sixteen

The next day seemed to drag on and on for Sarah. At breakfast, everyone had asked how Karen was, and Sarah had pasted on a smile and lied, saying how much fun the two of them had shopping and spending the day together. Her answer seemed to mollify them, which only served to increase Sarah's guilt.

When she became tired of sitting around the house, she asked Leah if she could borrow a book. She was distracted for a time as she sat in the living room and read for the earlier part of the day. But by midafternoon, she had become bored with the lofty language of her book and began to wonder if the next day would ever come.

And then it finally arrived.

She spent a good part of the morning debating how she should broach the subject of the ball with Ruth. She even considered leaving without saying anything so she wouldn't have to explain how she was going as Will Taylor's guest, but she decided against it; she knew that she needed to tell Ruth what her plans were, even if that meant upsetting Seth. Her opportunity came after breakfast while the two women were cleaning up after the meal.

"Mrs. Jones?"

Ruth looked up at her, and when she saw the expression on Sarah's face, she set the plate she had been scrubbing back in the basin and pulled a chair out for herself.

"I can tell that I'll be needing to sit down for this one."

Sarah smiled fondly at the older woman and sat in the chair beside her.

"I want to tell you something, and then I might need your advice." Ruth waited for her to continue.

"You know about the ball that's being held at the castle tonight, don't you?" Sarah asked. The older woman nodded. "Well, I was invited as someone's guest." She sucked in a breath and waited.

"Really?" Ruth raised her eyebrows in surprised pleasure. "By whom?"

Sarah paused. "Will Taylor. I'm supposed to meet him there tonight."

Ruth nodded, and Sarah thought she caught a note of concern in her eyes. "That Will Taylor is a fine man if I ever saw one." She patted Sarah's knee in a gesture of concern that only mothers do. "But do be careful, dear. As handsome as he is, the ladies tend to fawn over him. He doesn't ever encourage any of it, but I just thought you might like to be prepared so it doesn't come as a surprise to you."

Sarah nodded slowly; she wasn't sure she liked the idea of women hanging on Will's arm, though she refused to analyze her feelings on the subject.

"Thanks for your concern," she said sincerely, glad for the woman's honesty. "I think it will be fun to go and see the inside of the castle." She glanced down at her hands folded in her lap. "But my problem right now is that I'm not sure if I should tell Seth or not."

"Ah." Sarah looked up and caught Ruth's sympathetic smile. "Why don't you leave that to me? He will be a little disappointed, I know that. But he will not be mad at you, if that's what you're thinking."

Sarah was flooded with relief flooded at the knowledge that she wouldn't have to worry about that awkward conversation. A thought entered her head, and she voiced it hesitantly. "Would you mind helping me tonight? Help me get ready, I mean."

Ruth Jones looked surprised, and then she beamed. "Well, of course! I would love to help you prepare. It's not every day that one of my girls gets invited to a ball."

At that moment, the kindly woman reminded her so much of her own mother that Sarah had to fight back sudden tears. "Thank you," she managed to say past the lump in her throat.

Ruth rose to her feet. "After the noon meal, we shall get you ready. Now get out of my kitchen before I decide to put you back to work again!"

Sarah grinned as she jumped up from her chair. She bent down and hugged the older woman around the neck. Then she darted out of the kitchen, leaving the chuckling Ruth behind her.

She spent a bit more time reading the book she had borrowed from Leah, hoping it would distract her from her anxiety over the night before her, but she had a difficult time losing herself in the stilted language. She kept telling herself that they might not find Karen and that everything could go sour, but the inch of hope the opportunity had given her grew until she felt almost giddy with excitement.

Ruth brought her into the house after lunch, a meal that Seth did not attend, and told her to sit in one of the chairs by the warm fire. The older woman had insisted that all the men leave the house for the afternoon while they got Sarah ready for the ball. Leah stood in the corner, grinning from ear to ear as her mother instructed her and sent her on errands.

"Would you grab the iron from the fire?" Ruth asked her daughter. The young girl carefully pulled the hot, cylinder-shaped iron from the fire and handed it to her mother.

Sarah didn't have a mirror to see what they were doing, but she trusted them; she didn't much care how her hair turned out, anyway. She was just enjoying the time she had with them. She laughed every time Leah gushed at how pretty her hair was. Ruth would shush her every time, concentrating all her efforts on styling Sarah's hair as if she were performing brain surgery.

When at last they had pinned the last curl in place, the two Jones women started on her makeup. Ruth took a thin piece of charcoal and smudged it beneath each eye, rubbing it gently over her lashes to make them look fuller and darker.

I'll have to try that next time I run out of mascara, Sarah thought with a wry grin.

"Stop smiling and shut your eyes," Leah said sternly. Sarah felt like laughing at her serious expression, but she wisely remained silent and closed her eyes obediently. She felt Leah sweep a soft brush across her upper lids, moving carefully so she didn't smear the rest of the makeup.

"Where's the dress?" Leah asked excitedly, taking a step back to admire her work.

Ruth motioned with her head to the corner of the room while she adjusted some of the curls with her fingers. Sarah noticed the dress lying on the chair in the corner for the first time and recognized it as one of Karen's. She swallowed nervously. Had Ruth wondered why Karen hadn't taken any of her clothes with her when she looked for this dress?

"Do you like it?" Leah held the gown up for her inspection.

Sarah nodded sincerely. "It's beautiful. Where did you get it?" she asked, trying to keep her tone casual.

"Karen left some dresses behind in the barn," Ruth answered. Sarah breathed a sigh of relief.

"Mama and I picked out jewelry too!" Leah exclaimed. Sarah couldn't remember ever seeing her so exuberant, and she didn't bother to hide her smile.

As they helped her out of her dress, Sarah was glad that she had worn a white underdress beneath her everyday apparel. It was made from breezy fabric and had shorter sleeves and a neckline that dipped low enough that it wasn't visible beneath her regular dress. Karen had said that the women here wore the dress as an extra layer in the winter, but they also wore it in the summer because it was lighter than a petticoat.

As Leah and her mother slipped the dress over her head, they were careful not to displace a single curl. She was relieved to find that the dress was lighter than she had expected; she didn't want a heavy dress to weigh her down as she and Will snuck around the castle. The younger girl volunteered to tie the back while Ruth picked up the gold bracelet and matching earrings they had set on the table earlier. She helped Sarah put them on and dipped her finger in a bowl of red berries that Leah had dutifully crushed earlier. She dabbed the juice gently over Sarah's lips and told her to rub them together.

"Go and fetch your full looking glass, love," she told her daughter. Leah ran up the stairs with a giggle and returned a few seconds later, straining to carry a large oval mirror. She stood before Sarah and held it up so she could see herself, a giddy smile on her face.

Sarah rose from the chair carefully so she wouldn't step on her dress and looked in the mirror. She caught her breath as she stared at the girl standing before her. She had never considered herself very pretty. She wasn't plain or ugly, but she knew she would never win any beauty contests. However, as she examined her reflection in the mirror, for the first time she felt elegant and graceful, and she certainly looked the part. Her auburn hair had been curled and piled stylishly on top of her head. A few stubborn curls that had refused to be confined under the thin gold hairband now framed her heart-shaped face. The charcoal lining and pale gold on her lids accentuated her eyes and made them appear bluer.

And the dress! It was nearly the same style as the green one she had worn when she first went into town, but it was far more extravagant. Sarah ran her hands over the elegant red fabric, her fingers grazing the delicate gold braiding that encircled her waist and the scooped neckline. The gold braiding accented each of her long sleeves and brushed the floor as it ran along the hem of the full skirt. Loose gold thread held the sleeves to the bodice; the same white fabric that peaked out from beneath the thread was visible behind the thin gold cords that crisscrossed just under her bust, creating an elegant corset-like structure that slimmed and made her look more well-endowed than she really was. The long, droplet-shaped earrings lay delicately against her tan neck, and she touched them gingerly. Her red-tinted lips parted, but nothing came out.

"Do you like it?" Leah asked quietly, looking uneasy over Sarah's long silence.

"It's perfect," she whispered.

Leah's grin looked like it might split her face in two. "You look like a princess!"

"Aye, you do at that." Ruth smiled.

"It looks . . . it looks so . . ." Sarah shook her head, trying to find words.

"You look beautiful," Ruth said.

"I feel like Cinderella."

"Who?" the older woman asked, her brow furrowed in confusion.

"Oh, um, never mind. What did you use for my eyes?" she asked, referring to the pale gold shadow on her lids.

"Oh!" Leah clapped her hands in excitement. "That was my idea. I crushed some yellow and gold flowers that had dried in the garden until they turned to powder." She looked very proud of her cleverness.

Sarah smiled and hugged each of them in turn, careful not to damage their hard work. "Thank you both so much."

Ruth looked as though she might cry as she waved a hand in the air. "Now you had better go before I start blubbering."

Sarah laughed and hugged the woman one last time before collecting her skirts and heading outside, her dress swishing with her every move.

⚮

Mr. Jones stood in front of the wagon facing the house, his hands clasped in front of him while he waited. When he saw her, he smiled and took a step forward. Taking her hand, he bent over it in a low bow and then looked up at her. He winked. "Your carriage awaits."

Sarah laughed at his antics and allowed him to help her into the wagon seat, which had been covered with a quilt. He hopped in beside her and folded the other half of the quilt over her lap to keep her warm before taking his seat beside her. They waved at Leah and her mother as they emerged from the house to see her off. Then Mr. Jones flicked the reins, and the horses responded quickly, as eager to be off as Sarah was.

Sarah was so anxious and excited that she could barely sit still. The man beside her laughed every time she asked how much farther it was to town, which was very often.

When at last they arrived at the castle gates, the descending sun had already cast an orange hue to the underside of the clouds that lingered in the sky. She hoped that Will was inside already and that she would have no trouble finding him. A well-dressed servant stepped up to the side of the wagon when they came to a halt and offered his hand to her. Sarah leaned up and quickly kissed Mr. Jones on his cheek.

"Thank you," she said, unable to contain her smile. He winked at her, his own grin stretching across his face. She turned back to the servant and accepted his proffered hand, waving over her shoulder as she walked through the gate and up the stone pathway leading to the front entrance. A man waited just outside of the hulking front door and asked for her name.

"Sarah Matthews. I'm a guest of Mr. Taylor." He scanned the parchment he held in his hand and nodded once.

"Enjoy your evening," he said without emotion as he bowed.

She curtsied in an attempt to hide her goofy grin before she walked through the large entryway and into the castle.

Chapter Seventeen

Sarah tried not to gape at the intricate carvings and statues, the colorful ribbons and banners strung from pillar to pillar, and large oil paintings that hung from the walls. She tried to act like she was accustomed to such opulence, but her awed expression gave her away.

She stepped through the archway leading into the ballroom and found it to be more extravagant than anything she had ever seen before. The domed roof was set high and had been painted with angels strumming harps and sitting on clouds, their hands poised gracefully. The artist had used a lot of gold and white as well as many other colors that gave the scene a subtle elegance that complemented the wall hangings and fixtures around the room.

Sarah dragged her eyes away from the ceiling and glanced at the people around her. The women wore fine dresses of every color, fabric, and design; not one of them looked the same. The sight of so many swishing skirts made Sarah's head spin. The men were clothed in their finest pants and dinner jackets, some wearing flamboyantly colored shirts with ridiculously puffed sleeves. Servants walked through the crowds offering drinks on silver trays, and long tables covered with a hundred desserts Sarah had never seen before lined each of the four walls.

A band was set at the back of the room, and they began a song that Sarah thought she remembered from her music appreciation class last semester. Groups of guests danced to the sound of the music on the polished stone floor, moving fluidly across the floor as one body. To Sarah, it seemed as though she had just entered a fairytale, and she suddenly felt nervous and out of place. People around her began to glance at her—the strange newcomer—and she self-consciously touched her hair.

A young man made his way through the crowd and stepped in front of her, blocking her view. His brown hair was slicked back, a fashion that Sarah wasn't too fond of it. He looked nervous as he stood before her.

"I was wondering if you might like to dance, miss?" he asked, and his voice betrayed his youth.

"Oh," Sarah said, trying to mask her surprise. She pressed her lips tightly together. Was it her imagination, or did he look younger than her? Sarah scanned the crowd, trying to buy time. She desperately hoped that Will was nearby. She spotted him on the other side of the dance floor surrounded by a group of girls, all of who appeared younger than Sarah. He looked disinterested in their conversation, and his gaze wandered over the crowd, though he nodded politely every now and then.

His gaze landed on Sarah briefly, then continued on. Then suddenly, his eyes came back to where she stood, and he stared. She couldn't read his expression. She felt flustered by his steady gaze and looked down at her dress, wandering if she had gotten something on it. Or maybe her makeup had smeared, causing her to look like a well-dressed raccoon. When she glanced back up, he had excused himself from the group of clingy girls and was making his way toward her.

The song had ended, and he walked straight across the dance floor, maneuvering around couples and servants until he stood before her. Will looked dashing in his black coat and crisp white shirt. Unlike most of the men present, he had let his hair wave naturally around his temples. Sarah couldn't help feeling sorry for the girls he had left behind, but she was not sorry enough to send him back to them.

When Will glanced at the young man, Sarah felt her cheeks grow warm. She had completely forgotten he was there.

"The woman is with me," Will said. His words were not unkind, but his message was clear enough.

The boy looked flustered and hastily muttered his apologies before ducking his head and disappearing into the crowd.

Will took Sarah's hand in his calloused one and bowed over it like she had observed some of the other men in the room do with the other women. He looked up at her from beneath a dark veil of lashes, and the torchlight cast a glow on his blue eyes. "You look lovely this evening, Sarah Matthews."

Sarah curtsied, trying to hide her nervous smile. "Thank you. And you look very nice tonight, as well."

He straightened, his eyes locked on hers. "I was wondering if I might have the pleasure of dancing with you?" he asked, and Sarah was still very aware that her hand was in his.

She leaned in and lowered her voice. "Won't that draw attention to us?"

He shook his head slightly, causing a wavy strand of dark hair to fall over his brow. "We would draw more notice if we slipped away now." He held out his right arm. "Now, shall we?"

Sarah thought the gesture gallant, but she hesitated to take his proffered arm. She gnawed on her lip and admitted shamefully, "I don't really know how to dance."

His eyes sparkled, and she thought it was more from mischief than the flickering torchlight. He placed her hand in the crook of his arm and leaned down to whisper in her ear, "Just follow my lead." He straightened back to his full height and looked down at her. "So, may I have the pleasure?"

She smiled, enjoying her chance to play the part of Cinderella. Fortunately, unlike the maiden in the story, she did not have to be back by midnight.

"Why, yes, you may."

He looked pleased with her answer and guided her smoothly toward the dance floor, her skirt swishing about her ankles like a noiseless bell as they navigated around the crowd. Those who were ready to dance got into their positions: men on one side, women on the other. Will dutifully brought her to the end of the line of women and then moved to join the men opposite her.

As the band practiced a few notes, Sarah suddenly realized with alarm that these were choreographed dances. Before she had a chance to back out, the musicians began to play, and Sarah was relieved to find that every other couple broke away from their group, which meant she could watch the first couples before attempting it herself. She paid close attention to the dancers as they circled slowly around their partners and walked backward to their former positions. It seemed easy enough.

Sarah took a deep breath and tried to mimic their moves with as much finesse as possible when her time came to step forward. She walked toward Will and was surprised at how graceful and fluid he was in his movements as they twirled around each other and stepped back to their places. She smiled with pleasure over the fact that she hadn't fallen on her face or tripped over her dress.

The music struck up again and the dancers performed the same move, this time facing each other with their hands raised together in the air. Sarah followed as best she could as the dance became more complicated. Will helped her when she didn't know a step, spinning her around in the right direction before anyone could notice that she was going the wrong way and then whispering the next steps in her ear when she bit her lip in indecision. He nodded in encouragement when she missed her footing and would have stumbled had it not been for his firm grip on her hand. Once she got the hang of it, though, she began to enjoy herself and felt disappointed when the music ended.

Will placed her hand on his arm again and guided her away from the other dancers. They walked toward one of the open doorways at the back of the room and stood near a long table covered with delicacies.

"That was a lot of fun," she said with a grin, trying to catch her breath. "Thank you."

He nodded, and his dark blue eyes shone with pleasure. "I cannot remember having that much fun in a long time." He stared at her for a moment, and she shifted nervously beneath his gaze. "You know, I almost didn't recognize you tonight."

She gave an uncertain smile. "I don't look ridiculous or stick out too much?"

"In answer to your first question, no, you look far from ridiculous. But if I were to judge by the looks you are receiving from the gentlemen here, well, I doubt that I am the most envied man present because you blend in." He tucked a strand of hair behind her ear and smiled softly—the first smile she'd seen on him since coming here. Sarah quickly took note of the faint dimple in his right cheek, his perfect white teeth, and the way the gesture transformed his features. He was definitely handsome, but when he smiled, his features softened and it made him look boyishly innocent.

Sarah took in a shaky breath, feeling like she had received a small blessing; he had let down his guard enough for her to see a part of him that he didn't show very often.

Will cleared his throat, and his smile faded. He glanced over the whole room, looking everywhere but at her.

The moment was over.

"We should slip away before the next dance begins," he suggested to the dessert table beside them.

Sarah sighed, knowing that he had closed her off again.

"Lead the way," she said, disappointment lacing her words. He didn't seem to notice as he gave a quick nod and a glanced around the room before slipping through the doorway.

She followed silently behind, glancing over her shoulder occasionally to make sure they weren't being followed as they walked quietly through the dark hallway. When they reached a dead end, Will pressed his ear to the wood of a closed door. After a second, he nodded in satisfaction and opened it. A steep flight of stairs spiraled downward into utter blackness.

He motioned her down first, and she hesitated. She wasn't sure she liked the idea of scrambling down stairs that led into the unknown.

"Here," Will whispered, taking her hand. His hand was rough from hard work, and it was also strong and reassuring. Sarah gathered her courage and her skirts with her free hand, following him as he guided her onto the stairs. When he reached back to close the door behind them, they were plunged into complete darkness. Sarah froze and squeezed his hand tighter. He brushed past her to lead, feeling his way along the walls with one hand. He stopped abruptly, and she ran into his back.

"What is it?" she whispered, unable to see in front of her.

He didn't answer, and she waited. She heard a creaking noise and realized that their progress had been halted by the door Will was slowly opening. He stuck his head out and motioned for her to follow him.

They crept out into a dimly lit hallway. It was vastly different from the main hall, with its ornate decorations and paintings. With the exception of a few tapestries and flaming torches, these walls were completely unadorned. Will and Sarah hastened through the windowless corridor. Another stairwell sat at the end of the hall. There was no obstacle that would suggest they were unwelcome, but Sarah still cringed at the sight of the stone stairwell and the eerie shadows that the torches threw on the walls.

"We have to go down *there*?" she asked, her voice barely above a whisper. He nodded silently and slowly descended the staircase. She followed behind reluctantly, wanting to turn back and pretend like this had never happened. Maybe if they left now, they could make it back to the ballroom without anyone noticing that they had ever been gone.

She could see the light from the end of the passage ahead of them and heard clanging noises coming from below, then the sound of chains dragging. She shivered. Now was as good a time as any to make a run for it.

"Will—"

He placed a hand over her mouth and pulled her against the wall beside him. Her eyes widened, and her heart began to beat rapidly at what unknown danger he'd sensed. A dark shadow passed over the doorway and stopped. A man, who was fortunately facing away from them, began to chuckle at something.

"That's what you get for stealin' from the king," he spat in a gruff voice. "Now quit your begging. It's pathetic!"

The man moved past them, muttering something unintelligible as he walked away. Will slowly removed his hand from her mouth, and Sarah breathed a sigh of relief.

That was close, she thought, adrenaline pumping through her veins.

Together, they edged closer and peered through the doorway. No one was in sight, and they stepped tentatively into the corridor. Three hallways led out of the small space, one in front of them and the other two on either side. Will paused for a second before selecting the one on the right and heading in that direction. Sarah grabbed his sleeve and pulled him back.

"What is it?" he whispered.

"How do you know where you're going?" she asked impatiently. "Are you just selecting random rooms and stairways to enter?"

"My father worked in the castle when I was a boy, and I would stay with him while he worked." He glanced down the hallway. "I know this castle better than the king himself."

"But that was a long time ago," she whispered. He looked back at her, the first time they'd made eye contact since coming down here.

"Yes, a lifetime ago." Never before had she seen a look of pain like the one that crossed his features just then. She wanted to take back her careless words and simply follow him down the hall. He looked like he was a million miles away, so she stepped in front of him and began leading the way down the torch-lit hallway. She heard his footsteps behind her but didn't turn around.

"What are you doing?" he asked as he came up beside her.

"Trusting you," she said simply and risked a glance at him. The soft smile on his lips caused her to feel flustered, and she quickly turned back around. The sound of dragging chains and bone-chilling moaning grew loader the further they went into the passage.

"What is this place?" she whispered, as though the sounds of torment and suffering ahead might be alerted to their presence and come for them if she spoke too loudly.

"Hell," was Will's answer, and his voice sounded heavy with emotion.

That was when she saw the cells lining the walls on either side. As they passed, she noticed that some of them were empty. The filth covering the floors and walls made her gag, and she covered her mouth to block out the fetid stench of unwashed humanity.

The cells that caused her heart to clench were the ones housing families—women, children, and young boys. The prisoners came up to the bars when Will and Sarah walked by, sticking their hands through the slats and pleading for food and water. They were dirty from head to toe, and their clothes were torn.

Sarah's hand hung limply to her side at the disparaging sight. Children shivered in their rags as undrinkable water dripped from the crumbling ceilings and fell on their heads. It was a horrible sight, and Sarah stared in shock at the weeping mothers and a girl no older than seven crying in her father's arms. She would have frozen in place had Will not pulled her along past the awful scene. Her throat burned from unshed tears of compassion. She couldn't believe the conditions these families were made to live in. Had they really done anything to deserve treatment as bad as this?

"Here we are," Will suddenly whispered beside her. They stopped before one of the cells, and Sarah peered inside. A girl with knotted red hair sat huddled in the back corner of the small room. She looked up at them, and Sarah's hand again flew to her mouth to stifle the sob of shock that threatened to escape.

Karen's eyes widened when she saw them. She jumped up and ran to the bars on unsteady legs, a joyous smile lighting her grimy face.

Sarah felt tears run down her cheeks. She grabbed Karen's dirty hands as sobs racked her body.

"Don't cry, Sarah," Karen whispered comfortingly. "It's okay." She ran a hand over the younger girl's head like a mother trying to reassure her child.

"It's so awful in here," Sarah managed to gasp. "I shouldn't have left you."

"None of this is your fault," Karen said sternly. A mischievous glint lit her eyes. "Besides, the guards are too afraid to beat me or withhold food; they think I'll get angry and turn them into toads."

Sarah's laugh sounded choked as she stared at her friend, wishing that it were possible to switch places with her.

Karen smiled slightly as she looked her over. "You look beautiful. I'm glad that dress finally got out of the old trunk and could be put to use."

Sarah shook her head, unable to speak. An idea suddenly flashed through her mind. She turned to Will, desperation burning in her eyes. "We have to get her out."

"Sarah," he said slowly.

"You can't do that," Karen said urgently. Her eyes widened. "If they found out that you helped me escape, they might put you in here too. Then we'd never figure this out, and we would both be stuck here." She leaned forward, pressing her face against the bars. "You need to get out of here before the guard comes back."

"No, I won't go!" Sarah said stubbornly. There had to be some way they could help her escape. Her eyes darted over the bars, looking for some gap or rusty piece that they could pry open.

Karen looked at Will for an ally. "Please get her out of here."

He nodded without question and took Sarah's hand again, pulling her away. She tried to wrench free from his grasp, but his strong grip was unbreakable. She spun around to face him and gripped the front of his shirt in desperation, her eyes entreating him to understand.

"Please, just give me a minute." He looked torn between throwing her over his shoulder and making a run for it and letting her go.

"One minute," he said, releasing her slowly. She turned to Karen.

"I *will* get you out of here. I promise."

Karen smiled sadly. "It's probably best if you don't make that kind of a promise." She grabbed the younger girl's hands through the bars and held tight. "Just keep praying and remember that whatever happens, it will be all right."

Sarah nodded as fresh tears clogged her throat. She stepped back and took hold of Will's arm, raising her hand in silent farewell. She reluctantly ran behind him back the way they'd come. When she risked a glance behind her, she caught sight of tears running down Karen's pale cheeks.

Chapter Eighteen

Desperate pleas from the prisoners followed Sarah and Will as they ran down the hallway. They didn't even bother with stealth as they raced up the stairwell, hoping that speed would be enough to help them avoid being spotted by the guard. Sarah breathed a sigh of relief when they managed to reach the top without anyone calling out for them to halt. They had almost reached the door leading to the next level when they heard footsteps coming down the corridor toward them. A long shadow spilled over the floor at their feet just as a guard appeared around the corner.

Will suddenly grabbed her hand, spun her around, and pressed her back against the wall. Her eyes widened in shock as he placed his other hand on the wall and leaned his face close to hers, *too* close. She caught her breath, and her heart beat wildly against her chest. What on earth was he doing?

"You are not supposed to be here." Sarah jerked her head in the direction of the voice. A well-dressed guard stood with his feet spread apart and his arms folded across the royal seal on his chest; he was looking at them in agitation.

Will grinned at the man and slowly straightened, though he remained close to her and kept a hand on her arm. "Can I help you?" Sarah had never heard the slightly arrogant tone his voice now held.

The guard looked surprised. "I didn't expect to see you here tonight, Mr. Taylor."

Sarah looked between the two, her mouth slightly parted in bafflement. Did they know each other?

Will chuckled. "Well, I decided to get out this evening."

The man nodded, and his face became stern again, but this time his expression looked more like a father reprimanding a child than the threatening look he had taken on a moment ago. "You know you're not supposed to be down here."

"Come on, Lawrence," Will said, nodding his head in Sarah's direction. "She said she was interested in the castle, so I decided to show her around. Thought it might excite her." He winked at Sarah, whose face flushed with embarrassment. What on earth had gotten into him?

The guard frowned. "I'm surprised at you, Mr. Taylor. I never expected . . ." He shook his head and looked at Sarah. "Would you like me to escort you back out, Miss?"

"I think she would rather come with me," Will said hurriedly and glanced at her. "Wouldn't you?" She could read the urgency in his gaze and nodded her head slowly, though she felt more confused by the minute.

"Yes, I'll go back with you. Thank you for your kindness, sir." She nodded politely to the guard. Although he still appeared unconvinced, he allowed them to pass without further comment.

Will pressed his hand to her back and fairly pushed her up the stairs. She kept walking and told herself not to look behind her to see if the guard was following them. They reached the top and slipped through the door into the lighted hallway. Only then did Sarah begin to breathe normally again.

"That was close," Will murmured beside her. She nodded silently as they entered the ballroom. No one paid much attention to either of them, since most of the people were busy watching the couples dancing to the music. The twosome slipped quietly through the crowd and into the main hall. They were surprised to find it empty, save the man who held the door open for them when they approached the entrance. Out in the cool night air, Sarah's head cleared and her mind began working again.

"For a minute, I wasn't really sure what you were doing back there," she said when they had exited the main gate and were out of the doorman's earshot. She had meant the words to sound casual and teasing, but her voice quavered.

"I'm sorry," he said sincerely. "I did not mean to frighten you. You should know that I have not and will not ever take advantage of a woman."

Sarah almost gave a snort of derision, but she managed to refrain. "I don't think you have to worry about that. I'm sure they'd be very willing."

She was startled at the note of bitterness lacing her words and looked over at Will to see if he had noticed. She caught his expression of surprise that quickly turned to one of amusement. Hoping to avoid any questions and further embarrassment, she quickly changed the subject.

"Did you know that guard?"

"I have known him most of my life," he answered, going along with the different topic smoothly. "He has worked at the castle for some time."

They arrived at the livery, and Will unlatched the lock on door and swung it wide. Sarah suddenly placed a hand on his arm to stop him. Gazing into eyes that reminded her of the ocean at night, she smiled slightly. Her appreciation was genuine.

"Thank you."

He blinked once in surprise. "For what?"

"For taking me to see Karen."

He shook his head, causing that stubborn wisp of hair to fall over his eyes again. He ran his hand back through the wayward locks, looking aggravated with himself. "But it only upset you. I thought it would encourage you that she was all right if you could just see her. I was wrong, though, and I apologize."

A small laugh escaped her. "Please don't apologize. I really am grateful. I'll admit that it was hard to see Karen like that." She inhaled a shaky breath. "But wondering where she was and how she was doing was killing me."

"And now that you have seen the circumstances that she is living under?" he asked in the quiet way she'd become accustomed to.

"I want to get her out of there more than ever," she answered honestly. "Seeing Karen gave me hope that we can still save her."

His lips stretched into a grin. "'We,' huh?"

Sarah felt her cheeks turn pink. "Oh, I shouldn't have assumed that you'd want to help. I'm sorry, I just—"

He chuckled. "You worry too much, Sarah," he said before disappearing into the building.

She waited outside for him to bring the wagon out, busying herself with counting the stars in the sky. She hadn't tried this since she was little, and somehow it made her feel closer to home. She could hear Will approaching from behind and turned around, nearly coming nose to nose with the large brown horse he was leading. She almost released a frightened yelp as she jumped back to put some space between her and the large bay. Sarah glanced behind it, but she couldn't spot the wagon anywhere.

"Aren't we riding?" she squeaked.

"Of course," he answered matter-of-factly and patted the mare's neck. "I apologize, though. I lent out my wagon and was supposed to have it back before tonight, but they are a little late in returning it. I have her saddled up and ready to go, though. Give me your hand, and I can help you up."

Sarah gawked at him. "You can't be serious."

He appraised her for a moment. His eyes were so intense that she felt as though he were peering inside her and reading her thoughts. "You're terrified of horses, aren't you?"

She cringed. "I wouldn't go so far as to say *terrified.*"

He walked the horse slowly past her and tied the reins to a hitching post beneath a canopy of elms. When he motioned her over with his hand, she edged forward hesitantly, wondering what he was up to. She stopped several feet away from him, and Will walked over and placed a reassuring hand on her arm.

"I promise she won't hurt you," he whispered in her ear. She shivered and told herself it was because of the cool night air. "I'll be right here."

He gave her an encouraging smile, and she felt herself moving toward the horse as if an invisible hand were pushing her forward.

Will followed her, and they made a wide arc around the animal, coming within a few feet of its long face. Sarah stared at the dark brown main, silky coat, and large brown eyes that stared intently back at her. This mare didn't look as threatening or gigantic as horses usually seemed. Maybe she was getting over her fear. Or it could have to do with the comforting presence standing beside her.

She took a tentative step forward, and Will followed close on her heels. She took another step and another until she was within inches of the mare. Sarah slowly reached out and let her fingers graze its soft head. A mixture of fear and excitement raced through her veins. She ran her hand gently over the silky fur, warm nose, and soft mane. She smiled in wonder and noticed the way the animal's eyes watched her.

The mare nickered quietly, and Sarah jumped back in surprise, bumping into Will's chest. He chuckled softly and placed his hands on her shoulders. She looked up at him.

"It's all right. That is just her way of saying she likes you," he said.

Sarah squared her shoulders to cover her embarrassment. "I knew that."

He covered his grin by turning his gaze to the dark sky. "We should be going. I don't want to get you back too late." He looked at her. "Are you ready?"

She stared at the ground and nudged a pebble with her slipper-clad foot, too embarrassed to meet his gaze. "I don't know how to ride side-saddle," she admitted quietly. When she glanced up, he nodded his head.

"Good. Neither do I."

Sarah laughed at his answer, feeling at ease once again as he began instructing her on how to mount the horse. It didn't look that hard. She confidently placed her left foot in the stirrup, hoping the horse wouldn't suddenly decide to make a break for it. When she tried swinging her other foot over the saddle, she realized that she couldn't reach; the dress weighed her leg down, and the horse was too tall. She struggled to lift her right leg over the saddle, but to no avail. She could hear Will cough behind her to cover his laugh.

"It's not as easy as you make it look, Mr. Taylor," she grumbled, holding onto the horn for dear life, still trying to hoist herself onto the saddle. She no longer cared about mounting the bay with dignity and grace; she would be satisfied if she could do it without first falling on her backside in front of Will.

He walked up behind her. "Here, let me help you." He wrapped his hands around her waist, and with his help she was able to lift her foot over the saddle. It seemed much higher from up there, and Sarah suddenly felt insecure. Her feet dangled against the horse's side since they couldn't reach the stirrups.

"Um, maybe we should walk," she said quickly, glancing down at him. Will shook his head.

"You are the strangest woman I have ever met," he said.

She furrowed her brow in confusion. "Exactly what do you mean by that?"

He looked surprised and then appeared to think about it for a moment. He stared off into the distance as he spoke.

"Well, no woman that I have ever known would have suggested walking several miles in the dark alone with a man to avoid riding." He glanced her way, then continued. "You say what is on your mind and follow you heart. You are also stubborn, and I sense you don't follow orders very well. Although you have a fiery temper, you are kind almost to a fault and find joy in the smallest of things. You are unique, naïve, determined, passionate, and confusing. You never cease to amaze me."

He looked into her eyes, his gaze intense. "You are beautiful, and you don't even know it." He shrugged. "You are different."

Sarah laughed to cover the feelings he'd stirred with his appraisal. She had only expected a simple explanation for his comment; she hadn't expected him to give such a full description of her character. "Definitely different. And"—she wagged her finger at him playfully—"I need to learn to hold my tongue more, so don't encourage me."

Will's face was serious. "Never let anyone ever make you feel that you cannot voice your thoughts. You speak the truth without meaning to insult anyone; I admire you for that."

"Thank you," Sarah said quietly, staring at the back of the mare's mane as tears suddenly pooled behind her eyes. Why did his words mean so much to her?

"You are welcome." Before she could think of something to say to lessen the seriousness of the conversation, Will grabbed the saddle horn in front of her, placed his foot in the stirrup, and pulled himself up behind her in one fluid motion. He wrapped his arms around her waist, and her body went rigid at his touch.

"What are you doing?" she asked, pushing his arms away and turning in her seat to face him. He had to lean back slightly so her nose wouldn't touch his. Their faces were mere inches apart, and Sarah felt her breath catch. Dark hair had fallen over his forehead, and his blue eyes seemed to twinkle in the pale light as they stared back at her. The moonlight outlined his broad shoulders and made his square jaw look more defined. His lips had parted in surprise at her sudden movement, and her eyes absentmindedly drifted to them. Her cheeks flamed in humiliation when she realized that she had been staring, and she quickly spun back around.

He cleared his throat after a moment of uncomfortable silence. "I'm sorry. I simply needed the reins," he explained calmly.

"Aren't you going to ride your own horse?" she asked with her back to him, irritation edging her words to cover her embarrassment; anger had always been her shield, though even in the moment she knew her response was irrational.

"You don't know how to ride a horse, and I am not going to chase after you in the dark because it gets spooked." Now he sounded upset.

"Fine," she said with an indifferent shrug, feeding off his own frustration. "But I guess it's my turn next, then."

"What do you mean?" he asked suspiciously.

"It's my turn to assess you." She felt him stiffen behind her and found the courage to shift her position so that she could look at him when she spoke. His expression was guarded. "May I?"

"If you must." His voice was tight, but she ignored his obvious discomfort and began anyway.

"When I first met you, you were very hard to read, and you still are. You close people out and try not to get too close. So you don't get hurt, I guess. You think with your head instead of your heart, which I presume has served you well in the past after some major heartache. You're difficult and stubborn. You hide your emotions because, for some reason, you're afraid to show them." He looked away, and she found herself softening at the vulnerability in his eyes. She suddenly realized how childish she was acting after he had praised her character only minutes before.

She sighed in exasperation at herself and softened her tone to sound less abrasive.

"You're also intelligent, understanding, thoughtful, and kind when it suits you." His gaze returned to her once more, and she found the boldness to continue, though her voice was even softer than before. She cocked her head to the side as she examined his face in the moonlight. "I believe that you were deeply hurt by someone or something a long time ago, and that is why you've pushed people and God away for so long. You cut yourself off from emotion so you don't get too close to people or feel too much. You're afraid to let others see who you really are and the pain that you've been through so that you can avoid being hurt again. Am I right?"

His eyes stared intently into hers. He spoke after a few seconds of silence. "It's easier that way."

His honest response cooled any remaining defensive anger she had left. Sarah shook her head adamantly, compassion for this man filling her heart. She gestured with her hands as she spoke. "To stop yourself from feeling is like ceasing to live; life no longer holds meaning. Hurt, anger, pain, desire, compassion, love—they're what makes us human. They're what living is all about. Being able to *feel* is something that we shouldn't take for granted or push away when offered. Our lives aren't perfect, Will, but it all depends on how you face a situation, whether you're willing to look at something bad with a positive outlook."

He frowned. "Not all things are good."

"No, that's not what I meant." She silently prayed for the right words that would help him understand. "It's about being thankful in our circumstances and trying to look for the good in something, no matter how hard that might be."

"Optimism," he whispered. She nodded.

"Yeah, that's part of it. But it's also faith that God will always work it out for good."

He smiled slightly, and she thought she detected a hint of sadness and regret in his expression. "I envy your faith."

She knew it would be a waste of time to tell him that he, too, could have that kind of faith, so she remained silent. He lightly heeled the mare in the sides to get her moving. Sarah stiffened as the horse began walking and remained rigid for several minutes until Will, obviously sensing her discomfort, told her to relax. She tried to do just that, and when her cramped muscles began to unwind, she found herself enjoying the ride.

Somewhere along the road, though, her body started to give in to exhaustion, and her eyelids began to droop. She leaned her back against Will's strong chest, relaxing. The stars blinked behind tree limbs as they rode on, and the moon ducked behind wispy clouds. The sight began to soothe her, and Sarah felt herself drifting off to sleep.

CR&SO

John waited patiently behind the barrel until Will Taylor and the girl left the dungeon. Then he raced up the stairs in his excitement.

The captain had been livid when the poisoned chalice had failed due to the Shadow's interference, but this was John's chance to redeem himself. He had been lucky to spot them talking to the witch. He wasn't sure what had transpired, since the view from his hiding spot was too far down the corridor for him to hear their hushed tones, but what they said was of no importance to him; it only mattered that they had talked to the prisoner.

John slowed as he entered the ballroom, leaning with his hands on his knees for a moment to catch his breath. They needed a plan to trap them, but he had never been known for using his head. Straightening, he made his way across the ballroom toward Captain Dunlivey. He would know what to do.

CR&SO

Someone was speaking to her, and Sarah fought against consciousness, wanting to remain asleep in her warm bed for a few minutes more. When the person persisted to nudge her shoulder, she gave up on her blissful dream world and opened her eyes reluctantly, half expecting to wake up in her room back home. Instead, her eyes opened to the sight of the Joneses' house surrounded by twinkling stars.

"You need to wake up, Sarah," Will whispered in her ear. She realized that she was leaning against his chest and quickly sat up, feeling the heat of embarrassment burn her cheeks.

"I can't believe I fell asleep," she said, touching her hair to make sure that it was still in place. A few strands had come loose and tickled her cheek. She tucked them behind her ear, hoping she didn't look too disheveled. Will dismounted behind her and offered his hand to help her down.

"You were tired," he said with a shrug of dismissal. She stared at his outstretched hand, wondering how she could get safely to the ground without being unladylike or falling off the horse altogether. A look of understanding crossed Will's features. He reached up, took hold of her waist, lifted her backward off the saddle so her skirts wouldn't hike up, and set her gently on the ground as though she weighed little more than a feather.

She gaped at him and felt her knees buckle beneath her, unaccustomed to solid ground. Will's hold tightened and remained that way until she was able to stand on her own. Then he released her and took a step back.

"Eventually, you get used to riding," he said casually, and she felt grateful that he didn't make a big deal about it; he never belittled her or made her feel incapable, and she appreciated that after enduring four years of high school boys with no sense of courtesy or subtlety.

She ducked her head and hoped he couldn't read her thoughts as she dusted the dirt from her dress. She felt irritated with herself for acting like some damsel in distress who became weak in the knees from a little ride through the woods. Well, maybe it wasn't the ride that had made her weak, but she didn't want to consider that possibility.

"I believe they are waiting for you," Will said, inclining his head in the direction of the house.

Sarah nodded, and he walked her to the porch steps. She turned to him when he made no move to leave. "Thanks for dropping me off."

His eyes twinkled, and amusement was evident in his words when he spoke. "So, you survived your first ride. It wasn't all that bad, was it?"

A slow grin pulled at the corners of her mouth. "Oh, the part that I was awake for was very exciting. The rest I'm not so sure about." Her smile faded, and she became serious. "Thank you for your help tonight. I couldn't have done any of it without you."

His face became expressionless. "It was no trouble." His voice was devoid of any emotion, and Sarah felt rather than saw him take a mental step back.

She took a step closer to him to bridge the gap he had just put up between them. She shook her head. "Don't do that."

"What?"

"Shut me out," she said, motioning helplessly with her hands. "Just when I feel like I'm getting through, you close up." She stared at the wood beneath her feet and heaved a frustrated sigh. "Everyone needs someone that they can trust in, Will, and if you keep pushing everyone away, you'll eventually find that you don't have anyone left at all." When he was silent for a long moment, she looked up at him to find him watching her intently.

"Are you that person? Someone I can trust?" Though his expression looked guarded, to her he appeared to be that same lost boy he had revealed earlier. Her heart softened.

"You can trust me," she assured him, her voice soft in the moonlight. She stared at him, wondering if her eyes conveyed the emotional turmoil going on inside her. "But only you can decide if I'm someone that you can confide in. I can't make that decision for you."

He nodded. "Thank you."

He surprised her by spinning around and walking quickly to his horse, leaving her to stare after his retreating form in surprise. He looked at her for a long moment atop his mount; she was too surprised at his abrupt departure to say anything. Then he turned the mare around and rode away, quickly disappearing into the darkness.

Chapter Nineteen

When Sarah entered the main room, she saw Leah, Seth, and Joshua sitting on the floor playing some kind of game that required two wooden dice, a thin, flat piece of wood, and hand-carved wood figures.

When Leah spotted her, she jumped up and ran over to Sarah, smiling infectiously.

"How was the ball?" she asked, shifting her weight from one foot to the other in her excitement.

Sarah smiled at the girl. "It was very nice. I had a wonderful time."

Seth and Joshua rose from their sitting positions. Josh grinned at his sister's antics, but Seth stared at Sarah. She began to feel uncomfortable with everyone's attention on her and tried to think of a way to shift the focus away from her. Leah seemed to sense her discomfort and smiled knowingly.

"You're probably tired," she said. "I'll tell Mama and Papa that you got back safely.

Sarah nodded her thanks. "I think maybe I will go to bed now. I'll tell you about the ball in the morning," she said to Leah. She smiled at each of them before leaving the house, relieved to be away from Seth's penetrating gaze.

❦

The next day was uneventful, and Sarah wondered if she should go to town to see if Will had learned anything more. Her pride kept her from going. She felt disappointed in herself for the angry words she had said to him on the horse and the way she had revealed a small portion of her feelings and opened herself up to him. What on earth had possessed her?

She sat on the grass at the rear of the barn, her back resting against the wood as she watched the sun slowly descend over the treetops. As she sat there in the quiet, she was able sort through some of the jumbled thoughts in her head and think of ways to succeed in releasing Karen. However, every scenario she thought of ended badly or failed altogether.

And then there was the matter of Will.

She hated to admit it even to herself, but she was falling for him.

Sarah knocked the back of her head against the wood again and again, as though the pain might give her some brilliant insight, or at the very least a better idea.

Nothing.

"You're going to get a headache if you keep doing that." She glanced up at Seth and caught his easy grin.

"That's the least of my worries," she said dryly, though her head stilled against the wood. He sat down beside her, and for a while neither one spoke.

"What were you banging your head about?" he asked after several minutes.

She sighed and stared at the trees, imagining the woods beyond. "I'm just feeling a little helpless right now," she answered honestly.

"Do you want to talk about it?"

She smiled at his sincerity but shook her head no. "Not right now."

He nodded in understanding and turned his face to the sun. She studied his profile for a moment before asking the question that had nagged at her for the past three days.

"Are you mad at me, Seth?"

He looked genuinely surprised by her question. "What made you think that?"

"You've been avoiding me a lot lately," she answered quietly.

"No, I'm not mad at you. I'm sorry you thought I was."

Sarah smiled. "That's a relief. I was worried I had done something to upset you." She looked at him for a moment and noticed that he seemed uncomfortable. "What was it, then?"

He stared at the ground, seeming embarrassed. "It wasn't that I was angry with you, Sarah, but I will admit that I was trying to avoid you." He took a deep breath. "I didn't want to sit back and watch you fall for another man, so I hid away from you and my feelings. But it didn't work." He stared into her face as though he could find the answer to his questions there. Sarah's mouth went dry. He sighed at her expression.

"I know you don't feel the same way. Don't worry, I'm a big boy."

"Oh, Seth," she said softly, sitting up straighter. "I'm sorry. I didn't . . . I never wanted to hurt you."

He forced a smile. "I know; we're just friends. I can live with that."

She leaned the back of her head against the wood again and sighed. "If it makes you feel any better, I'm not sure I'll ever fall in love with any guy."

He shook his head. "Yes, you will. If not Taylor, then someone else." They were silent as they watched the sun dip behind the treetops and cast long shadows across the lawn.

Sarah stood suddenly, feeling restless. "I think I want to go for a walk." She needed time to think and clear her head, and a walk through the forest seemed like the best way to do it.

Seth stood as well. "Do you want company?" She shook her head, and he seemed to understand, though he looked reluctant to let her go alone. "Be careful, then; it's almost dark."

"I will." She smiled at his concern and turned to leave. "Don't wait up," she called over her shoulder as she made her way toward the tree line.

CRSO

He didn't know why he was out here, simply waiting in the forest with his green cloak about his shoulders. It was just now becoming dark; he usually wasn't this careless, but he couldn't help feeling that something dreadful was going to happen. His instincts had very rarely been wrong in the past.

A twig snapped behind him, and before he could react, he felt something hard slam into the back of his head. Pain exploded through his skull, and bright spots appeared behind his eyes, blurring his vision. He landed on his knees, fighting to remain conscious as the blackness pulled at him, trying to take his mind from this world.

When he refused to go down, someone kicked him from behind, sending his body spiraling to the ground. He fought against the darkness long enough to hear someone chuckle menacingly. A familiar voice sneered above him, "Don't worry, I'll take care of her."

Then he blacked out.

CRSO

Sarah stepped over a fallen log and tried not to panic. She looked to her left and saw only trees. She glanced to the right: nothing but trees. It was the same in front and behind her. *So much for a quick stroll to clear my head.* How had she gotten so turned around?

"Which way?" she mumbled, looking from one identical tree to the other. She would never admit that she was lost. That would mean defeat, and then she would really freak out.

"It's okay," she told herself out loud, trying to break the quiet closing in on her. "I'm not lost. I'm just taking a little stroll through the woods by myself. There's nothing to panic about."

Except for the bears, bandits, man-eating animals, and whatever else is out here. She pushed the disquieting thoughts aside before she started to buy into them.

"Left," she said randomly and turned in that direction, hoping she was heading back toward the house. After a few minutes, she came to a clearing.

It was the same clearing she had been in moments before. She let out a disparaging groan. She immediately felt shame over her fright. She'd been preaching to Will about faith and optimism the night before, and here she was, immediately giving in to despair and self-pity at the first sign of a difficult situation.

"Okay," she said, taking a deep breath. "It could be worse. I could have gotten even more lost, but instead I can try a different way." She nodded her head decisively, as though the action made it true. She bit her lip in indecision, unable to recall which way she had just come from. If she had gone north, then maybe she should try heading east.

But which way was east? She threw her hands up in a gesture of exasperation. "I don't even know which direction north is!"

She kicked at a pile of dry leaves in her frustration and mumbled, "Why couldn't compasses have been invented now? Or better yet, GPS navigation."

She turned around and started, halting her ramblings at the sight of the figure standing at the edge of the clearing. Her eyes adjusted to the darkness, and she realized with relief who it was.

"You scared me," she said breathlessly. She took a step toward him, feeling her hope rising. If anyone could find a way out of the forest, it was the Shadow.

"I'm a little lost. Could you maybe show me the way back to the Joneses' house?" she asked.

When he didn't say anything, she took another step closer to him. He just stood there. What was wrong with him? He lifted his arm slowly and pointed behind her. She turned around quickly, half expecting to see some kind of danger lurking behind her.

He ran up behind her before she had time to react, wrapped one arm around her waist, and held a wet cloth over her mouth. She tried to scream, but the cloth prevented her cry from getting very far, and the smell of it nearly caused her to gag. Her arms and legs flailed as she tried to escape. She heard her assailant groan in pain as she elbowed him between the legs.

Her victory was short lived. She began to feel the effects of whatever he had put on the cloth, and her body sagged as she lost consciousness.

Chapter Twenty

Sarah's eyes opened slowly, and she blinked several times to clear the fog that had settled over her vision. She felt groggy and had to fight off a wave of nausea and panic as she realized she was being dragged along the forest floor. She didn't know exactly how long he had been pulling her along behind him, but from the way her backside ached, it had been awhile.

She was about to attempt to stand and break free from him when she heard her captor panting as he strained to pull her along. Thinking quickly, she closed her eyes and made her body as heavy as possible. Her attacker groaned at the sudden weight, and she smiled to herself. If she played the part of the fainting damsel, he might let his guard down long enough for her to overpower him and escape.

When he dragged her body over a pile of small rocks, she ground her teeth to keep from crying out in pain. This went on for several minutes more as he pulled her over twigs and sharp rocks on the forest floor. She was just wondering how much more she could take when he stopped abruptly and dropped his hold on her. She lay silently on her back, hoping that playing dead might grant her a few moments while he caught his breath.

She carefully opened one eye and saw that they were in front of an old shack surrounded by a copse of trees. The ground was wet where she lay, though it hadn't rained since the day Karen was taken.

The man had his back to her as he fumbled with the large sliding lock on the front door of the shack. Sarah watched him closely and rose shakily to her feet. Her pulse sounded like a wild drumbeat in her ears, and she ignored the pain that stabbed through her back with every movement. She backed up slowly with her eyes still on him and then made a mad dash though the trees, swatting branches and leaves out of her way as she ran for safety. She had no idea where she was going, but she knew she had to get out of there. Thunder rolled through the sky, and gray clouds moved in the breeze as her captor's feet pounding on the earth just behind her.

The man quickly caught up to her and grabbed her arm. She screamed at the top of her lungs, and his hand closed over her throat to choke out the sound. He squeezed her neck until she wasn't able to get enough air into her lungs to make any noise at all. Her mouth worked silently, and she could feel her pulse in her cheeks just before they went numb.

He jerked her around and shoved her toward the shack. He pushed her hard enough through the open doorway that she lost her footing and fell to the floor inside.

Looking to the side, she kept her eyes on her captor, but he remained by the door and made no advance toward her. Sarah ran a shaky hand through her wind-whipped hair to get it off her face and gave a cursory glance around the room. Decorated with only a wooden chair and the bearskin rug that she lay on, the shack looked like it had not been lived in for some time.

Her gaze wandered to the crumpled figure in the corner a few feet from her. She thought her heart might stop as she scrambled to stand on her wobbly legs. She half-ran, half-stumbled to the still form and dropped down beside him. Her hand hovered over his bloodstained forehead as silent tears clogged her aching throat.

"Is he dead?" she managed to say in a small voice, staring at Will's closed lids, willing him to open his eyes.

"Not yet," her captor said behind her.

Sarah breathed a sigh of relief. She grabbed his arms and shook him gently, casting a frightened look over her shoulder at the hooded man to ensure that he was still a safe distance away. He stood guard by the door, and his silent presence was disturbing.

"Will?" she whispered, patting his cheek with her hand. "Will!" she said, louder this time, though it hurt her throat to speak. It was as though the man's hands were still constricting her vocal chords.

She continued to shake him and call out his name. "Please wake up, Will," she whispered in desperation when he refused to stir.

Still feeling the effects of whatever the man had drugged her with, she leaned her forehead against his chest in exhaustion and waited for the tears to come. But her eyes remained dry. It was as if she had shut down.

Will couldn't die—not like this. How was she going to survive this without him? She knew the thought was selfish even as it passed through her mind.

She closed her eyes tightly to shut out the world. When had it become so cruel? She was shaken by the realization that it had been this way for a long time; she had just never paid much attention to how evil the world had become, perfectly content in her cocoon of safety back in Oklahoma.

"Please, Father, we need you," she whispered against Will's shirt, feeling broken and frightened.

"Sarah?" She bolted upright at the sound of her name. Though his eyelids drooped with the effort to remain conscious, his eyes were open and staring right at her.

"Oh, Will!" she cried and threw her arms around his neck, not giving thought to his injuries.

"Gently," he murmured against her hair. She quickly pulled back.

"I'm so sorry," she said, her hand fluttering above his neck in fear that she might hurt him again if she touched him.

Will smiled, though it looked like the action pained him. "It was worth it."

"Well, this is sweet," the man said sardonically behind them. Sarah turned her head in time to see him remove the hood. She gasped when she saw the man beneath the cloak.

"Allan." She said the name in surprise, staring at Will's hired hand. She shook her head. "Wait, *you're* the Shadow?" It didn't make sense. There had to be a mistake.

He laughed. "No, but it was pretty fun convincing you that I was. Next time don't put up such a fight, sweetheart." He winked at her, and she felt Will stiffen beside her as she recoiled from Allan's open gaze.

"I swear," Will said, narrowing his eyes, "if you so much as laid a hand on her—"

"You'll what?" Allan asked with a twisted grin, looking obnoxiously arrogant and comfortable with the situation. "I don't think you're in a position to be making threats. This time, I have the upper hand. It's a good thing she's so fond of you and your little charade. She practically ran into my arms when she got lost in the forest."

Will sat up slowly, his eyes darker than she had ever seen them. "You're pushing it, Allan." His voice had dropped to a low growl.

Sarah couldn't remember ever seeing him so angry, and she could only stare at him. The silent and calculated way he held his anger and regarded Allan unnerved Sarah. Somehow, his silence made him more intimidating than if he had simply lashed out.

"Lucky for me," Allan said, drawing Sarah's gaze back to him, "I don't work for you anymore and don't have to listen to you. I got a better offer from Dunlivey and took it. Apparently he's not too fond of either one of you." His upbeat tone grated. "Little did we know that in catching the girl and the Green Do-Gooder, we'd get you, too, Will. I'm sure Dunlivey will be thrilled to hear that I got rid of all three of you in one fell swoop."

Sarah looked between the two. Allan laughed again at her confused expression. "She doesn't know, does she? Well"—he leaned forward and rested his palms on his knees as though he were addressing a child—"it's obvious that your gentleman caller here got it into his head that this town needs a savior, so he picked up this little charade to do his good deeds without all the unnecessary attention. He's been lying to you this whole time."

He straightened, removed the cloak, and threw it toward them, revealing a sheath tied around his belt. The cloak landed in a limp pile at Sarah's feet. She stared at it and didn't bother to look up as he continued on his monologue.

"The best part is that even with all your secret meetings, neither one of his personas can save your friend." Allan paused dramatically, obviously relishing the power he held over them. "The witch burns in two days."

Sarah's surprise quickly melted away as disgust and hatred burned through her. Somewhere in the back of her mind, she registered that what she was about to do was foolish. Sarah rose to her feet and lunged at the traitor. He was faster than her, though, and shoved her back to the floor.

In a split second, he unsheathed the dagger that had been concealed by the cloak. Amber-colored liquid dripped off the point as he held it above her, wickedness burning in his eyes. He grabbed her arm and sliced the blade across the top of her hand in one quick motion. She gasped in surprise and pain as the cut burned. It felt as if her whole hand were on fire.

Allan smiled sinisterly. But his menace faded, and his face registered shock as Will's body slammed into his, heaving him across the room. The dagger flew from his hands and landed noiselessly on the rug. Sarah rolled onto her side and watched Will wrestle the younger man to the ground. Allan was soon pinned to the floor as Will sat atop him. The smaller man grunted as he tried to free himself, but Will was stronger.

He raised his fist to strike Allan, but it stopped in midair and he swayed slightly. He shook his head as if to clear it, and Allan took advantage of his opponent's broken concentration. He punched Will hard in the side of his face and rolled to the side, sending Will sprawling to the floor.

Allan made a run for the door. Will found his feet and charged after him.

"Good luck," Allan called out before closing the door soundly and bolting it behind him.

Will rammed into the door. It didn't budge.

Sarah stood and held her injured hand tightly against her chest, trying to abate the throbbing pain. It wasn't bleeding excessively, but the burning was almost unbearable.

Will backed up and tried ramming the door with his shoulder several more times. Sarah realized that he was going to hurt himself.

"Just stop. It's not going to budge."

Will slammed his fist into the door in frustration and leaned his forearm against the wood. Sarah watched in compassion as his chest heaved from the effort of trying to break the door down. He straightened and walked over to her; regret, sorrow, and anger glittered in his gaze at once. A small trickle of blood from the cut above his right brow had dried on his temple, and she could tell from the cut on his upper lip and the welt on his cheekbone that he'd been beaten before coming here.

"Are you hurt?" he asked, and his eyes drifted to the blood seeping through her fingers. Will frowned. He went over to where Allan had thrown the cloak and tore off a thin strip of the fabric. He dropped the garment at their feet and looked into her eyes.

"This might hurt," he said, seeming to search her gaze for some sort of indication that she couldn't handle it.

She nodded solemnly and held her hand out to him. He was careful, his hands gentle, but the mere touch of the cloth upon her hand caused searing pain to course through her entire arm. She clenched her jaw to keep from crying out and focused her eyes on his hands as he worked. He had numerous scrapes on both of his palms, but they couldn't have been from his fight with Allan since they had already begun to heal.

When he had finished, Will tied the bandage securely, which caused her to wince. She looked up at him plaintively.

"Is his plan just to starve us to death?" she asked quietly.

He averted his gaze. "Possibly."

Sarah watched him closely. She had come to know him well enough to tell when he wasn't speaking the whole truth.

"You know what he's going to do, don't you?"

He looked at her then and nodded reluctantly. "Do you smell that?"

She sniffed the air. At first, she didn't smell anything, and then she thought she caught the faint scent of gasoline, though it smelled sweeter.

"It's a mixture of tar and oil," he said quietly. "It burns very quickly."

What hopes of survival she had left plummeted as his words sunk in. Maybe starving to death wasn't so bad after all.

"But he'll burn down the whole woods!" Sarah cried in protest, as though she could reason with the man that was no longer there.

"He probably wet the dry brush first," he said. Sarah suddenly remembered the wet ground outside. Thunder clapped overhead, and she flinched at the sound.

"Besides," he continued, "it appears that it is going to rain, which is added insurance; he chose a good time to do it."

As if on cue, smoke began to seep beneath the cracks in the floor, filling the room with a gray haze. Sarah coughed and covered her mouth with her good hand. Quick on his feet, Will ran to the center of the room and snatched the dagger off of the rug, tucking it safely in his belt. He grabbed the bearskin and ran swiftly to the door, stuffing the rug against the crack to stop the smoke from filtering in. He put his ear against the wood and waited.

"What are you doing?" she asked, sending herself into another coughing fit.

"I am waiting for him to leave. It's better if he thinks we are dead," he said as he jerked the knob repeatedly to open the door. When that didn't produce fruitful results, he tried working the door free from its hinges, but the heavy bolt on the outside prevented him from lifting it even an inch. He kicked the door in frustration, breathing hard from his efforts. He covered his mouth with his sleeve and coughed as smoke filled his lungs.

"It's no use," she said loudly, hoping to be heard over the crackle of the flames outside. This only seemed to fuel his determination, and he began kicking at the door with all his might. The wall at the back of the shack smoldered as the fire began burning through the wood. Flames appeared overhead as the roof caught fire, sending a dusting of sparks cascading to the floor.

Oh, God, help! Sarah prayed silently. The fire was spreading too quickly. She ran over to Will and grabbed his arm. "Will, stop it!"

He ceased beating the door, and his chest heaved as he tried to breathe deeply without coughing. He leaned his back against the wood and slid down until he was sitting on the floor. He looked up at her in anguish.

"I have failed you, and I'm sorry." Sarah crouched down beside him and laid her hand on his shoulder. He looked like a soldier that had been unsuccessful in his mission.

"You haven't failed me," she said, blinking against the haze. "We're going to find a way out of this."

As if to back up her claim, rain came down in a slow shower and pelted against the wooden roof. She sent up a prayer of gratitude and smiled at him in reassurance. "See? Everything is going to be—"

The roof groaned loudly, and they both looked up just as a support beam fell to the floor in a flaming heap. Pieces of the ceiling fell down around them, and Sarah covered her head with her hands. She felt Will protectively wrap his arms around her to shield her body from the falling pieces of ceiling. She peeked out between his arms and saw a large hole in the roof, which allowed rain to pour into the room freely. But the oil in the tar prevented the water from squelching the hungry flames.

Sarah looked quickly down at her foot and saw that her shoe was on fire. She shrieked and swatted at the embers with the hem of her dress. They were extinguished quickly, unlike the rest of the raging flames that seemed to grow with each passing minute.

"Heavenly Father," she cried out in terror and tried to pray, but no words came. She watched in horror as the back wall crumbled and was reduced to smoldering remains, revealing the dark night outside through a screen of flames. The room was going to fall apart at any minute.

Sarah started as Will suddenly jumped up and ran to the middle of the room toward the smoldering logs that had fallen from the ceiling. He snatched the cloak up from the floor and dashed back to her, narrowly avoiding a large chunk of ceiling that fell just inches from his head. He threw the cloak around his body and pulled the hood over his head. He held his hand out to her.

"Come on," he shouted above the roar of the flames.

Dazed, she grabbed his hand and allowed him to help her to her feet. He surprised her by lifting her into his arms and facing the fallen wall.

"What are you doing?" she cried, realizing his intent. They were going to go through it!

Sarah stared at the open passage leading to safety. The flames leapt up from the floor and came down from the ceiling, nearly shrouding the night from view. But it was their only chance. She looked back at his expectant face.

"Trust me," he said. She nodded slowly, knowing it was their only hope. "Cover yourself." She followed his orders and pulled the cloak around her body, burying her face in his chest and praying they would live to regret this.

She felt Will take a deep breath and begin running to the other side of the room. He jumped over burning logs and ducked under fallen beams. She could hear the shack crash to the ground piece by piece around them. She squeezed her eyes closed as it became unbearably hot inside the cloak, but she didn't dare open it for fear of what she would find. Will leapt forward and kept running, holding her tightly against his chest.

Cool air suddenly enveloped them, and Sarah realized that they were outside. Will stopped abruptly, setting her gently on her feet and throwing the cloak to the grass. The embers on it began to dim as the rain soaked the garment.

The duo looked upon the burning shack from a safe distance as it caved in on itself, leaving a pile of smoldering wood as the only evidence that a building had ever existed there. Rain poured down on their heads, but they barely took notice.

"We made it," Will whispered in amazement, staring at the ashes in disbelief.

Sarah's throat and eyes burned from the smoke. She noticed again the searing pain in her hand. The rain had already soaked through her dress, and she shivered. Her heartbeat sped up and then slowed considerably, leaving her feeling light headed. She blinked several times and fought to keep her head upright. Her body swayed to the side, and the image of the smoldering building blurred as she felt herself falling.

Will caught hold of her just before she hit the ground. He laid her down slowly on the soft, wet earth.

"Sarah, what's wrong?" he asked worriedly.

"I don't feel good," she mumbled, and her heartbeat slowed once more. The slow, sporadic beat seemed to be the only thing that she could hear now, though somewhere in the back of her mind she registered Will's voice trying to bring her back. His urgent words seemed to blur together and became nothing more than a deep, garbled noise.

Her head lolled to the side uncontrollably. The sight of the body made her want to scream, though the only noise she made was a small gurgling sound.

Allan lay on his stomach a few feet from her, his mouth open and his wide eyes staring at her lifelessly. Her breathing became labored, and she succumbed to the blackness, but not before she saw the blood coating the arrow in his back and the way it glistened in the light of the flames.

Chapter Twenty-One

Will watched her eyes close and felt his face drain of color, much like hers had done just before she collapsed.

"Sarah?" He shook her gently, eliciting a soft moan from her parted lips, though her eyes remained closed. He glanced to the side and saw Allan's body lying on the ground. He turned away in revulsion and focused back on Sarah.

Her usually rosy complexion had turned so pale that Will feared he might have lost her already. He placed a finger against her throat and breathed a sigh of relief when he felt the faint, sporadic beat of her pulse.

She felt so limp and frail as he hoisted her into his arms, running as fast as he could without stumbling. Will held her body close to his chest to shield her from some of the rain and hoped he wasn't jostling her too much. He knew these woods better than anyone and cut a straight path to the only place he knew to go. He just hoped he wouldn't be too late by the time he got there.

The rain made it difficult to keep sure footing, but he made it to his destination quickly and without mishap. Shifting Sarah's body in his arms to balance her weight, he lifted his leg and banged on the large door with his boot until the person he was looking for opened the portal. The man held a lantern in front of him and appeared to be disheveled from sleep.

"Will, what are you—?"

Thomas Greene caught sight of the limp girl in Will's arms and stepped back silently, allowing the younger man to enter.

"What happened?" he asked, following the couple to the bedroom in the back. He threw the quilt back and placed the lantern on the bedside table. Will set Sarah carefully down on the mattress, breathing heavily after the entire ordeal.

"I'm not sure," Will said. He raked a shaky hand back through his damp hair, sending droplets of water falling to the floor. His cloths dripped on the woven rug, but he didn't care. He stared at Sarah's unconscious form, ignoring the cold that seeped into his bones.

"Will," Thomas said firmly, gripping his shoulders until the younger man looked at him. "You need to tell me what happened."

Working on calming his emotions, he spoke softly, reliving the night as he explained. "We were attacked. I woke up in that abandoned shack near the lake north of here, and she was there. He attacked her and cut her hand with this." He pulled the dagger from his belt and tossed it onto the floor in disgust. "He locked us inside, and then he burned the place down. We escaped just before it came crashing in."

He swallowed convulsively. "Then she collapsed outside. She does not seem like the type to faint, so I can only assume that it's smoke inhalation that caused her to pass out."

Thomas looked at the dagger and his eyes widened. He rushed to the side of the bed and threw open the door to the small cabinet there. Looking over the bottles inside, he selected several, grabbing a small dagger off the shelf as well. He dumped everything on top of the cabinet and began pouring carefully measured amounts of the liquids into an empty bottle. He placed the stopper in the top and shook it quickly to mix the concoction.

"Go make a fire," he commanded.

"But—"

"Do as I say!" Thomas said gruffly, grabbing the dagger off the floor and handing it to Will. "Clean it thoroughly and then stick the point in the flames when you get it started. And hurry!" He followed Will to the bedroom door and closed it behind him.

Will worked for several minutes at building a fire with the wood beside the hearth. His fingers were numb and shaky, but he managed to get the flames going. He stripped off all of his unnecessary clothing and warmed himself by the fire as he wiped all remnants of the amber liquid off the blade and then carefully held the tip of the dagger to the flames. Seeing the roaring embers reminded him of the ordeal they had just been through, and he shook his head at the unwanted memories that seemed to consume him suddenly.

He had been in countless scrapes before and had sometimes even wondered if he would survive some of his reckless escapades, but this night was the closest he had ever come to losing his life—and Sarah's. He pushed aside the feelings of guilt and rose as soon as the tip of the dagger began to glow with the heat. He knocked softly on the closed door.

Thomas quickly opened the portal and took the knife from Will's hand. "Give me a few minutes to clean the wound." Without waiting for his reply, Thomas closed the door in his face.

Will felt like ramming the door in his anger, but his logical side prevented him. Thomas was a skilled physician and knew what needed to be done; he certainly did not need Will interfering.

"You can come in now," Thomas said softly from the other side of the door a few painfully long minutes later.

Will entered tentatively. Thomas sat on the edge of the bed; he was holding Sarah's hand up to the lantern light so he could examine it more closely. The quilt had been pulled up to her chin, and her soaked dress lay over a chair in the corner.

"What's wrong with her?" Will asked quietly. Thomas looked up at him and shook his head slowly.

"You said he cut her hand?" he asked. Will nodded. "I can only surmise that he poisoned her when he did it."

He paused. Thomas had always believed that being straightforward when giving a diagnosis was the best approach—be considerate of their feelings, but don't lie. Will could tell that he was about to give his honest opinion.

"At this point, I'm not sure that she will survive."

Will felt as if all the air had been sucked out of the room. He gripped the doorjamb for support. "What do you mean poisoned?" he demanded.

"He must have soaked the knife in some sort of potion and cut her with it to guarantee she wouldn't survive, even if she did manage to escape."

He shifted the covers aside and held Sarah's hand up for Will's inspection. The cut had turned a ghastly shade of green, and the poison had caused her hand to swell considerably. Beads of sweat glistened on her forehead, and her lips were nearly the same shade of white as her once-tan face. The moan that came from her was the most heart-wrenching sound Will had ever heard.

"What can we do?" he asked, never taking his eyes from her ashen face.

"I gave her something to counteract the poison, and I cleaned the wound, removing as much of the toxin as possible. But there's no guarantee," Thomas said softly and rose from the bed. "And look at this."

He was gentle as he rolled Sarah onto her stomach and pulled the blanket down her back, resting it just above her hips. He undid the ties and pulled open the back of her underdress.

Before Thomas had ended his practice, Will had assisted him with many patients. But he usually helped with the male patients, and the sight of Sarah's bare back caused his neck to heat. As he came closer, he saw the gashes and bruises along her exposed skin. Several cuts ran along her lower back and trailed under the quilt. He clenched his fists as anger boiled inside of him.

"They are on her legs, as well, but not as severe," Thomas said softly. "Do you know how she might have received them?"

A muscle in Will's cheek twitched, and he wondered if he might break his teeth from clenching his jaw so tightly. "Are they just on her back?" he asked, his throat tight with repressed anger. Thomas nodded. "Then he must have dragged her through the forest all the way to the cabin."

Thomas nodded again and walked toward the door. "Stay with her until I'm back," he said over his shoulder.

Will felt uncomfortable being alone with her and kept his eyes focused on the wood floor. He heard the older man's footsteps as he reentered the bedroom a few minutes later, and Will exhaled in relief.

"This should cleanse her wounds and keep them from getting infected," Thomas said, handing Will a handkerchief and a small bowl filled with a murky white liquid that smelled of lavender and peppermint. "I'm going to collect some rainwater. Apply that to each cut and let it dry." He turned again to leave.

"You want me to do it?" Will had applied disinfectant a hundred times before without embarrassment. Why did it cause his hands to shake nervously at the mere thought of doing so now?

He looked up and caught Thomas staring at him questioningly. "You're blushing." Will glanced at the floor while the older man continued to study him. "You've helped me many times before with this kind of thing. What's so different now?"

Will looked up at Sarah's still form and clenched his fists, angry with himself. It was his fault she was here and lying unconscious after nearly being killed in a burning building. He should never have brought her into any of this. He should have turned her away the minute she entered his livery nearly a week ago and never looked back. His throat tightened at the thought.

"She's special, isn't she?" Thomas said quietly behind him. Will said nothing but looked at the wise man with pain-filled eyes. Thomas nodded slowly in understanding. "I truly hope your friend lives. I would like to meet the girl who stole my nephew's heart." Then he left the room.

Will walked over to the bed and sat down, holding the bowl in his lap. He dipped the cloth in the pale liquid and gently dabbed at a cut running over her right shoulder blade. She whimpered softly, and his hand froze on her skin. He hadn't considered the fact that she might be able to feel all that was going on, but the painful sound was evidence that she could sense everything around her.

Working up his resolve and swallowing the lump in his throat, he went about cleaning her wounds as gently and quickly as possible. A silent tear trickled out of the corner of her eye and rolled over the bridge of her nose, though she made no more sounds.

"I am sorry," he whispered brokenly, knowing she would be better off if he continued with his work. When he was finished, he sat on the floor with his back to the wall and waited for the ointment to dry. He rested his arms on his knees and laid his head on them, completely exhausted.

I need you. Her words echoed in his ears. She had spoken them with such faith, trust, and hope, and he had only let her down. He squeezed his eyes closed.

"No, you don't," he whispered to the still room.

"How is she doing?" He raised his head to see Thomas standing in the doorway holding a large pale of water and a cloth.

"She cried while I tended her wounds," he said quietly. "She can feel everything, Uncle. Did you realize that?"

Thomas nodded solemnly. "It needed to be done, and I wasn't sure you would do it if you knew." He set the pail down beside the bed and went about tying the strings of the gown loosely over her raw shoulders and back. Then he carefully rolled her over, pulling the sheets up to her chin once more. Leaning close to her, he listened as she inhaled a trembling breath. Then he shook his head and straightened.

"She's having trouble breathing," he said. Will rose to his feet and came to stand beside his uncle.

"The poison has affected her lungs, and her fever is growing worse. Normally I would have a large number of remedies for congestion that would dissipate the discomfort and essentially heal her body, but it's not a matter of simple congestion; her lungs are just shutting down. I can give her something to numb the pain, but it will also dull her defenses against the toxin."

Will felt torn, understanding the troubled look in his uncle's eyes. He had the choice to end her pain now and allow his uncle to give her something to dull her senses, but he knew it would also destroy any chance of survival. Somehow, he knew that she wouldn't want to give up so easily, and he was not ready for her to let go.

He shook his head. "I don't think she would choose the easy way simply to make herself more comfortable."

His uncle seemed pleased with his response and was silent for a moment before he spoke softly. "You must understand that I'm not sure if she will make it through the night. Even with our best efforts, I cannot guarantee that."

"There must be something that we can do," Will said desperately, though he knew the answer from the look on his uncle's face. Thomas had worn that sympathetic expression every time he told someone that there was nothing he could do to save their loved ones.

"We can keep her as comfortable as possible and try to get her fever down." He placed his hand on his nephew's shoulder. "And we can pray."

"Why don't you get some rest and I can watch her," Will snapped. Thomas's hand fell away at the younger man's obvious irritation. Will could see his uncle's dejected look and felt remorseful over being the cause of it, though his pride kept him from apologizing.

"I can stay in here while you dry off," Thomas said quietly, setting the pail on the ground and soaking the cloth in the cold water. He rung it out and laid it on Sarah's forehead, keeping his back to Will.

Will knew it was no use arguing with the man, so he left the room without another word. He stretched out on the ground in front of the flames and stared at the ceiling. His body felt heavy with exhaustion, but his mind continued to keep him awake. He wondered what he could do to help Sarah and how he was going to fulfill the promise he had made to her to try his best to release Karen. Now he only had two days to keep his oath.

He squeezed his eyes shut, trying to direct his train of thought to something else. Surprisingly, his thoughts turned to his uncle. When they were together, it always amazed him how alike they were. Though Thomas and Will's mother had been identical twins, their personalities had been very different.

Sophie Greene had been outgoing, quick to laugh and smile, and had always said what was on her mind. Thomas tended to keep to himself and think through what he was going to say before he spoke. A quiet spirit, his mother had often said. Though Will had inherited his father's physical characteristics and his mother's dark eyes, he had a "quiet spirit" like his uncle, though he knew he wasn't nearly as humble.

He admired Thomas for the way he seemed to take everything in stride and always had the right words to say. Will constantly became angry with himself when he didn't know what to say or do. He was well aware of the fact that he could stand to learn a few things from his uncle. The older man never seemed to fail, and failure was the one thing Will truly feared. He had failed before, and the consequences had haunted him every night since.

Chapter Twenty-Two

"Will?" His uncle's voice startled him from his sleep. Will bolted upright, fully alert, wondering if something was wrong. He hadn't meant to drift off, but judging by the dim light pouring through the window near the door, the sun was already beginning to rise.

"You fell asleep," Thomas said with a small smile as he stood over the younger man.

Will rose to his feet and raked a shaky hand through his hair, his heart beating fast. "Is everything all right?"

Thomas nodded. "I was wondering if you would mind staying with her while I rest in the back room for a few moments."

"Of course." His heartbeat began to slow with the realization that there was no emergency.

"Here." Thomas held a damp cloth out to him. "You can use this to clean that cut above your eye."

Will touched a finger to the dried blood on his brow. He had completely forgotten about the cut. He accepted the cloth and walked almost mechanically into his uncle's room while Thomas made his way to the room opposite. When he'd still had his practice, Thomas had used that room to house his patients while they recovered. There was a single bed in the back corner, and Will hoped his uncle would be able to get some sleep.

He used the damp cloth to wipe the blood from his forehead and watched Sarah sleep, standing just outside the doorway. He made no move to enter the room even after the bloodstained rag hung limply from his hand. He simply stood there, staring, unmoving. Being in the room with her, unable to do anything but stand idly by and wait for some improvement, made him feel helpless and useless. He didn't like feeling that way.

Forcing his feet to move, he entered the room slowly, his eyes locked on her face. Thomas had pulled the quilt down so that her arms rested atop it and she could breathe easier without the added weight of the bedding.

Will stood there for a moment, indecisive, and then sat down on the side of the bed, suddenly wanting to be closer to her. He needed to feel that she was still with him. When he laid a hand on her forehead, he found she was still burning up, so he grabbed the cloth Thomas had left on the side of the bucket and proceeded to brush it lightly over her face. The water in the bucket was still cold, but when he touched the cloth to her warm forehead, she didn't seem to notice. Her mouth hung open slightly, and he could tell her breathing was labored. How much longer?

William Taylor was not one to give into feelings of helplessness, but at that moment, that was exactly how he felt. He laid the cloth on her forehead and found himself pleading with the One he had tried to ignore for so many years.

She trusts You, he cried silently, fury and despair lacing his unspoken words. *Are You just going to let her go? Has she not been faithful to You, just like my parents were? Is this how You repay people who trust, who have faith?*

Will clenched his fists and tried to force down his anger. Growing angry with God was not going to solve any of his problems. He sighed, feeling his frustration drain from him as he expelled his breath.

She believes in You and does not deserve to die this way. I am the one who has doubted and questioned. I felt like You deserted me that day and had to stop believing so I wouldn't get hurt.

Will stopped abruptly, realizing that he was pouring out his heart to a God he hadn't trusted for so long. His throat tightened as he closed his eyes and found himself praying earnestly. *If you will save her, I will never doubt you again. You may be ready to have her, but I am not ready to let go just yet.*

When he opened his eyes and saw that her condition had not changed, he felt strangely disappointed. He hadn't expected an immediate miracle, but a small part of him had hoped.

Will spent another hour washing her face with the cool rag, hoping for improvement. He could smell breakfast cooking, but he had no appetite for food. A few minutes later, Thomas came into the room carrying a wooden plate filled with ham and scrambled eggs.

"I'm not hungry," Will murmured. His uncle nodded in understanding and set the plate on the night table.

"Just in case. How's the patient?" he asked, laying his large hand on her pale forehead. A smile lit his face, and he turned to Will. "Her fever is down."

Will stared at his uncle in surprise. "What?" He touched a hand to her cheek and realized the older man was right; her skin felt normal.

Will stood and walked to the other side of the room in a fog, leaned against the wall, and slid down slowly. He watched Sarah's face closely for any sign that she was in pain and still fighting for her life. There were none.

"Will." His uncle crouched beside him. "Look at me," he prodded. Will turned his head and stared at the man.

"I prayed for her, Uncle," he whispered, feeling an odd mix of emotions course through his body. It couldn't have been that. It had to have been something else. But there had been no hope left for her, so what other explanation was there?

Thomas tried to keep his expression neutral, but Will could see the joy in his eyes as he nodded. "You did well, son."

He shook his head, denying the evidence before his very eyes. "No. It must have been what you gave her," he said, trying to ease his conscience. After all of the things he had said about God, the curses he had cried in the night, the hate and bitterness he'd held within, his pride kept him from acknowledging the fact that the Almighty might have been the one to save her.

"Will," his uncle said slowly in the tone he used when he was about to tell someone they were wrong. "I know that you want to believe that so you don't have to face the fact that a God who you think abandoned you years ago might have listened to you. But it's true, son."

Will shook his head again, vehemently this time. "She must have gotten enough rest, that's all."

Thomas placed a hand on his nephew's shoulder. "You know that's not true. I know that it's easier for you to deny Him than face the fact that He heard you. What's more, He answered you." He paused, as though wondering if he should say anything more. "She was going to die, Will, whether I did something or not. There was nothing left to be done."

"But you said—"

"I said those things so that you might have some hope that she would improve. I was speaking in faith that maybe God would perform a miracle and save her." He smiled. "And He has, but I don't believe that it was anything I tried to do for her."

"But why would He listen to *me*?" Will asked quietly, his words full of guilt and grief. "Why would He choose to hear me now?"

His uncle's eyes filled with compassion. "He heard all along, son, but He finally got you to a point where you would listen." He seemed to read the unspoken question in the younger man's gaze because he shook his head. "I don't know why He took your parents to be with Him, but I do know that they are happier than this world could ever make them. They're just waiting for you to join them someday."

Will stood abruptly, feeling uncomfortable with the direction the conversation had taken. "The family that she is staying with is probably worried. I should go and make up an excuse so they don't come looking for her."

Thomas rose to his feet. His steady gaze seemed to penetrate the carefully erected mask that Will had disguised his face in for so many years. "Is that the whole truth?" he asked.

"Not exactly," Will said slowly, trying to ease his guilty conscience. "But if I tell them that she is staying with a friend, which she is, technically, then it will not be a lie at all. Besides, I am not sure when she will awaken, so I don't want to give them a return date. This seems like the easiest solution."

"Would you like me to go for you?" Thomas asked, following his nephew as he hastily walked to the front door.

Will shook his head. "They don't know everything that she has been up to, so it might be hard to explain why you came to deliver the news." He gripped the doorknob. "If she wakes up before I get back, please tell her that I will return shortly."

With that, he swung the door open and walked quickly away from the cabin.

CRSO

He found Seth outside of the Joneses' barn chopping wood on a large stump. Seth had his back to him, so he walked around in front of him, giving him plenty of distance. He had learned that you should never startle a man wielding an axe.

Seth raised the blade over his head and brought it down hard on a piece of wood. He pulled his axe from the log and looked up. Will thought he gripped the handle a little tighter when he spotted him. The two stared at each other from a distance, assessing the other with his gaze.

"What are you doing here, Will?" Seth asked impatiently.

"I have a message from Sarah."

Seth's eyes widened, and he took a step closer to Will, though he still held the axe. "Is she all right?" he asked, concern and suspicion apparent in his gaze. "Mama and Leah have been worried sick."

"She's fine," Will said quickly. He took a deep breath and wondered why he felt so uncomfortable. Maybe it was because he knew that Sarah wouldn't want him to lie for her. But he convinced himself that he was doing the right thing, so he pressed on. "She gave me a message for your family."

Seth raised a brow. "Really?"

"She said that she met a friend in town and is staying with them for a little while, though she is sorry that she was unable to get a message to you sooner. With the rain and all . . ."

Seth nodded, relief apparent in his gaze. "I understand. Tell her not to worry. I'll pass the message on to everyone else."

"All right. I guess I'll just—"

"How did she find you to pass the message along?" Seth asked. He tried to sound nonchalant, but Will wasn't fooled.

I was hoping to avoid this, he thought to himself. Luckily, years of side stepping people's questions had trained his mind to work quickly, and a response was on his lips almost before he had time to think about it.

"I met her in town this morning and was headed this way, so she had me stop by here so I could assure you that she was all right."

Seth seemed to consider his answer for a moment. He leaned the axe against the chopping block and walked over to where Will stood. It looked as though he were trying to read the older man's expression while he studied him. After a long pause, he asked slowly, "So she isn't staying with you?"

Will tried to look amused as he spoke. "You know how small my cabin is, Seth. I can barely fit myself inside."

Seth grinned slightly. "You're right. I'm sorry I even considered that." His expression suddenly became thoughtful. "We used to be such good friends when we were kids. What happened to that?"

"We grew up," Will said matter-of-factly.

"And now we're letting a girl get in the way."

Will feigned incredulity. "What are you talking about?"

Seth eyed him for a moment. "You mean you don't have feelings for her?" he asked slowly.

"Who?"

"Sarah, of course. Don't you like her?"

Will waited a moment too long to answer, which caused Seth's grin to widen.

"That's what I thought." He clapped his hands together. "So, what are we going to do about it?"

"Nothing," Will said with an indifferent shrug.

"Or we could let her choose."

Will shook his head. "I'm not sure I like that idea."

"I'm not saying that we'd come right out and ask her to pick. We should make a pact right now that whichever one she chooses, there will be no hard feelings."

"Or she could choose neither of us."

"We're the only single men of age in this town who aren't twelve years older than her," Seth said with a chuckle. "I think we're our only competition. Unless, of course, you'd rather just step back and let me court her."

Will did not like that proposal. "What are the conditions?" he asked against his better judgment.

Seth brightened visibly. "There's no trying to woo her; that would be cheating. We just have to act normal around her. Then we'll know that the best man won and there'll be no hard feelings. Deal?" He extended his hand and waited.

Will didn't like the idea, but he liked backing down from a challenge even less. He gripped Seth's hand firmly in his and shook it.

"Agreed."

∝≫∽

On his way back to his uncle's cabin, Will wondered why on earth he had agreed to something as juvenile as a race to see whom Sarah would fall for. His conscience gnawed at him as he remembered that the girl whose attentions they were vying for was unconscious, the threat of death still looming over her head.

He shook his head at himself as he stepped onto the porch of his uncle's cabin. The next time he saw Seth he would tell him that the deal was off and that they should focus their attentions elsewhere. Although, he admitted to himself, he most likely would not take his own advice.

Will opened the door and stood at the threshold for a long moment, listening for some kind of sound coming from inside. The cabin was eerily quiet. He had expected his uncle to be bustling about the small house, or at the very least come to greet him with encouraging news about Sarah's recovery.

He swallowed hard and stepped into the main room, closing the door quietly behind him. While he walked slowly to the back room, he grew afraid of what news might await him. He stopped in the bedroom doorway, and Thomas looked up from his perch on the side of the bed. The older man stood and came to stand in front of him.

"She's stable now," Thomas said. Will felt the air whoosh out of his lungs and realized that he'd been holding his breath.

"Good, very good," he murmured. He cleared his throat to dislodge the lump that had formed there. "Has she regained consciousness or said anything?"

His uncle shook his head. "I'm afraid she has not come to just yet. However, for a few moments while you were gone, she kept mumbling something about days. Two days, or something like that. Does that make any sense?"

Will felt his chest tighten, knowing exactly what his uncle was referring to. Even while unconscious, she remembered her promise to Karen. He remembered his pledge to help her, and he had no intention of letting her down.

"I need to go," he said suddenly. Thomas looked surprised at his sudden declaration.

"What do you mean? You only just arrived."

"I will explain everything later, Uncle, but I really must go now," he said as he turned around and jogged toward the front door. He was back in the small room a moment later, though.

"Uncle?"

Thomas was standing in the same place he'd left him.

"Yes?" he asked.

"Do you have a cloak I could borrow?"

Thomas smiled.

Chapter Twenty-Three

Sarah felt like she was floating. Though she couldn't see anything, she could feel the world around her. At first, she wondered if she was dead, but she knew that couldn't be true because this certainly wasn't heaven, rather somewhere in between. She felt a cool hand upon her forehead, then her body tipped dangerously to the side. She tried to reach out for something to steady her, but her body wouldn't respond to her command.

Something poked at her back, and pain seared through her body. Words were whispered in her ear as they continued to cause her undue pain, but she couldn't make out what they were saying. Sweat broke out on her brow and a tear slipped down her cheek as the discomfort continued.

Just as abruptly as the pain had started, it faded away, leaving in its place the feeling that she was drowning. She felt like she had been thrown into the ocean as her lungs began to fill and contract rapidly in her panic to find air. Her breathing became labored, and she tried to fight her way to the surface, but her limbs refused to cooperate. She thought of Karen and how she had failed her.

And then all feeling slowly began to grow weaker until she felt nothing at all.

CRSO

Sarah's hand brushed against something soft. The urge to open her eyes was so intense that she focused all of her energy into that action. Her tired lids obeyed slowly, though they felt like they weighed a hundred pounds. It took a moment for her eyes to adjust to the dimly lit room; the lone candle on the bedside table was the only source of light. Where was she? She tried to move, but her body was too weak, and she only managed to lift her hand slightly. It brushed against something again, and she managed to roll her head to the side to see what it was.

A moment passed before she could make out Will's features. He was sitting on the floor, eyes closed, back against the bed, with his head resting on the edge of the mattress. Sarah's hand lay on the bed, the back of it just touching his hair. Without thinking, she raised her hand and brushed her fingertips through his thick, wavy hair. She was surprised at how soft and warm it was against her cold fingers, and she felt a tingle race up her arm.

Will moaned softly. The sound startled her and she quickly jerked her hand away, causing the bed to shift slightly. Will stirred and his head lifted from the mattress. She froze, feeling like a kid caught with her hand in the cookie jar, unsure of what she should do.

Will reached up and massaged the back of his neck with his hand for a moment while he glanced about the room, as if he were trying to get his bearings. His gaze came to rest on her face, and his eyes widened.

"Hi," she offered weakly. She realized that her throat felt dry and swollen, and she blinked several times to rid her eyes of their gritty feeling.

Will rose from his sitting position and came to his full height. He fairly towered over her as she lay in bed, but she didn't feel frightened or even intimidated by his large presence. Actually, it was strangely comforting to know that he had been there while she slept.

"You're awake," he whispered, his voice revealing his surprise and relief.

Sarah nodded against her pillows. "Can I have some water?" she asked, her voice hoarse.

"Of course." He picked up the water glass on the bedside table and leaned over her. He tucked his free arm underneath her shoulders, cradling her like a small child, and helped her sit up so she could swallow easier. She was touched by his thoughtfulness and eagerly took a drink from the glass he lifted to her lips, though she was careful not to spill any on herself. She could feel his gaze on her while she drank but forced herself not to look up. When she was finished, he laid her head against the pillows and set the glass back on the table.

"How are you feeling?" he asked.

"I'm fine," she whispered against the tightness in her throat and tried to smile. She was caught by surprise when Will placed a hand on either side of her and leaned toward her so his face was only a few inches from hers. She felt her heart beat wildly against her ribcage and wondered if he could hear it.

"What are you doing?" she breathed, pressing her body further into the mattress to put some distance between them.

"I am trying to see if you're telling the truth, but I couldn't see well enough in this poor light," he explained logically, his brow furrowing as he tried to read her expression by the candlelight. Sarah told herself that her reaction to his nearness was silly and tried to calm her breathing. Will's eyes softened for a moment and seemed to caress her face rather than study it. Then he pulled back abruptly.

Sarah felt an odd mixture of disappointment and relief.

"You should rest," Will said quietly. "I will leave you now." He turned to go.

"Wait," she grabbed his hand, halting his movement. He stopped with his back to her. "I don't even know what happened or what I'm doing here." She looked over her unfamiliar surroundings. "Wherever here is."

He moved away from her, breaking her weak hold. She assumed he was going to leave and was surprised when he walked to the wall and lifted the chair there off of the floor. Setting the chair down close to the head of the bed, he folded his large frame in the seat, leaned forward, and rested his forearms on his legs.

"What do you want to know?"

Sarah was momentarily taken aback by his compliance. She stared at him for a moment, trying to remember exactly what it was that she had wanted to know. The dim light allowed her to see Will's face as he returned her stare, and she could see that the cut above his brow had begun to heal. He seemed to be perfectly content to wait for the questions she had, but for the life of her she couldn't remember what he had asked just a moment ago.

She swallowed hard and found it difficult to concentrate as the candle flame glowed softly on his face, accentuating his strong jaw and the breadth of his shoulders. His dark eyes appeared black and seemed more mysterious than she remembered. The scene felt far too intimate, and Sarah opened her mouth to speak so that the spell might be broken, but she couldn't force any words past her lips.

Will's intent gaze softened once more, and he leaned toward her. "Sarah? Are you all right?"

She shook her head gently, feeling foolish. "I'm sorry. What were you saying?" She hoped he wouldn't notice the squeak in her voice as she spoke.

"I asked you what you wanted to know about what has happened over the last few days."

"Last few days?" Realization crept in, and a thick blanket of dread seemed to choke the breath from her. "How long have I been asleep?" she asked with a calm that surprised her.

"Three days," he answered.

She was too late.

She turned her head away from him so he wouldn't see her eyes grow misty with the sudden realization. Karen had been executed already, and Sarah had been asleep when it happened. She had been completely powerless to do anything, and that knowledge left her feeling disheartened and drained.

She cleared her throat to dislodge the pain there and knew she had to change the subject before she broke down. "What happened, Will?" she asked, watching his face closely.

"You mean with the fire?"

"Before, actually, like how you got there." She waited for him to speak.

"I was waiting for you when he came up behind me and knocked me out."

"You mean, waiting for me as the Shadow, right?" It was still difficult for her to digest this newest bit of information.

He nodded, and she thought he looked remorseful. "The next thing I remember is waking up to find you there. And you know about the fire, but after you collapsed I carried you here to get help."

Sarah felt heat flood her face at the thought that he had carried her through the rain. She hoped he hadn't hurt himself by bearing her weight for however long it took him to get here. She looked up at him again.

"Where are we, exactly?"

"My uncle's house. He was once a doctor, so I thought he might be able to help you, since I did not know what to do."

She could hear the self-condemnation in his voice and gave a small smile. "You saved my life, Will. Don't ever think that you did anything less or that you didn't try; I wouldn't have made it without you. God used you to get me here."

He stared at her silently while he let that sink in. "I prayed for you." He spoke the words so quietly that she almost didn't catch them. Her pulse quickened.

"You did?"

He looked down at his hands clasped in his lap. "There was nothing more that we could do. My uncle and I tried everything that we could think of, but nothing seemed to work; you were getting worse. I began to give up hope, and I directed my anger at God, blaming Him for every prayer He didn't answer and every request that He didn't seem to hear."

"He heard," she whispered, keeping her tone gentle. "He always hears."

Will looked pained. "I think I have always known that. But when the answer was no, I pretended it was not an answer at all and that He had not heard or simply chose to ignore my request. But I found myself praying for you to recover anyway."

He looked up at her, his eyes glowing with a mixture of awe and confusion. "When I woke up, your fever was down. I knew that was my answer, but—"

"You didn't want to accept it," Sarah finished with a soft, knowing smile.

Will nodded. "I couldn't believe that He had even listened after all the accusations that I had thrown at Him. I thought I had been cast aside, yet there I was, receiving the exact answer I was looking for."

"God is a god of forgiveness," she said quietly, speaking the words to comfort him as well as remind herself of this fact. "We're never deserving of it, but I guess that's the beauty of Christ's sacrifice, isn't it?" She looked at him. "Thank you for praying for me, Will."

He looked down, appearing embarrassed. "It gave me a lot of things to think about."

There was a lull in the conversation. Because Sarah had never been very comfortable with long silences, she spoke the first thing that came to mind.

"What happened to your parents?"

She felt like clapping a hand over her mouth as soon as the words left her lips. His head jerked up sharply, and he stared at her. She could tell that she'd either surprised or upset him, and she immediately wished that she hadn't been as forward as she always was.

"I'm sorry, I shouldn't have asked. I overstepped my bounds." She looked down and busied herself with pulling at a loose thread in the wool blanket that had been laid over her. She suddenly wished she had some duct tape to cover her mouth so she wouldn't have to worry about her rash and thoughtless words. When would she learn to keep her mouth shut?

"They died in a fire," he said softly, which surprised Sarah, since she hadn't expected him to speak to her at all. His eyes looked pained with remembrance.

Sarah laid her hand on his forearm. "I'm so sorry," she said sincerely.

He stared down at her hand as he continued, his voice strained. "My father was the king's personal guard. I came with him some days when my mother did not need help around the house. I followed the servants around and even helped them with their chores on occasion. They never complained about my pestering them and allowed me to explore the castle, so long as I didn't wander too far." He gazed across the room and out the window where the sun was just beginning to rise. His thoughts seemed to take him a million miles away.

"There was a corridor I had never been down before, and my curiosity got the better of me. I got lost after a while, and then I heard my father's voice. I thought that I was saved until I realized that he was arguing with someone, so I hid and waited for the man to leave. I didn't catch the whole conversation, but it was apparent that the man my father was with had approached him with a proposition. When my father refused, the man threatened him . . ." His voice trailed off.

"Who was the man?" Sarah asked.

"Dunlivey." He shook his head as if coming out of a dream. "I had never really met him before, but I knew from what the servants said that he was a scoundrel. I never knew how right they were until that night."

"What happened?" she prodded softly, completely involved in the story.

Will shifted uncomfortably in his chair. "I had been angry with my father because he had allowed the man to talk to him the way he did. But my father was the most levelheaded and kind man I have ever known, so I knew he would do nothing, which only fueled my anger. I refused to return to the house with him later that night, choosing to walk home well after dark. I was too hot-tempered to notice the smoke until I was nearly upon the house."

His Adam's apple shifted as he swallowed convulsively at the memory. "When I saw the fire, I ran inside to find my parents and drag them to safety. But a beam fell from the ceiling and hit me in the head. That was the last thing I remembered until I awoke outside. My uncle was standing over me; he had followed me to make sure I got back safely, and then he ran inside after me when he saw me go in." His eyes took on a faraway look. "He hadn't realized that my parents were inside as well. By that time, there was nothing either of us could do."

Sarah's heart squeezed in pain for him. "How old were you?"

"Fourteen."

She couldn't imagine losing her parents so tragically at such a tender age. "I'm so sorry," she said again. It seemed to be the only words of comfort she could offer. She swallowed hard and tried to speak. "Is that why you became the Shadow? To avenge their deaths?"

Will smiled without humor. "I thought that I could save the world in a way I had not been able to save my parents. If no one knew who I was, I could bide my time until I could figure out some way to get the man responsible for their deaths."

The pieces suddenly seemed to come together in her mind to complete the puzzle surrounding Will. She stared straight into his eyes and saw the answer to her question even before she asked it. "You think Dunlivey set the fire that took your parents, don't you?"

"I *know* he did," he said vehemently, his eyes intense. "Or at the very least he sent someone to do his bidding. Every time I see him, it takes every ounce of self-control within me to not walk over and strangle his thick neck." His desire to do just that was evident in his voice and darkened gaze.

"That's what this whole masquerade is all about, isn't it? A score that you feel is your job to settle."

"And who will give him what he deserves if I don't?"

The answer came to her without having to think it over. "God."

Will's shoulders sagged in defeat as his anger left him. The room was silent for some time while she allowed him to think over what they had discussed. He seemed to grow calmer with each passing minute.

"Will," she said slowly, not being able to hold back her curiosity any longer. "Do you think Allan had time to tell Dunlivey who you were before he was, um, you know?"

A muscle in his jaw twitched, which she had begun to notice was a sign that he was trying to hide his anger.

Oh, great. Here we go again.

"No. The maggot was killed from a distance."

Sarah shook her head against the pillow. "Oh, Will," she said sadly, sensing his hatred.

His eyes darkened as he stared at her, and she shrank back from his gaze. She didn't think that she had ever seen someone look so menacing. "You don't actually feel sorry for what happened to him, do you? He got what he deserved!"

"Just because he did wrong by me, doesn't mean I wish him dead."

"But he tried to kill you. How can you not be angry about that?"

"Well, at first I was," she said slowly, choosing her words carefully. "But now that he's dead . . . I just don't think I can hold a grudge against someone who isn't even alive anymore. And now he's lost for all eternity."

Will rose to his full height. She shrank back, wondering why his height seemed to make him more threatening now than before. Maybe it was because his anger was obvious in the imposing stance he took.

"I do not hold a grudge," he said, clenching his jaw. "However, I do not see how you can so quickly forgive what he did."

He made it sound like she was the one that had done wrong! Sarah felt her own frustration rise. She pulled herself into a sitting position, wincing as pain sliced through her back. She sucked in a deep breath through her teeth and jutted her chin defiantly, trying to ignore the fact that the simple movement had taxed her. "I forgave him because I know it's what I am *supposed* to do."

"Well, my job is to protect people from men like him and seek justice for those who have been wronged."

A verse suddenly popped into her head. "That is *not* your job, Will," she said firmly. "Our job is to forgive and leave the judging to God."

The muscle in his jaw twitched again, and Sarah wished she had bitten her tongue instead of responding to his anger in kind.

"The next time that you look in the mirror, tell me if you still feel the same way about that traitor's eternal soul."

She glared at him questioningly. "What is that supposed—?"

The bedroom door opened, and they both turned to see a man with salt and pepper hair peek his head into the room. He brightened when he looked at Sarah and opened the door all the way. He entered the room, and his smile faded as he looked between the two of them, obviously sensing the dark mood permeating the room.

"Am I interrupting something?" he asked carefully.

"No," they replied in unison, neither one looking at the other.

"I'm glad to see that the patient is feeling better," the man said, his eyes crinkling at the corners as he smiled. He walked over to the bed and stood next to Will, looking very pleased. Sarah felt uncomfortable that he had come in during their disagreement. She was able to take a closer look at his face since the sun was now up, and she couldn't help but feel that she had seen him before.

"I don't believe that we have ever had the pleasure of being properly introduced. I am Will's uncle."

A switch seemed to go off in Sarah's head as she listened to his voice. Her eyes widened in recognition. He had been the tracker in the woods the first day she had arrived. What had Karen said his name was? Thomas . . . Thomas something. Then it hit her.

"Thomas Greene," she blurted out. "You're Will's uncle?"

Both he and Will appeared surprised at her sudden outburst.

"I'm sorry, have we met before?" Thomas asked.

"Well, no. Not exactly." She glanced at Will and, seeing his skeptical stare, quickly turned back at the older man.

"Thank you for letting me stay here these past few days," she said, changing the subject as smoothly as possible.

"It was our pleasure." Thomas smiled kindly. Sarah noticed for the first time that his eyes were the same shade of dark blue as Will's. They even crinkled at the corners when he smiled the way that Will's had done on the rare occasions that he had allowed any joyful emotions to show.

"We thought that you might leave us for a while there," Thomas said, bringing her thoughts back to the present. "But you are a fighter, aren't you?"

Sarah shook her head slowly. "I don't think it was my fight to win." He seemed pleased with her response, but out of the corner of her eye she saw Will's body stiffen.

"I need to make preparations for the day," Will said, his voice tight. Without waiting for a response, he quickly left the room. Both pairs of eyes followed him as he exited.

Sarah sighed in frustration, wondering why he was fighting it so hard.

Thomas turned back to her, and his grin surprised her. "What on earth have you done to my nephew?"

She glanced back at the now empty doorway.

"I have absolutely no idea."

Chapter Twenty-Four

Thomas brought breakfast to her in bed, saying that she needed to save her strength for the day's travels. She wasn't exactly sure what he meant by that, but she chose to simply remain silent for once. Her tongue had gotten her into enough trouble for one day.

It was nearly two hours later, and Will still hadn't shown back up. Sarah was beginning to worry. She didn't know how long they should wait before going out to look for him.

Thomas appeared completely unfazed by his sudden disappearance as he strode into the room with a dress draped over his arm. "I thought you might like to put this on."

Sarah glanced down at the gauzy underdress she wore in surprise and wondered where her clothes had gone.

"I didn't even realize that I was wearing this." A hot blush heated her cheeks with the realization that someone had removed her dress sometime while she was unconscious. She prayed that it had been the doctor, not Will; just the thought was mortifying.

Thomas laid the garment out on the end of the bed and left the room, closing the door behind him so she could change in private.

Sarah threw the covers aside and stood on shaky legs. Her muscles ached, and each movement seemed to take more effort than the last. It took a moment for the dizziness that clouded her vision to pass. Casting a quick glance over her shoulder to make sure that the door hadn't opened by itself, she caught a glimpse of the back of her dress in the full size mirror that was set in the corner by the door. Though the glass was foggy with age, her reflection was still very clear.

The white underdress she wore dipped low in the front so it wouldn't be obvious underneath most gowns, and the back drooped even lower to accommodate some of the more revealing dresses she had seen at the castle ball. The cut of the dress allowed her to clearly see the slashes that were just beginning to heal and scab over, crisscrossing over her shoulders and upper back.

She reached behind her, wincing with the movement, and loosened the tie holding the back of the dress together. She held the front of the gown to keep it from falling off as it hung loosely on her shoulders, allowing her to see the full extent of the cuts and bruises that trailed along her back. She gasped and quickly retied the strings, facing the mirror as she did so, as though hiding the markings from view would make them disappear.

When she finished tying the dress back together, she stared at her reflection for a moment, wondering if the old mirror was playing tricks on her. She hadn't noticed the yellow-green markings on the sides of her throat before and took a step closer. Sure enough, a large, yellow bruise was healing on the right side of her neck, and on the left were four more matching bruises. Her hand fluttered against her throat as though to cover the unsightly marks. It took several seconds for the image of Allan trying to strangle her in the forest to come to mind.

"That's what Will was talking about," she whispered to herself in the empty room. Even if she could cover her scarred back, it would be hard to disguise the proof of Allan's chokehold on her neck.

Someone knocked quietly on the door; the sound nearly caused Sarah to jump out of her skin.

"Just a minute," she called. She tried to pull on the dress Thomas had brought as quickly as possible while still avoiding rubbing some of the new skin off her back.

"Don't rush," Thomas said from the other side. "I simply wanted to tell you that you need to leave within the hour."

"Thank you." She heard him walk away from the door and released her breath. She had managed to pull the dress on, but she didn't have the strength to reach behind her and synch the ribbons to secure the gown.

She collapsed onto the bed, feeling completely exhausted from the simple act of putting on a dress. Closing her eyes and allowing herself to melt into the soft mattress, her thoughts began to fade one by one until the blessed blackness that comes with sleep enveloped her.

CRSO

A hand gently nudged her shoulder. Sarah wished that the culprit would stop bugging her so she could get back to her perfect, dreamless sleep. But the nudging persisted, and the person began to softly call her name. She forced her eyes open and was surprised to find Will bending over her. She was relieved to see that his expression seemed to have softened since he'd left earlier.

Sarah sat up slowly and shook her head to clear the fog that had settled there. She had forgotten that she hadn't tied her dress in the back. She felt the gown hang loosely on her shoulders and quickly pressed her palm to her chest to keep the gown from slipping any further.

Will stood abruptly, appearing embarrassed as he avoided her gaze.

Sarah could tell he was going to run from the room at any moment, but she knew that she still couldn't master all of the ties herself. Swallowing her pride, she looked at the floor and said quietly, "I wasn't able to pull it closed by myself." She hoped he would take the hint so she wouldn't have to embarrass herself by asking him outright to help.

The room was silent for a long, uncomfortable moment.

"Fine," was all he said before taking a step back from the bed to give her some space.

Sarah stood and turned her back to him, feeling the heat creep up her neck as he quickly and dutifully tied the ribbons, being careful not to pull them too tightly over her raw skin. She wouldn't have been embarrassed about her appearance back home, since the underclothes covered her lower back and the dress still modestly hid her shoulders from view. However, she knew that Will wasn't accustomed to so much exposure and must have felt very uneasy. This knowledge caused her face to heat again.

She was surprised when he paused with the last few ribbons still undone.

"Did you see these?" he asked, his voice soft.

Sarah nodded stiffly, aware that he was referring to the scrapes and cuts on her back.

"And yet you still defend him." Before she could comment, he quickly fastened the dress the rest of the way, though he lingered behind her when he had finished. Sarah glanced over her shoulder at him and caught his thoughtful expression.

"This was my mother's," he said, his eyes filled with a sadness that he tried to hide.

She turned around to face him, feeling like she was intruding on some private memory. "I can put on my own dress, if you would rather I didn't wear your mom's."

He shook his head slowly. "Your dress is torn. Besides, it's not as though my mother is here to wear it."

A thoughtful pause passed between them. Sarah was the first to break the silence.

"What was your mother like?"

Will's eyes searched hers for a long moment. His lips curved in what seemed to be a wistful smile of remembrance. "She was much like you, actually. A little outspoken at times, kind, and forgiving to everyone. She had a wonderful sense of humor. And she was very beautiful." Sarah watched as his Adams apple bobbed up and down nervously, as though he had revealed too much.

He took an abrupt step back from her, hiding his feelings behind the familiar expressionless façade that had masked his features so many times before. "We need to be going before it gets too late."

"Where are we going, anyway?" Sarah asked, respecting his desire to change the current topic of conversation, though she felt disappointment, nonetheless.

"Back," was all he said before ushering her out of the house with a gentle hand at her elbow.

Thomas was outside and, to Sarah's relief, was hitching a horse to the front of a small wagon. He looked up and smiled when he saw her.

"I thought you might have a better time in this than on horseback." Sarah nodded her gratitude.

"I need to grab something from the house," Will said suddenly, surprising them both. He walked back inside before either of them could object.

Sarah stood there awkwardly, staring at the ground and trying to come up with something to say. When she glanced up at Thomas and saw that he was grinning at her again, completely at ease and unaffected by the silence, she relaxed.

"I wanted to thank you for all that you did for me," she said at last, staring into eyes that looked so much like Will's, though this man was far better at breaking a smile every now and then. "I really appreciate your kindness."

To her surprise, Thomas chuckled. "I don't believe I really had all that much to do with it, my dear."

Sarah smiled at his comment, knowing exactly what he was referring to. "Still, thank you."

Will emerged from the house and strode toward them.

"Are you ready?" he asked. Sarah nodded, and Thomas offered her his hand to help her into the wooden seat, holding on even after she was situated. He used his hold on her to pull her down toward him while Will walked around to the other side.

"Don't give up on him yet," Thomas whispered so only she could hear.

"What?" she asked quietly, confused.

"He's closer than ever because of you. Don't lose hope; hang in there."

Sarah glanced at Will over her shoulder as he climbed into the wagon. She turned back to Thomas and nodded reassuringly.

"I won't."

He smiled and squeezed her hand gently before letting go and taking a step back. "It has been a pleasure meeting you, Miss Sarah," he said, genuine joy shining in his eyes. Will flicked the reins to get the horses moving. Thomas called behind them as they rolled away, "You must come back and visit sometime."

Sarah didn't respond. Instead, she forced a smile to her lips and waved over her shoulder in farewell, knowing she couldn't make any promises.

Chapter Twenty-Five

They rode in silence for what seemed like an eternity. Every few minutes, she shifted uncomfortably in the hard seat. She sat up with her back straight because every time she leaned against the seat, it rubbed at the new skin on her back. They hit a rut in the dirt path, and the wagon dropped and rose quickly. She grimaced. Will must have noticed because the wagon slowed, and he pulled the horses to a stop.

"You should have told me that you were in pain," he said, laying the reins down and turning so he could look at her.

"Would it have mattered?" she asked with a raised brow.

"Yes," he answered without hesitation.

She was taken aback by his quick response. She instinctively straightened her back and stuck out her chin. It was something that her dad always said she did when she was being stubborn or prideful, but she pushed those thoughts aside.

"I'm fine," she said, taking deep breaths in through her nose to help keep her focus off of how uncomfortable she was. "We need to keep going." She kept her gaze focused on the trees ahead. When he remained silent and the wagon didn't move, she turned to look at him. His grin was filled with amusement.

"What are you smiling about?" she asked, feeling herself growing more irritated.

"I am smiling over the fact that you and I are not so very different, Sarah."

"Of course we are," she argued, knowing that the full extent of their differences included a few hundred years, something he had no clue about.

Will shook his head, still clearly amused. "I believe that we are more alike than you are willing to admit, especially where our tempers are concerned. My uncle would say that we both have chutzpah."

She sighed in frustration. "What does that even mean? You know what, never mind," she hurriedly added, raising a hand in surrender. "Let's just stop disagreeing and keep going. I can make it the rest of the way." She flicked her hand in the air as though she were signaling a cabby to drive on.

Will eyed her for a moment, then leaned back and pulled a thick blanket out from behind the seat. He folded it until it was the right size and gently stuffed it behind Sarah's back. She leaned against the blanket and was pleased at how much more comfortable the seat was because of it.

"Thank you," she said to him. "*Now* we can go."

His crooked grin returned. He slid down in the seat and leaned casually against the side, his knees nearly brushing hers as he closed his eyes. He threaded his fingers together over his chest, looking far too comfortable for Sarah's liking.

"That would be a 'no,' I presume," she said, obvious irritation lacing her words. What had happened to the dark, brooding fellow who had matched her anger earlier? He seemed completely relaxed and at ease.

His eyes remained closed as he chuckled softly. "I promised my uncle that I would not make you overdo it."

"I'm not *overdoing* it. See?" She relaxed against the back of the seat and managed not to wince. He peeked one eye open and looked at her, then closed it again, all the while grinning like a fool.

"We rest here," he said.

Sarah glanced around them at the narrow dirt path. "But we're blocking the road. What if someone needs to get by?" she asked in a last desperate attempt to motivate him.

"Then we move," he said, seeming completely content to rest there all afternoon. He shifted, and his knee bumped hers and remained there; Sarah wondered if he did it to keep tabs on her while he rested.

Sarah glared at him; his closed lids prevented him from seeing the silent daggers her eyes were throwing at him. She heaved a frustrated sigh for effect.

"Fine. But just for a few minutes." He grinned silently as she settled back against the seat and closed her eyes.

CR80

She awoke sometime later and forced her tired eyes to open. She blinked several times and raised a hand to shield her eyes from the blinding sunlight. How long had she been asleep?

She looked at the man in the seat beside her and grinned, her earlier frustration having faded. Will's mouth hung open slightly, and his chest rose and fell rhythmically as he slept. She hated to wake him, but she knew that they needed to be on their way.

"Will," she whispered and poked him gently in the arm. Sarah gasped and jumped back as his eyelids flew open and he sat straight up.

"What's wrong?" he asked, appearing surprisingly alert for having just woken up as he scanned their surroundings for anything out of the ordinary.

Sarah put a hand over her heart, trying to keep it from popping out of her chest. "Don't ever do that again," she said breathlessly.

His expression relaxed as he realized that there was no real danger. He actually had the nerve to grin. "I'm sorry. I should have told you that I am a light sleeper."

"Yeah, well, I'm a light sleeper; you're something else entirely."

"Sorry," he said again, not sounding the least bit regretful.

"Whatever," she mumbled before remembering where they were. "How long do you think we've been asleep?"

Will squinted up at the sun and appeared to assess its placement in the cloudless sky.

"Only about an hour or so," he said.

Sarah glanced up at the bright afternoon sun and had no idea what he was talking about. She couldn't even tell that it had moved at all.

"So we should be going?" she asked slowly.

He nodded, grabbed the reins, and prodded the horses forward. They shook their heads in protest but moved forward without too much encouragement.

Sarah focused her attention on the horses as they rode along. Their manes danced in the light breeze, and their heads bobbed up and down as they pulled the wagon. They seemed to banter back and forth as they nickered to each other. Like she had so many times before, Sarah imagined what it would be like to ride bareback—nothing but a silky mane to hold on to as she rode through a grassy field with the wind whipping through her hair and tickling her face. The image caused her to smile.

"Don't worry, you will get your chance," Will said beside her.

"Huh?" she asked, peeling her eyes away from the horses and forcing herself to focus on what he was saying.

"You will get to ride one someday," he repeated without taking his eyes off the road ahead of them. "I mean *really* ride. I can teach you."

"Really?" she asked, growing excited at the mere thought of learning to ride. "You would do that?"

He nodded.

Sarah felt like hugging him, but instead she wrapped her arms around her waist.

"Thank you," she said with a small smile.

He looked at her in surprise and then smiled in return. The tension from earlier that morning seemed to have faded completely, and Sarah felt that they were starting fresh.

They rode in comfortable silence for a while before coming to a clearing. She was about to ask where they were going when she recognized the barn they were headed toward. She looked at Will questioningly, but he avoided her eyes and pulled the horses up behind the wood building.

"Why didn't you just tell me that we were coming back here?" she asked, keeping her voice low in case anyone heard them. Not that she was worried about what the Joneses would think of Will driving her back, but she didn't want anyone to interrupt them and give him a reason to escape before she got an explanation.

"Why is it important?"

"It isn't necessarily important. I just . . ."

Being back on the Joneses' property suddenly brought back the thoughts of Karen that she had tried ignoring all day. It reminded her of the promise that she had made and broken, and the fact that she had failed miserably. She swallowed. "Never mind. It doesn't matter."

They were both quiet for a long moment.

"I have something for you," Will said suddenly. She looked up at him. "What?"

Instead of answering her, he reached into his coat pocket and extracted a long silver chain. He let it dangle from his finger so that she could see it fully. On the end of the chain hung a delicate circular pendant. As Sarah leaned in for a closer look, she noticed that the center of the pendant had been carved out to look like a tree. Its trunk wound up the center of the circle and bloomed into thin branches that grew out to the sides. The necklace was utterly breathtaking!

When she was silent for what must have been too long, Will hurriedly explained.

"My father made this for my mother as an engagement present. I thought . . . because—what I mean to say is that I have no use for it. And, well, I don't know that many women who would appreciate it." He shifted nervously in his seat.

Sarah couldn't remember ever seeing him so frazzled and couldn't resist the urge to tease him a little.

"Are you proposing to me?" she asked with a grin, raising her brow in question. His eyes widened in alarm, and she couldn't help laughing at his expression of panic.

"I'm sorry. I was only teasing you."

He breathed what she could only assume was a sigh of relief. "Oh," was all he said.

Now she felt bad about having made a joke at his expense. She put her hand on his arm and smiled, hoping to smooth things over.

"It's beautiful, Will," she said sincerely. "But are you sure you want to give it to me?"

He nodded quickly and held it out to her. "Like I said, I have no use for it, and you are the only woman who, well, who might appreciate such an item. I realize that I might have waited until you were settled back here, but for some reason I felt I needed to give it to you now. I had my uncle keep it for me all these years."

Sarah hesitantly took the delicate necklace from his hands and stared at it for a moment before looking back up at him and smiling her gratitude.

"It is absolutely beautiful. Thank you." He seemed relieved that she had accepted the gift and visibly relaxed in his seat. Sarah held the pendant up at eye level and let the chain hang from her finger.

"Your father was very skilled. I've never seen anything like it."

He smiled slightly, as though remembering. "He was good at what he did and took great joy in it. He could make anything, and everyone in town loved him because of his skill and the kind man that he was."

They heard the barn door suddenly swing open, and both grew silent. Footsteps could be heard rounding the corner on the soft grass, and Sarah stared in shock at the person standing before them.

"Hi, Sarah," Karen said with a smile.

Chapter Twenty-Six

Sarah stared in shock at the young woman; her mouth was working, but no words were coming out. She wondered for a long moment if her sanity should be questioned and if Karen was just a ghost coming back to haunt her—not that she believed in that kind of thing, but these days, nothing seemed impossible.

She noticed that there were dark circles under Karen's eyes from lack of sleep, and she looked as though she had lost a little weight, making her appear weak. However, she appeared far healthier than when they last saw her, and Karen's green eyes still sparkled when she smiled, which caused her whole face to glow with life.

Sarah looked at Will to see his reaction and ascertain whether she was simply seeing things. He smiled kindly at Karen and nodded once.

"I am very pleased to see that you are back safely."

Karen laughed. It was a sweet, almost bell-like sound. "You and me both."

She turned to Sarah and offered a hand to help her down from the wagon. Sarah took it mechanically, grasping the necklace tightly in her other hand as she stepped down. She continued to stare at the friend she thought had been lost forever, her mouth hanging open slightly as she fought for words. Finally, she found her voice.

"You're really here?"

Karen grinned and hugged her. "Yes, I'm really here."

This announcement brought tears of relief and joy to Sarah's eyes.

"But how?" she managed to ask past the unshed tears that clogged her throat.

Karen pulled back and smiled in amusement.

"You'll never believe me." She looked as though she was about to elaborate when she paused and waved at something behind Sarah. Sarah turned around to see Will driving the wagon in the direction of the forest, leaving the two of them alone to talk privately. She smiled softly. He always seemed to know what was needed before anyone spoke, and she was beginning to realize how much she appreciated him.

Trying not to let her thoughts wander too far, she focused her mind back on the present and remembered what Karen had said a moment ago. She turned back to her.

"What won't I believe?"

Karen grasped her arm, glanced quickly around their surroundings, and then pulled her into the barn. She closed the door and walked over to a pile of hay in an empty stall in the corner. They both sat down in the hay, and Sarah waited.

"No one should bother us for a while," Karen said. "I don't want them to know that you're back just yet, otherwise we'll never get a chance to talk."

"Do they know that *you're* back?"

"Of course," Karen said lightly and tucked a piece of hair behind her ear. "I told them that the reason why I was so delayed was because I got sick, which I did. Ruth has been babying me ever since I arrived and insisted that I sleep in the house." She grinned. "This is the first breath of fresh air I've had all day. I'm not used to being smothered."

Her eyes narrowed in scrutiny as she leaned closer to Sarah, staring at her neck. "What happened there?"

Sarah suddenly remembered the bruises on her neck; she used her left hand to quickly pull her hair over her shoulders to cover the unsightly marks.

"I can tell you about it later. So how did you escape?" Sarah could not contain her curiosity any longer.

Karen's green eyes fairly sparkled as she leaned toward her, taking the bait.

"The Shadow." She whispered the words so quietly that it took Sarah a moment to realize what she had just said. When she did, her eyes widened.

"You mean . . . ?" She let her voice trail off.

Karen nodded enthusiastically.

"But how? When?" Her mind reeled as she absorbed what she was hearing. How had Will done it? She hadn't been asleep for *that* long. She suddenly felt frustrated that he had kept this from her. At the same time, though, she wanted to hug him and tell him how much she appreciated what he had done. Sarah forced the confusing emotions away and focused on her friend.

"It was yesterday morning," Karen was saying. "A few hours before sunrise. He must have broken into the castle somehow—I'm not sure how he managed that. But then all of a sudden, he was in my cell and carrying me through a secret tunnel that led us to the forest." She sighed dreamily. "It was the most romantic scenario I could possibly imagine, saving me just before the clutches of death tried to take me."

Sarah felt something akin to jealousy stirring inside. No, that couldn't be right. Why should she care if Will, correction, *the Shadow*, miraculously saved the damsel in distress from almost certain death? It was only the perfect setup for every romantic novel that she had ever read. Big deal.

Sarah forced a smiled for her friend. What was wrong with her that she had to force herself to be happy that Karen was alive?

No, I am happy that she's okay, she reasoned with herself. *I'm just not too pleased about the circumstances leading up to it.*

"What happened after that?" she asked, trying to muster genuine excitement. She must have asked the right question because Karen smiled again, looking like a woman in love. Sarah swallowed hard.

Karen raised one of her perfectly arched brows and leaned forward slightly. Her red hair slipped over her shoulders, and she grinned. "He set me on his horse and we rode out here. He didn't say anything, and I was too shocked to say anything, so we rode in silence. Then when he got here, he hopped off the horse, helped me down, and rode off into the sunrise."

Sarah couldn't help wondering if she had left something out, so she decided to come right out and ask her. "So nothing else happened between the two of you?"

Karen pulled back, a look of surprise crossing her features. Her quick laugh caused her shoulders to rise once in amusement. "What do you mean? Of course nothing happened between us! Why would you even think that?"

"I just wondered," Sarah mumbled. "I mean, it did sound pretty romantic. You said so yourself."

"I said it was a romantic *scenario*, mostly because I envisioned Seth being the one to save me and sweep me off my feet."

Now Sarah was the one to look surprised. "You were imagining Seth saving you, and *that's* why it was so wonderful?" She suddenly felt like laughing in relief. But then again, she didn't care; why should she be relieved?

Karen stared at her for a moment, looking like she was trying to read her expression. "Why do you ask?" she asked slowly.

Sarah averted her gaze. She focused on an invisible wrinkle on the front of her dress and busied herself with smoothing out the nonexistent crease.

"No reason, really," she murmured, hoping her cheeks were not as red as they felt. When she looked back up, Karen was grinning from ear to ear.

"You like him, don't you?" she asked, leaning closer.

Sarah's ears heated with embarrassment, but she decided to play dumb. "Who? Seth? Of course I like him. As a friend, I mean." Her voice sounded unusually high to her own ears.

Karen looked slightly smug. "You know who I was talking about. You wouldn't have asked if anything happened between the two of us if you didn't care, Sarah. Come on, give me some credit here. I'm not stupid. What happened while I was gone?"

Sarah shifted uncomfortably under Karen's scrutiny.

"Trust me, nothing happened between me and him." That was true. Technically, no secret romance had been kindled with the Shadow. Will, however, was another story.

Karen seemed to believe her, but her next question caught Sarah off guard.

"What about you and Will?"

Was she that transparent?

For the first time since entering the barn, Sarah remembered the necklace clasped in her hand. She hid her fist under the folds of her skirt, unsure whether she wanted to tell anyone about that just yet—especially since she wasn't even sure what it meant.

She sighed and decided to answer honestly. "I have no idea what's going on there; do you mind if we drop it for now?"

Curiosity was apparent in Karen's eyes, but she nodded reluctantly.

"Fine. But I want to hear about it eventually." She inclined her head toward the opening of the pen. "We should head up to the house and let everyone know that you're back."

Sarah smiled her gratitude, and they both stood. Karen led the way to the barn door. She opened it and didn't bother to close the large door. Sarah slipped out into the open and glanced down at the necklace as she followed Karen. How was she going to hide it when they came to the house?

Seeing that Karen was looking straight ahead and that there were several feet in distance between them, Sarah made a quick decision. She grabbed both ends of the chain and tried to fasten them at the back of her neck. It took her a moment, but she was able to clasp them together without too much effort.

She had just tucked the pendant into the neck of her dress so that only the chain was visible when the front door of the house burst open. Leah ambled over to the end of the porch, a large fur rug slung awkwardly over her arm. When she looked up and saw them coming toward her, she flashed one of her beaming smiles at them, threw the rug over the railing, and fairly skipped toward them. As soon as she reached Sarah, she grabbed her hand and pulled her in the direction of the house.

"I'm so glad you're back," she said, her copper curls bouncing as she talked. "How is your family doing? Have you eaten yet?"

Sarah laughed at the string of questions and answered them as simply and quickly as they had been presented. "Thank you, fine, and no."

"Mama will want to fix something up for you as soon as she hears that. When Karen got back, Mama was like a mother hen trying to force feed her little chick." Leah covered her mouth with her hand to stifle a giggle before she opened the front door.

"Mama," Leah called out as they entered. "We have a late arrival for supper tonight."

Ruth Jones emerged from the small kitchen looking flushed. She appeared surprised when she spotted Sarah, then her face stretched into a warm smile as she came forward to embrace her. Sarah accepted the older woman's hug. She swallowed back the lump in her throat that seemed to have taken up permanent residence there recently. The sweet woman had only know her for a week and greeted her as though she were one of her daughters, even after she had been gone for days without so much as a word.

Ruth pulled back, still smiling.

"Welcome back, dear. Now, have you eaten yet?" Sarah shook her head. "Well, then you must sit down in the kitchen and tell me all about your trip while I fix you some supper."

"Oh, you really don't have to," Sarah protested. Ruth seemed not to have heard her as she bustled back into the kitchen like a woman on a mission. Leah followed close on their heels.

"I would like to hear the real story about your trip later," Karen said so that only she could hear as they walked into the kitchen. Sarah nodded silently.

"We've already eaten," Ruth was saying as the two entered the small kitchen and found her stirring a pot on the fire. "But it shouldn't take too long to warm this up for you." She waved a hand at them and motioned to the chairs around the table. "Now sit and tell me about your time with your family."

The three younger girls sat down, and everyone waited for Sarah to speak. She cleared her throat nervously.

"There really isn't much to tell. It was fairly uneventful." She would have to ask forgiveness for that one later.

"Did you at least enjoy your time with your family?" Ruth asked as she sliced a large loaf of homemade bread.

Sarah shifted in her seat, wondering how she could get around that one without lying. "It was very enjoyable. I'm glad to be back, though." Ruth Jones appeared extremely pleased at this, and Sarah found herself growing even fonder of the woman.

Hoping to divert the conversation away from her travels, Sarah asked Leah about her week. Leah brightened and chatted away happily. Ruth set a bowl of beef and vegetable stew and a large slice of fresh bread in front of Sarah and pulled out a chair for herself. Sarah ate contentedly while she listened to the younger girl talk, occasionally nodding her head and smiling when necessary. By the time she finished the meal, her eyes were beginning to droop. Ruth must have noticed because she stopped her daughter midsentence as she was telling them in great detail about the new baby goat she had helped deliver.

"Why don't we let our guests sleep for a while, and then they can hear about the rest of your week later, love?"

Leah seemed to realize that she had been dominating the conversation and appeared embarrassed.

"I'm sorry, Sarah," she said, looking sheepish. "I didn't think about how exhausted you must be after traveling all day. We can all talk later if you're feeling up to it."

Sarah smiled her thanks. "Maybe I will take a quick nap." She paused. "Um, where are the boys?"

Ruth Jones took on that knowing look that only a mother can wear. "They're felling trees with their father in the forest."

Sarah tried not to let her relief show as she nodded. At least she could put off that awkward reunion for the time being.

"Well, we'd best be going," Karen said, speaking for the first time since they had sat down. "We'll probably see you in the morning for breakfast."

"Do you want a lantern? It's getting dark."

Karen shook her head. "It's not that far of a walk. Thank you, though."

They stood, and all four of them walked to the door. Leah grinned as Ruth embraced Sarah and Karen in a hug.

"It's so nice to have you girls back." She smiled, and Sarah couldn't help smiling in return.

"You have a pretty nice home here," Sarah commented as they walked the short distance to the barn.

Karen's face took on a wistful look.

"Yeah, I do." She looked at Sarah. "And as soon as we get inside, I want to hear the whole story. When Seth told me that Will had stopped by to tell him that you were staying with some family or a friend for a little while, I admit that I was a little worried."

"Will stopped by?" This was news to her. "I didn't know that."

Karen shrugged. "I guess he must have come over to let them know that you were fine. But it got me pretty curious, and ever since I heard that, I've been dying to get the rest of the story."

"I'll tell you everything so long as I can lie down while I give you the recap. I feel like I'm going to collapse." Karen nodded her head as they entered the open barn door.

Sarah gratefully fell onto the pile of quilts stacked on top of the mound of hay that she had used as a bed before. She sighed contentedly as her aching body relaxed into the soft bed.

Karen sat in front of her cross-legged.

"Okay, I can't take it any longer," she said after a full five seconds.

Sarah grinned at the ceiling. "Fine, but there isn't a whole lot to tell because I was unconscious for most of it, though Will filled in some of the missing pieces."

Sarah looked over in time to catch Karen raise a brow in question. Sarah recounted the story as best she could, telling Karen about the fire, Allan's death, and the poison that had rendered her unconscious. She filled in the gaps while she was unconscious with what Will had told her. However, she decided it was best to leave out the part where she discovered that Will was the Shadow. She knew that after so many years of tactfully keeping his secret from everyone, he would not want her broadcasting it all over town as soon as the opportunity presented itself. It was his secret to tell or keep, and he could do with it as he chose.

When she finished describing the past couple of days, she turned her head to the side to catch Karen's reaction and saw that she was grinning broadly.

"He saved you from a burning building, huh?" she asked, her brow raised once more, this time in friendly teasing. "That's really heroic. He must be a great guy to have done all that."

"Well, it was pretty heroic, I guess. And he is a great guy." Sarah eyed her redheaded friend. She narrowed her left eye suspiciously. "What are you thinking?" she asked cautiously.

Karen shrugged nonchalantly, though her eyes betrayed her interest. "Oh, nothing."

Sarah used her elbows to prop herself up. "Hold it right there, missy. I know what you're thinking, and it isn't like that. Not at all."

"Mm hmm."

Sarah sighed. "All right, fine. Obviously it's no use arguing with you. I'll get some shut eye, and then we can resume this conversation another time." She didn't wait for a response before easing herself back down on her pallet and closing her eyes.

"Besides," she continued, "there are several hundred years between our realities. It never would have worked out." She couldn't help wondering exactly who she was trying to convince, Karen or herself.

Karen was silent for a long moment, and Sarah was almost asleep when her friend whispered into the silent room, "Maybe it can."

Chapter Twenty-Seven

Because her body felt so exhausted, Sarah had assumed that she could simply shut off her brain and sleep peacefully and undisturbed for hours. However, her mind refused to comply as a constant flood of thoughts and confusing emotions caused her to toss and turn all night. Even when she did manage to fall asleep for a time, nightmares of a burning building crumbling around her disturbed her slumber.

Sarah fought against the dark nightmare that haunted her subconscious, trying to break free from the frightening images that threatened to consume her. She jerked her eyes open just as the ceiling broke free and crushed both her and Will.

She awoke to the stillness of the barn, half expecting to see flames bursting forth from the beams above her. She was breathing heavily from the vivid dream and had to remind herself that it was just that—a dream. But the terror she felt while she was asleep had been so real that her body now trembled from genuine fear.

It was only a dream, just a dream. She repeated the words over and over in her head to convince herself of the fact and calm her frayed nerves.

She lay there for a long time as she tried to still the tremors shaking her body, debating whether she wanted to fall back to sleep and risk having another nightmare, or if she should she just get up and start her day. Feeling too restless to lay still another moment, she sat up slowly and massaged the kink in her neck that she had received from having slept wrong. She had no idea what time it was, but she forced herself out of bed anyway, wrapped one of the quilts around herself for warmth, and crept quietly out of the barn so she wouldn't disturb Karen.

The sun was not yet up as she made her way outside, but the paralyzing darkness of night had passed, and she could see well enough to find her way, though she didn't have any particular destination in mind. Her lungs filled with the coolness of morning as she found herself wandering to the outer fields; it felt as though something were drawing her there. It had rained in the night, and the grass felt dew kissed beneath her bare feet. The sensation helped the grogginess to pass and made her more alert.

She walked for some time before she found a patch of grass dry enough to sit on. She lowered herself to the ground and wrapped the blanket around herself tightly to stave off the morning chill, tucking her feet inside to warm them. She sat there for several minutes, staring off into the distance. An immense feeling of helplessness nearly overtook her.

"I know that I should be relieved that Karen is okay and that Will and I are even alive," she whispered to the dark sky overhead, her eyes searching for unseen answers. "But how much longer, Father? How long do I have to be a stranger in this place? Whenever I'm around this family, it makes me long for home. Will I ever get to go back? Am I going to be stuck here forever?" She winced as she realized that she sounded like a needy child.

"Sorry," she murmured, casting her eyes downward as if she had just received a gentle reprimand. "I just miss Mom and Dad. I even miss my old, dull life that I complained so much about. And I have no way of knowing if Lilly got back safely or if I'll ever get to see my family again. I worry that I'll never get home."

She raked a shaky hand through her sleep-tangled curls, suddenly reminded of something her mom always said. Sarah recited the words from memory in a voice barely above a whisper.

"When in need, pray. When in doubt, have faith. When faced with difficult circumstances, be content and give thanks. Then you shall receive your heart's desire."

The words came so easily to her, it was as if her mom had spoken them herself. Sarah absorbed the meaning of those words. She breathed in deeply, enjoying the crisp, earthy scent that hung in the air, and she smiled. She loved how everything always smelled so refreshing and clean after it rained, seeming to bring with it the promise of a new day for those who were looking for a fresh start, those in search of happiness.

"That's kind of like what You do, isn't it?" Sarah whispered as she twirled a piece of grass between her fingers absentmindedly. "Because of Your love and mercy, You wash away all the bad that we've done and grant us a second chance at a new day and whatever joy comes with it."

She smiled up at the sun as it began to make its ascent over the hills in the distance, casting an orange hue on the horizon. "I guess this is my new day, isn't it, Lord?"

The last stars yet to fade in the sky seemed to twinkle their agreement.

Pray, have faith, give thanks, and be content, she silently reminded herself, and she did just that. By the time she had finished her humble prayer, the heaviness that had weighed down her heart for days had lifted. She felt suddenly renewed.

❦

Sarah sat there for some time watching the sunrise, a contented smile upon her lips, nothing in particular occupying her thoughts. At that moment, she didn't care what anyone thought of her if they saw her sitting alone in the middle of the field in her nightgown. She didn't mind the fact that the moisture from the grass had begun to seep into the bottom of her quilt; she hardly even noticed. And the worries that had been plaguing her heart and mind for what seemed like a long time were nowhere to be found, lost somewhere in the distance. They seemed to have fled with the passing darkness.

Reluctantly, she rose to her feet; she didn't want to leave her haven of peace, but she knew that Karen would come looking for her soon enough.

Her spirit continued to feel invigorated as she took her time walking back to the barn. The morning sun warmed the top of her head, and she savored the sensation, imaging that it was God's hand resting upon her. The thought caused her to smile once more.

She was still smiling several minutes later when Karen climbed down from the loft and found her neatly folding her quilt.

"You're up early," Karen observed groggily, covering her mouth to stifle a yawn. She stretched her arms over her head and rotated her shoulders to loosen her tight muscles.

"Good morning," Sarah said cheerily. She couldn't help wondering if this was how Scrooge felt after waking up on Christmas morning, wanting to spread joy to all.

Karen eyed her warily. "You were humming."

"Was I? I didn't even realize I was doing that."

Sarah laid the quilt at the end of her pallet and waited patiently for the question she knew would come. She did not have to wait long.

"What did you do this morning?"

Sarah heard the note of incredulity in her friend's voice and turned around to face her, trying to suppress her giddiness long enough to explain.

"I wasn't able to sleep very well, so I got up early and ended up wandering out in the fields," she said. "I started complaining to God about how I missed home and just wanted to get out of here."

Karen's eyes widened in surprise, and Sarah held up a hand to keep her from speaking.

"I don't blame you in any way, but I just felt so frustrated. I ended up venting my anger and confusion at God for allowing me to get stuck here. Then I realized how ridiculous I sounded, telling God how He should do His job, when I was neglecting to do what I was supposed to. So I decided that I will be content with where I am and try to make the best of it until He sees fit to do otherwise with my situation."

Karen's face had turned unusually pale by the time her explanation was finished. She looked uncomfortable as she shifted from foot to foot.

"What's wrong?" Sarah asked, concerned that she had suddenly become ill. She took a step closer.

"You aren't exactly stuck here," Karen said, wincing as she spoke.

"What do you mean?" Sarah asked, knitting her brows in confusion.

The older girl was silent for a full minute before everything came spilling out at once.

"It's just that I was really enjoying having you around, and I know the Joneses did too. It was selfish, I know that now. I think I knew it then, but I wasn't quite ready to lose you. I know it wasn't my decision to make, and I shouldn't have taken that from you. I'm sorry—so sorry." Karen took a deep breath and waited.

Sarah paused, her heart skipping a beat as the meaning of Karen's hurried words began to sink in. Did this mean what she thought it meant?

"So they didn't find your watch when they took you?" she asked slowly, wanting to clarify Karen's hurried confession. Karen shook her head, looking as if she were preparing to be slapped at any moment.

"When was it ready?"

"The night after they caught me."

Sarah collapsed onto the pile of straw that she had slept on and stared at the floor, not really seeing anything. She hardly noticed when Karen sat beside her.

She could have been home almost a week ago! She felt like she should somehow be angry with Karen for keeping her here all this time, but then she wondered if she really would have wanted to go back. A few days ago, she would have jumped at the chance to leave this foreign land. But now, after all the trials she had overcome, the people she had come to know and adore, and especially the lessons she'd learned, she wasn't sure how she should feel. Could she really be upset with someone for allowing her to experience the greatest adventure of her life?

"Karen," she said gently and laid a hand on her shoulder. "I'm not mad. Actually, I should thank you for letting me stay."

Karen looked completely taken aback. Her eyes widened. "But you have every right to be upset with me after what I did."

"Listen," Sarah began, wanting to put her at ease. "I know that we haven't known each other very long, but I would consider you a good friend. I think some of the reasons why I felt such a quick connection between us were that we met under difficult circumstances and have had to rely on each other. It kind of forced us to bond, I guess. But I would like to think that it only cemented a friendship that was going to come about anyway. And since I think of you like that and have a hard time staying mad at my friends for very long, you have absolutely nothing to worry about."

Karen seemed to absorb her words for a moment. A slow smile made its way to her lips.

"You know," she said with a slight chuckle, "you are the most unique person I have ever met."

Sarah rolled her eyes heavenward. "So I've heard."

"I meant it as a compliment." Karen playfully nudged Sarah with her shoulder. "Seriously, though. I don't know anyone who wouldn't flip out at me for keeping them trapped in the past when they had the opportunity to return home. No one would have forgiven me on the spot for doing something so heinous."

"It wasn't heinous," Sarah said, and then grinned. "A little misguided, maybe, but I feel honored that you like my company enough to want to keep me around."

Her smile dimmed as reality hit her. "But, Karen, as much as I have loved being here and experiencing all these crazy adventures, I do have to go back. I don't belong here."

Karen sighed heavily. "I know. I just wish things were different."

"Me too," Sarah said quietly.

They were silent then, each consumed with their thoughts. Karen stood abruptly, startling Sarah.

"All right, that's enough moping around," she announced, hands on her slender hips. "You're going to enjoy your last day here if I have anything to say about it. And then tonight—" She paused, then shook her head. "Well, we won't think about that until the time comes."

Sarah laughed at her friend's speech as she rose to her feet. "You sound like you're running for president."

"If that's what it takes to get you off your behind and into the house for a normal, carefree breakfast, then so be it."

Karen walked to the front of the barn and swung the door wide, looking like a woman on a mission. Then she turned around to face Sarah as she waited for her to follow.

Sarah inhaled a shaky breath and steeled herself for the goodbyes she was about to say.

Chapter Twenty-Eight

When Sarah announced at breakfast that she was leaving early the next morning, she was surprised by the reactions of the family sitting around her at the table.

Ruth and Leah both looked genuinely upset with this news, while Seth and Joshua appeared surprised, glancing at each other every now and then. It took only a second for this announcement to sink in before everyone began asking questions and begging for her to stay for another day. The noise level grew at the table as each person tried to be heard over the other.

Sarah was taken aback at their sincere reactions, and her mouth worked silently, too stunned to say anything. Mr. Jones must have noticed the confusion on her face because he stood suddenly, his large presence demanding everyone's attention. The room went completely still as they waited for him to speak.

"I know that we all have been blessed with this young lady's company recently," he said as his gaze traveled over the faces of his family. "However, she has a home and a family of her own, and we cannot ask her to stay here any longer than she is able."

Ruth's face grew pink with obvious embarrassment, and the rest averted their gazes guiltily. Sarah felt gratitude that he came so quickly to her defense. If she had had to defend her actions to this family, she wasn't so sure that she would have declined their invitation, even though she knew she could stay no longer.

Mr. Jones smiled at Sarah as he continued. "But if you ever decide that you would like to visit or remain with us for a time, we would be more than willing to make you a bed in the barn."

Sarah grinned. He obviously sensed that she needed her space and liked to be able to come and go as she pleased. However, Ruth Jones appeared aghast at his offer.

"The barn? With the animals? That won't do at all. When she comes back, she must stay in the house with Karen and us."

Sarah shook her head slightly. "I really appreciate you offering to let me stay in the house, but I'm perfectly comfortable in the barn. Really, I am."

Ruth appeared unconvinced, but thankfully she let the matter drop.

Because it was her last day with them, Ruth and Samuel Jones announced after breakfast that their children could escape their chores for the day. Joshua was the first one to come up with an idea of how they could best take advantage of the perfect weather.

He ran back inside the house and emerged carrying a sheepskin ball. The two brothers began kicking the ball back and forth between each other as they explained the rules of the game to Sarah, which she realized was very similar to soccer back home. They split up into two teams, boys against girls, and each group decided where their goals should be. Leah declared that she wanted to sit out for the game and cheer the girls on from the sidelines.

Sarah followed everyone's example as they removed their shoes and set them on the ground near the side of the barn. She was surprised and slightly dismayed to find that Seth and Josh were excellent soccer players. They passed the ball effortlessly back and forth, making it difficult for the girls to steal it away. On one play, Seth became cocky and waited too long to pass the ball along, giving Karen enough time to kick it away from him toward her teammate.

Sarah stopped the ball with her foot and began to dribble it in the opposite direction toward the boys' goal. Leah clapped her hands and jumped up and down, yelling for her to keep going. Seth was delayed in reacting, most likely because he was so surprised that he had actually lost the ball and was too far behind to hinder her progress. Josh grinned as he waited in front of his team's goal. Sarah's breathing was erratic, but she kept running full force, adrenaline coursing through her veins.

Speed wasn't a problem for her; she had always been a fast runner. However, she had never been very good on her high school soccer team when it came to actually aiming the ball, so she knew that her judgment would be off. Deciding to just get it over with, she blindly kicked the ball as hard as she could in the direction of the goal and hoped that it would somehow reach its mark.

The ball sailed through the air, and Josh jumped to block it, his hands raised high. But he underestimated the speed of the ball and reached too early. The ball glided over his fingertips and landed between the sacks of grain with a dull *thump*. Sarah's mouth hung open in shock as she stood there, dumbfounded and too surprised to move. She had actually done it! She smiled victoriously at the astonished goalie as Karen and Leah rushed up to her, shouting their congratulations. The three girls jumped up and down, shrieking, giddy with excitement.

"You're supposed to block the ball," Seth called out playfully to his brother as he jogged over to the celebration, an amused grin on his face. Josh shrugged and held his hands up to quiet the laughing group of girls.

"That was a nice shot, but the game's not over yet," he called.

Karen grinned. "Let's see what you've got!"

CR80

Later that night, after everyone had gone to their rooms, Sarah laid on her bed in her jeans and T-shirt, staring up at the ceiling with her arms behind her head, a small smile lighting her face. Though the girls had lost the game five goals to two, she couldn't remember the last time she'd had that much fun outdoors. There had been no television or cell phone—no modern devices of any kind to provide distractions. The things she thought she needed every day had not been present.

And she'd had fun.

What a wonderful feeling to be free of technology and realize that she could be entertained without acquiring the latest gadget or gizmo! It was a simple life, free from the modern world she had grown up in. The freedom to have innocent and carefree fun with friends was wonderful.

She could definitely get used to this life.

Sarah's smile faded as she remembered that she wouldn't need to get used to it because she was leaving tonight and never coming back. She would go off to college, probably get some boring office job that she would be stuck at for the rest of her life, and marry some dull, unadventurous man who would lose all his hair and only wished to study his coin collection in his free time.

Will's face came to mind unbidden. He certainly wasn't unadventurous; he embraced life and sought adventure! Life with him would never be dull, and he also had a full head of hair.

Sarah rested her forearm across her eyes, trying to block out the images and stop her thoughts from running away with her. That would never happen. Not now. She heard Karen's voice in her head asking her if she would like to go into town to say goodbye to him. And, worse yet, she kept hearing her answer repeated again and again.

No.

She groaned softly, the sound breaking the stillness in the silent barn. When Karen had asked why she didn't care to go, she had said that it didn't matter if she ever saw him again. What had ever possessed her to say something so untrue? She knew the answer, but she tried her best to ignore it, though she couldn't push the thoughts away fast enough.

Because goodbye seems too final.

She sat up abruptly and shook her head to clear it of the nagging voice.

"It doesn't matter anyway," she whispered in the silence. "He'll meet some beautiful girl, and they'll get married and live happily ever after." She winced as she spoke the words, wondering at the fact that it stung so much to hear them aloud.

The door opened into the barn, and Karen stepped inside. She closed the door behind her and nodded at Sarah.

"Everyone's asleep," she said, her eyes searching Sarah's face for any sign of hesitation. "Are you ready to do this?"

Sarah took a deep breath and nodded once, then she stood. The two girls walked toward each other and met in the middle of the hay-strewn floor. Karen's eyes were filled with regret.

"I'm really sorry that I got you into this," she said quietly, dipping her head in remorse.

Sarah felt an odd mix of emotions churning inside her. She so desperately wanted to avoid this painful goodbye and get on with what needed to be done. She would find herself back in her room, back to her old life, and she could forget that this whole thing ever happened.

But that was the problem: she wasn't so sure she wanted to forget. While she was dying to go back home and see her family again, she was not so eager to leave the best adventure of her life just yet, nor the people and the places that had taken up a place in her heart. As soon as she stepped over that threshold leading her back to her world, all the joy and excitement she had experienced since arriving here would come to an end.

But all things must come to an end, she reminded herself despondently.

When Sarah neglected to answer her, Karen looked up, hurt evident in her face.

Sarah suddenly remembered her friend's words a second ago and gave her a small smile. "Don't apologize. Although there have been a few bumps in the road, I wouldn't trade this experience for anything."

"I'm just sorry it had to end this way," Karen said.

Sarah raised one shoulder in a shrug, wondering if her eyes reflected the sadness inside. "I am too."

She reached out, and the two girls embraced. Sarah felt tears burn the back of her throat and closed her eyes tightly to hold them back. They held each other for a long moment and then slowly pulled away. A silent tear ran down Karen's cheek and she sniffed quietly.

"I guess we should do this, then, huh?"

Sarah took a deep breath for courage and nodded. Karen pressed her finger to her watch and glanced back up. She smiled sadly.

"Goodbye, Sarah."

Sarah raised her hand in silent farewell, too emotional to speak. White light suddenly blinded her, and she closed her eyes and turned her head to block some of it out. She felt strange and weightless for a moment, then her legs crumpled beneath her, and she fell onto her back.

◌౭ఴ

The strange sensations stopped, and she slowly opened her eyes. It took a moment for her vision to adjust to the light. When it did, she blinked several times to make sure she was seeing right.

Sunlight spilled into her room through the window by her bed, hitting the crystal hanging there and throwing rainbows onto her cream-colored walls and bright purple rug. Her bed was still unmade, and dirty laundry littered the floor where she had left it. Everything was as it had been.

She was lying on the floor, as she had been when she bumped her head in the storm. She sat up slowly, feeling disoriented. Her eyes roamed over the room in awe as her mind tried to take in the fact that she was home, and she had just time traveled to get there. She glanced down at her hands to make sure that there were still ten fingers there and that they hadn't been lost in some other dimension. She sighed in relief when she counted the correct number.

Something out of the corner of her eye caught her attention, and she turned her head. Lilly lay curled up on her side, her back against the wall and her hands pillowed underneath her head as she slept. Sarah smiled at the sight and crawled over to her sleeping form. She shook her sister gently to wake her, though she hated to disturb her peaceful sleep. Lilly's eyes opened slowly at the persistent nudging, and she looked up at Sarah. Her blurry eyes took in the room and became suddenly alert as she sat up. Sarah had to jump back to avoid getting smacked in the head.

"But this, I mean, how—?" Lilly stopped and shook her head.

"It's okay, Lil, I'm here," Sarah comforted. It was probably a shock to wake up back in their house without her big sister around, only to have her reappear days later. It was no wonder she looked so surprised.

Lilly seemed to relax. She let out a slow breath and shook her head.

"But it all felt so real. I mean, I knew it seemed crazy at the time, but boy, that was some dream!"

Sarah stared at her sister in confusion.

"What are you talking about?"

"I had this crazy dream that we were transported back in time and there was this family that we stayed with. And someone was being poisoned." She squinted at the far wall, as if trying to conjure up the memories. "It's all kind of fuzzy, though."

Sarah's heart beat faster. Lilly thought it was a dream! Here Sarah had been worrying about how confused she would be, and her sister didn't even think any of it had happened. But that would mean . . .

"Lilly," Sarah spoke slowly, "you had this dream last night?"

She nodded. "It felt like we were there for a long time, though. It was so strange and real. I really didn't think that it was a dream at the time, but I guess I should have realized it, considering how farfetched it was."

Sarah sat back on her heels, her mind reeling. She glanced over at her nightstand and saw her cell phone atop it. She lunged for it, fumbling to open the phone. It lit up as she opened the cover, and she realized that her battery hadn't even died in nearly a week and a half of leaving it on. She stared in disbelief at the black letters on the screen that told her it was the sixth of August.

"Are you okay?" Lilly asked behind her. "You look like you're about to be sick."

"Yeah, I'm fine," Sarah mumbled absentmindedly, mentally counting backward. Not even a full day had passed since they had left. Was that even possible?

If Lilly didn't think any of it had been real, did Sarah really need to tell her? She felt the weight of responsibility upon her. It was her job to protect Lilly, and telling her would only confuse her. Besides, no one would believe them anyway, so what was the use in spreading that story around?

"I must have fallen asleep on your floor during the storm last night." Lilly's words pulled Sarah from her thoughts. She watched as the younger girl held the front of her nightgown and stared down at it. A suspicious frown clouded her features. Sarah held her breath as she realized it was the dress that Karen had lent her.

"Was I wearing this last night?" Lilly asked, then she shook her head at her own question, saving Sarah the trouble of coming up with an excuse for it. "I must be more tired than I thought," she mumbled, rising and making her way across the hall to her own bedroom, leaving Sarah alone.

Sarah lowered herself onto her plush rug and lay there for a while, staring up at the ceiling in contemplation. It would have been nice to have someone to talk to about all that had taken place, but Lilly was better off thinking that none of it was real. Then she wouldn't have to miss any of it. Although Sarah already missed the friends she had just left behind, she was struck by the realization that she was finally back home.

She smiled.

Home.

Epilogue

Sarah sat on her bedroom floor, loading all the novels and mystery books from her bookshelf into the empty box beside her. She was leaving for college in four days, and her mom had been after her all week about getting started on packing. With only a few days left, Sarah decided that she had put it off for long enough. She might as well appease her mother by getting a few boxes done this morning before it conveniently slipped her mind again. However, it was taking far longer than she had expected; she hadn't realized how much junk she actually owned.

She glanced around at the mess her room had become and wondered absentmindedly if it might help to use a shovel to pack. She had spent the last hour and a half sorting through her closet and deciding which things stayed and could be tossed out. The things she planned to toss in the trash were in a heap at the end of her bed, and the keepsakes she decided to take littered the floor here and there, making it difficult to walk without tripping or getting stabbed in the foot. Sarah had only managed to pack one box of her belongings so far.

She frowned as she realized the meager progress she was making. She began to work faster and reached for another book to add to the box. When she picked it up, something slid out from between the pages and fell to the floor. Tossing the book uncaringly over her shoulder, she heard the satisfactory thump as it landed in the half empty box. Without thinking, she reached for the silver chain and picked it up off the carpet. She almost tossed it back onto the shelf in her haste before she realized what it was.

Her unpacked books forgotten, Sarah stared at the necklace dangling from her fingertips, her eyes roaming over the delicate tree. The sunlight streaming through her window reflected off the pure silver chain and made it sparkle. She had completely forgotten she had hidden this away, so intent was she on making plans in the present in order to forget the questions of the past.

She was still unaware of why Will had given the necklace. What was the significance of it? Had he really only meant for her to have it because she was the only woman he knew who would care for it and appreciate it? Or had the gesture meant something infinitely more?

These were questions that she would rather not spend too much time analyzing, so she turned her attention to the necklace. Turning her hand slightly to better examine the pendant, her eyes caught site of the scar on her hand. Her breath lodged in her chest as she stared at the thin white line thoughtfully, not really seeing it, but rather remembering the circumstances surrounding it.

At first, she'd had a difficult time sleeping at night because the memories seemed to haunt her every time she closed her eyes. It was why she had hidden the necklace among the dusty books her second night being back home; if it was tucked away out of sight, then maybe the dreams and memories associated with it would disappear, as well. But then the memories were no longer as vivid as they had once seemed. And now, she wondered if all of it hadn't been some crazy fantasy she conjured up to keep herself entertained. But the skillfully sculpted necklace hanging from her fingers and the scar on her hand were proof enough that it had been real. A moment ago, all those memories seemed as if they happened hundreds of years ago in another lifetime. And in a way they had.

But now, those once-forgotten memories came back in a rush. Sarah stared at the scar, then closed her eyes and allowed her thoughts to transport her back to that day, only a short time past, yet so long ago. She remembered everything. Getting thrown into that old shack and the dread she had felt over seeing Will's body as she wondered if he was dead, the raging fire and the way Will had saved them both. The picture of Allan's cold face as he lay on the ground appeared on the back of her lids without warning, and Sarah opened her eyes quickly to dispel the image.

She buried her face in her hands, pressing the necklace against her face as she tried to keep herself from reliving that awful day. She could only hope that all the memories would fade away once again, and the pain over having to leave would do the same.

"Sarah, can you get the door?" her mom called, startling Sarah. She hadn't even heard the doorbell ring, so absorbed was she in her thoughts.

She rose slowly and took a steadying breath, hoping to calm herself. She realized that she was still holding the necklace. Not wanting to stir any questions from her mother, she reached behind her neck with shaking fingers and fastened the delicate clasp, dropping the circular pendant inside her T-shirt for safekeeping.

She carefully picked her way to the door, kicking an empty box out of her path as she made her way down the hall. Her dad had gone out of town Sunday to look at a possible location for a new hardware store, and he wouldn't return for at least three more days. Lilly was sleeping over at a friend's house that night, and she wouldn't be back until late tomorrow evening. That left just Sarah and her mom.

As Sarah walked past the kitchen on her way to the door and saw her mom wrist-deep in bread dough, something occurred to her: if she could just throw herself into her school and not think about anything else, then she would eventually forget about her little adventure in the past. Everything would go back to the way it had been. But did she really want it to return to normal?

She grabbed the handle of the front door and pulled it open with more force than she intended. Her eyes widened as she stared at the person standing on her doorstep.

"What are you doing here?" she managed to ask after her initial shock had passed. "*How* did you get here?"

"It doesn't matter," Karen said, glancing around her warily. Sarah followed her gaze, but she didn't see anything suspicious in the empty street. She directed her attention back to the redhead before her.

"Sarah, I need your help. I was right all along."

Sarah stared at her, squinting her left eye in confusion. She felt a mixture of excitement and suspicion.

"What are you talking about? What do you mean you were right?"

Karen shook her head from side to side. "There's no time to explain."

"I think I deserve a little bit of an explanation," Sarah said, folding her arms across her chest, unmoving. Silly her for thinking that she could simply forget about the past without it coming back to haunt her.

Karen shook her head, more insistent this time. Her green eyes were wide. "You don't understand, Sarah. The king is dead. You have to come back!"